MANGO

MANGO

PAULA R.R. BROWN

Introduction

The sound of a motorbike whizzing past jerked Val from her nap. She found herself in the back of a rickety taxi. The sixteen-hour flight from Phoenix to Taipei, then five-hour flight from Taipei to Georgetown Penang had left her so drained, that everything was putting her in a sour mood. Nothing more so than the loud-ass motorbikes speeding by. They were like mosquitos in her ear, waking her up every time she drifted off to sleep. Val let out a loud, bothered sigh, and stared out the window. It was all the same. Her taxi was still driving along a one-lane highway, an imposing rainforest surrounded her on all sides. This was the furthest from home Val had ever gone, and already she was doubting her decision to come all this way at all.

Val's phone buzzed in her lap, jarring her to jump in her seat. The too-bright-for-the-moment screen glowed white, with the word *"Facetime"* written along the top. She rolled her eyes, regretting how little sleep she had procured on each plane, and hoped that her muddled state of mind wouldn't be too obvious.

Val slid her finger across the screen to answer, grimacing at her puffy complexion before the call connected. "Hey mom, how ya doing?"

A middle-aged, dark-haired woman stared back at her with heavy eyes; looking as if she had slept even less than Val had. *"Me? Really? You're really asking how I'm doing? My baby's on the other side of the world, and I won't be able to see her for a whole year! How are you doing? How were the flights?"*

"They were good." Val lied. Truth be told, she was petrified the entire time, and the sleeping draught she had chugged didn't work in the slightest. Val had only taken a flight once before in her life, when she was nine to visit her dad in northern California. It was such an uncomfortable experience, both the flight and interacting with her dad; that she had vowed to never do either again.

"Where are you right now? Hold up the camera so I can take a look around. Are you there yet?"

"No mom," Val groaned, "I'm still on the way. There's nothing really for you to see right now. I'm in the middle of nowhere."

"Are you in the taxi? Does the driver seem... *safe?* Is anyone else taking the ride with you? Tell the Taxi driver you have a knife or pepper spray on you... just to let him know!"

Val's cheeks turned bright red. She caught the taxi driver glancing back at her through the rear-view mirror. "Mom, you're on speaker phone!" Val put the phone down, mouthing the words *"I'm sorry"* towards the driver. "He speaks English... you're really embarrassing me!"

"Well good — I want him to hear me! He better know nobody's messing with my baby!" Val's mom took a few deep breaths in and out, before cooing: "I'm sorry sweetheart... it's just, you've never been so far away from me before. I'm kind of freaking out thinking about it. Anyways miha, your abuela wants to talk to you."

In true grandma fashion, a pair of sunken grey eyes and skinny bifocals took over the whole screen. *"Aye — me bebe. Como estas? Todo bien?"*

"Si, todo bien... everything's good, I'm just tired."

"I'm sorry." Val's grandmother replied, in her thick Colombian accent. *"Aye, mi chiquita, jyou remember what I tell jyou."*

Val rolled her eyes again. Of course she remembered. Her grandma wouldn't stop reminding her of it. "Yeeeessss..."

"Jyou send me the mangoes — the dried mangoes — no too much sugar."

Before she had left, her Grandma had done a little digging online about Malaysia, and found out mangoes were a popular staple food grown locally. She had been nagging her nonstop ever since.

"Don't worry, I'll get you your mangoes. I promise."

"Okay mi chiquita, te quiero. Aye, I pray por jyou!"

Val was already starting to miss her abuela immensely. "I love you too."

The phone was handed back to her mom, who fretted just a bit longer before saying her final goodbye. Val disconnected the facetime call and rested her head against the back seat window.

The lush green of Malaysia felt so different from the Arizona desert where she had grown up. Almost too different... she didn't realize just how opposite the other side of the world would actually be. A large lump started swelling in her throat, as she questioned whether her quest for whatever the fuck she was trying to find had flung her too far from home.

Val had spent her whole life in a suburb of Phoenix. Even going to community college there for two years; before attending Arizona State, which was even closer to her family home than the community college.

She dreamed of her life afterward, of a cushy job, and an even cushyer apartment. Of the adult work friends she would make at happy hour, and the vacations she could afford to take. Preferably with the mature, sophisticated men she would meet at posh adult social gatherings. But to her dismay, those expectations were quickly crushed nearly as soon as she walked off stage with her diploma.

Quite frankly, everything *sucked*.

Her entry-level position at a local bank had her doing little more than scanning and copying paperwork; stapling packets together that no one would ever read. The cute, potted plants and plush pillows at her cubicle did nothing to make the grueling, forty-plus hours a week at work more bearable. In fact, seeing them depressed Val more.

She didn't make anywhere near the type of money she had expected to earn; so settling into a nice apartment, or taking vacation was out of the question. Even sick days were a risk. Val's boss chewed her out in front of her colleagues when she took one to see a doctor over a particularly nasty flu. What did it matter? She wasn't really doing anything important anyways.

Her colleagues had organized only one happy hour together, and it was clear to Val that everyone attended begrudgingly. They seemed way more interested in getting home to spend the precious little time they could with their respective families. Val understood. It depressed her to see her co-workers try, and fail, to have a healthy balance in their lives. She'd never forget the softened cries of her cubicle mate for months after she returned to work, from her brief maternity leave.

She didn't *do* shit, she didn't *make* shit, and her colleagues were kinda shitty too. Soon Val would be one of them, if something didn't change.

To make matters worse, nearly all of Val's school peers got lame all of a sudden. They were alway too busy, too tired, or just too stressed to want to hang out anymore. Topping it all off, she had met *zero* eligible bachelors who came anywhere near reaching her standards. All of the pompous, cocky, shallow frat guys had not grown or matured one bit. And even the older gentlemen she met were just even pompouser, cockier, shallower, former frat guys — with receding hairlines.

Through all this, Val realized how much she missed the little things; like the freedom of taking walks in the dry, Arizona sun. She longed for the feel of sun on her face, and the peace that came with a scenic stroll around town. Val could only really make time to go out and take walks on the weekends, while wasting five precious days under the harshest fluorescent lights imaginable.

She more than needed a change, her *soul* craved it. Val considered returning to university to score a Masters degree, but immediately realized that was a dumb and temporary solution. She tried applying to other jobs, but none of them even bothered to send her a rejection email. There were too many unemployed college graduates who would kill for even her shitty job.

A stray Facebook advertisement popped up on her screen one night for English teachers wanted abroad, and Val decided to apply. After impulsively completing the two-month online TEFL certification course and agreeing to teach anywhere, she accepted a position in Malaysia. It was *far*. Real *far*, but she would get free room and board and a slightly higher paying salary. With her bags packed, flights booked, cubicle empty, student loans paid off, and Mom, Abuela and Abuelo kissed goodbye, she left the day after her twenty-fourth birthday.

Val hoped to feel anything other than empty, other than hopeless, hoping to feel at least *something* once again. Right now though, in the back of this taxi, seemingly in the middle of nowhere, all she felt was dread. Was she making the biggest mistake of her life? Did she fly all the way across the world, just to realize there wasn't anything for her here either? She peered outside at the endless jungle again, and never longed so badly to see her desert home once more…

CHAPTER ONE

The crunching of gravel underneath the taxi tires startled Val awake again. She glanced outside the taxi window, which had pulled in front of a midsize, two-story family home that was surrounded by palm trees. Before she could even catch her breath the driver had already parked, popped open the trunk of his car, and unloaded half of her bags.

Val clamored out as quickly as her sleepy stupor would allow, and helped him with the rest of her luggage. After settling her fare she turned around, and jumped at the sight of a petite middle-aged Chinese woman; who had bolted out of the house and was now standing directly behind her.

"You must be Ms. Palacio." She greeted cheerfully; with shining, welcoming eyes that seemed to almost smile. "I'm Yeo A'i, my husband isn't home yet, but let me help you with your bags."

Before Val had the chance to politely protest, Yeo A'i had already seized two of her largest suitcases and started lugging them up the front lawn; with awe-inspiring strength for a woman who must weigh no more than ninety pounds. Val trotted along behind until they reached the front door. She scanned the interior of the house. There was a lot of space, also a lot of ongoing, unfinished... *projects*.

"You're taking my daughter's old playroom, she's studying to be a dentist in London right now." Yeo A'i called back to her, as Val navigated around a half-finished bird house, and an unopened beer brewing kit. She pointed to one of several pictures leading up the staircase. "That's her right there."

Val glanced up at the photo. Inside the frame a big-boned Chinese woman had her arms wrapped around Yeo A'i and an older gentleman she didn't recognize. They all seemed so happy in the shadow of big ben.

"Cool." Val replied agreeably.

"Yup, we're so proud of her. We visit her in the UK every summer, but she's been gone for a few years now, and this house just seems too lonely sometimes... when the Semua Tangan school posted that they needed a host family, I signed up." Yeo A'i let out a loud huff, as she lugged the suitcases up the last stair. "They're great really, best public school in all of Malaysia I think. It feels like only yesterday I was dropping off my daughter there for her first day of school..." The mother's eyes fell to the floor, and the smile receded from her face. Val guessed that the summer trip couldn't come soon enough.

They reached the second-story bedroom. The brightly painted, lime green door complimented a spacious and cozy inside. A trundle bed rested against the window facing the backyard, while a large armoire, drawers, and a desk took up the other side.

"It was so nice meeting you Ms. Val." Yeo A'i grunted, as she swung Val's things towards an empty corner. "The bathroom is right here to your left. Don't mind me... make yourself at home. You're *really* doing a service to the people of this community. It's so important for our kids to learn English nowadays — but you'll find that most people are pretty good at it already since we're a part of the commonwealth. Anyways, I'll be downstairs if you need anything." With that, Yeo A'i trotted back down the stairs.

Val immediately undressed. Fear had a stench, and she wondered if the putrid smell from her armpits would actually wash off the shirt she'd worn on both flights. Val barely had enough time to wash, dry off, and dress, before the sound of a loud knocking at the front door echoed up her room.

"*Valentina — Valentina —* Eh-hem... I mean Ms. Val! Come downstairs when you're ready!" Yeo A'i called.

Val rushed down the creaky stairs in her hurry. At the last step her eyes met a pair of large black ones. An Indian girl, roughly her age, sat alone at the end of the kitchen table; sipping a cup of steaming tea. She peered up for only a second when Val entered, before checking her watch.

"Ms. Palacio... I presume?"

Val nodded her head.

"I'm guessing you forgot about our 14:00 appointment for your tour of the school this afternoon?"

"Um... no!" Truth be told, it had slipped her mind completely. Val had actually been hoping to continue her nap from the taxi ride.

Yeo A'i glided in from the kitchen. "Oh come on Ms. Nadar, the poor girl just got here thirty minutes ago. You know how flights work, they're never on time."

Ms. Nadar rolled her eyes, before sipping the last of her tea. "Well... I guess there's no point in *wasting* another fifteen minutes of daylight!" She sassed, before standing up abruptly and marching towards the front entrance. Only turning back around briefly to bark, *"Are you coming?"* as she was nearly out the door.

Val jogged to catch up with her, reaching her nearly at the end of the front lot. They veered right, and walked briskly down a sleepy road.

"So... Ms. Palacio?" Ms. Nadar sneered. "That's your last name?"

Val knew exactly what Ms. Nadar was getting at. Her name may be Valentina Palacio, but it always shocked people when she told them anything other than that her name was simply *Val*. They probably assumed her full name was something like *Valerie Smith,* or *Valerie Johnson;* since her complexion resembled her biological father's more so than her mother's.

"Yup." Val muttered back, through gritted teeth.

"That might be a hard name for your students to pronounce... Why don't you choose something... *different?* Perhaps Ms. Pal?"

Val Pal. That didn't sound right... "How about they just call me Ms. Val? That's what Ms. Yeo A'i has already started calling me."

Ms. Nadar checked her watch and picked up the pace again. "Whatever..."

Val struggled to keep up with Ms. Nadar, even at times trailing half a block behind. Val wondered what exactly the chip on Ms. Nadar's shoulder might possibly be? She looked to be around Val's age, and hadn't even bothered to share her first name.

After fifteen minutes they reached a compound of several large, two-story buildings, with orange roofs and white walls.

"This is the front entrance of Semua Tangan. Most of our students get dropped off by their parents or the school bus here, so it can get very crowded." She motioned towards the roof. "Here in Malaysia, we take protecting our environment *very* seriously..." Ms. Nadar growled as she shot Val a stern side-eye. "Over the summer we installed solar panels along each of our buildings, *and* starting this year we're banning all zero-waste plastics." She snapped. "As Chair of the Environmental Protection board of this campus, I won't hesitate to hand out fines to *all* offenders — Students *and* Staff!"

Of course this woman was in-charge of something stupid like this... Val rolled her eyes.

"As Vice Chair of the Committee of Modest Attire, I should also tell you that what you're wearing is *not* school dress code. Just because we're a girls school doesn't mean anyone gets a pass. I guess you haven't read chapters two through five of the school handbook?"

Val actually had. Female teachers had to cover their shoulders, chests, and backs; as well as have skirts reach below the knee. Val had flipped through some of her teacher friends' social media accounts for a point of reference. At the moment though, she sported an ASU tank top, leggings, and flip-flops.

"I have — you don't need to worry about that. There's a whole suitcase of mine full of teacher clothes."

Ms. Nadar eyed Val disapprovingly once more. "Well, right now we're just taking a tour of the facilities and your classroom... but afterwards I'll need help setting up for the *facility-parent safety meeting* tonight." She checked her watch again. "Normally, I'd send you home to change into something more... *appropriate*... but there's no time. You'll just be the most under-dressed person there." Ms. Nadar sneered, before turning abruptly towards the front doors. "We've gotta keep moving... let's go now!"

Val bit back several insults, before begrudgingly following along.

They entered the first large school house building. Val peered around. The floor plan was simple, it jetted off to her right and left. Massive windows at the back revealed an extensive courtyard that only ended where the rainforest began.

"As you can see, behind me is the courtyard where the students play. The halls to our right are for our primary school students... but you won't be here much, so we won't bother with it today." She turned on her heel sharply and strutted down the left hand corridor. Val was just about to follow her, when something caught her eye...

At the back of the entrance hall, a semi-circle nook stuck out into the courtyard, surrounded by six, menacing statues. Each stood with a sense of... something. Authority maybe? Whatever it was, she was intimidated. The longer she stared, the more they seemed to tower over her... even though none of them were any bigger than herself.

The one nearest her she recognized right away, an Anglican priest. To his immediate right, a Buddhist, then Taoist monk. The next two were some different types of Indian Holy men, and on the opposite side, a shriveled, hollow robe... but for a single sickled hook protruding from the left sleeve; poking through a Songkok cap.

Her body froze in place. She felt a sharp gust of wind blow through the stale air... a strong set of chills made her shiver.

Then she stopped.

Val couldn't move.

Not a muscle.

A warm, fleshy hand slid up her neck, and seized the back of her head!

Val shrieked and whirled on the spot! She swore, screamed, cursed at Ms. Nadar... but surprisingly, she wasn't there... nobody was there... Instead, Ms. Nadar was already down the hall.

"What?" Ms. Nadar barked.

Val pointed a shaky, timid finger at the statues; all the while trying to regain composure.

"What... What... Who are those?"

Ms. Nadar stopped dead in her tracks. She glanced over her shoulder at Val. Her eyes shifted to the statues, and her already sour face grew even more tart.

"That? Ugh... those are just some busts the town council set up a few years ago." Ms. Nadar's dark face grew a few shades whiter, and her voice shook a bit. "The buildings in this compound had several uses before they came together as a public school. One was city hall for a bit, another a hospital, but most were houses of worship." She glanced nervously at the statues once more. "The big kids like to tell scary stories about this place to scare the little ones. They think it's funny... personally, I don't think it's funny at all." She swung her head around so violently that her head scarf nearly flew off. "We need to keep moving!"

Val shot the ring of statues one last suspicious look, before surmising that it was a lack of sleep playing with her mind just now. Val bit her lip, regretting her lapse of reality; then swirled around, trailing after Ms. Nadar once again.

The pair nearly jogged the entire perimeter of the school compound. Val raced through a tour of the whole place.,. the canteen, the courtyard, the nurses' station, the blacktop, the main playground; even the graveyard from colonial times that was kept quite nicely for its age. Ms. Nadar mentioned how she *alone* makes sure the gardening staff pays attention to this area. *"Someone has to respect the dead laid to rest here!"* It was Ms. Nadar's sole redeeming brag in Val's opinion.

They reached the entrance of a long hall that stood cross ways to the entrance foyer.

"These two corridors on the right are for our secondary school students." Explained Ms. Nadar, who strutted up the outside staircase. "You'll notice we have an extremely diverse student body. We have Malays of course, but also a large chunk of Hokkien Chinese and Tamil Indian pupils as well. There are so many different languages spoken, it's important to make sure everyone's mouths are as pure as their spirits..."

"Er... what?" Val mumbled.

"Your teenage students will play games with you. They'll say as many curse words in their own language as they can get away with before you catch on. I'll email you a list of words and phrases you should censor."

Val snickered under her breath. Learning a few new choice words to describe Ms. Nadar right now sounded pretty nice. "Okay." Val mumbled.

They reached the top of the steps, turned sharply to the left, and walked what Val assumed to be halfway down; before stopping in front of a doorway.

"This is your classroom." She said sharply, while jiggling a set of keys from her side purse. Ms. Nadar unlocked the door, swinging it wide open. Several rows of single unit desks faced towards a cleanly swept chalkboard; while a large, wooden teacher's desk with several scratches mirrored where the students sat.

"Most of our teachers have already finished decorating their classrooms. I finished two weeks ago... I guess you won't have time before classes start monday..."

Val seethed silently to herself, damning having to spend a single second more with this arrogant *puta*. She rolled her eyes towards her classroom, which did look pretty depressing. Empty classrooms always were.

She mosied inside. Though it felt kinda lonely it was at least bright. A wall of windows opened up to a view of the courtyard outside. She would stay after class the next few nights to make sure that the room wasn't so bare.

"Here—" Ms. Nadar called, while tossing the keys in Val's vicinity, but out of her grasp. They landed on the ground several feet away, forcing Val to squat down awkwardly to pick them up. "Principal Arif wanted me to give you these."

"Thanks..." Val enunciated angrily; rolling her eyes for the thousandth time this afternoon.

"We really should be meeting Ms. Mawar and Ms. Dian in the auditorium to set up for tonight." Ms. Nadar rushed once more. "It's already 4:30."

They shut and locked the door behind them, setting off to the building furthest to the back of the compound. Val was glad to be heading somewhere inside for a while. The late afternoon sun was right on her back. It'd be a while before she'd wear long pants again.

Two stout Malay women were already at the front of the auditorium, setting up the first row of folding chairs.

"Um... excuse me? Didn't you two read my email?" Ms. Nadar barked. "I explicitly said don't start setting up without me. This is all wrong... there's supposed to be a gap in the middle to make room for a row down the center. Is *that* what you call a gap? It's entirely too skinny — it must be wider!"

The two women locked eyes, in what Val knew to be the: *"are-you-fucking-kidding-me"* glance. The gruffer of the two responded.

"We do this every single year... trust me, we have this under control. Why don't you make yourself useful somewhere else..."

Ms. Nadar grabbed a chair from the pile, unfolded it, and placed it along one of the rows. "It looks like I'm needed here Ms. Dian. Ms. Val, what are you doing? Grab a chair."

Val shook her head. She exchanged cordial greetings with the two sane women, and began unfolding and lining everything up exactly according to Ms. Nadar's specific directions — which still left her unsatisfied. Several times, Ms. Nadar came over and corrected a chair she didn't think was straight enough, or placed a certain chair in another spot altogether. Val clearly made out every blood vessel in Ms. Dian's forehead, when Ms. Nadar blew out the speakers while fiddling with the microphone. Even after this mishap she ordered them to place an itinerary of the evening's speakers on every seat. Of which, there were only two. By the time seven o'clock rolled around, they had dusted, mopped, swept, re-mopped, and re-swept every single square inch of the auditorium. Val hardly had a chance to sit down and relax before the first set of parents trickled in through the doors.

Less than a third of the chairs they had set up were occupied by the time the first speaker, a petite, sixty-year-old woman, took the stage.

"Good evening," the woman started, with a steady, soothing voice, "my name is Principal Arif. Welcome to the start of the 2023 academic school year."

The crowd remained silent.

"I understand that most of you are the parents of our youngest primary school students... and some of you out there are feeling a bit nervous about sending your little ones off to school for the very first time. I want you all to know that your feelings are normal, and that everything will be okay."

Val took another peek around. Besides herself, Ms. Nadar, Ms. Mawar, and Ms. Dian, there wasn't any other facility there. This wasn't as *mandatory* as Ms. Nadar was making it out to be...

"But just to give each of you nervous parents some peace of mind, I'd like to invite our wonderful groundskeeper, Ms. Dian, up to the stage. She'll go over our safety protocol, our training, and even a few tips to remind your children in case of an emergency."

Ms. Dian grunted, as she heaved herself from her seat and made her way up to the stage. She greeted everyone curtly with a casual salute. "Eh-hem, I'll start with the fire escape routes..."

Val rested her head on the back of her seat and closed her eyes. All she wanted right now was to try out her new bed; with its cozy comforter and all those fluffy pillows. This was a waste of time. Kinda. She *should* probably know this stuff. She *should* probably be paying better attention, but god was this boring.

The hard-plastic chair she found herself slouching in was much less comfortable than even her economy seat. At this point though, her mind and body were so exhausted that she could have fallen asleep on a pile of legos.

She had almost sunk into a dreamy nap... when a strange, cool, thickness enveloped the room; almost as if a fog had drifted in through the front doors...

Then, at once, all the lights burst in a fizzle of sparks that rained down around them!

Darkness enveloped the whole auditorium!

Ms. Dian's microphone fell silent, and parents gasped in horror!

A lone light from the back of the auditorium made its way towards the center.

"Everyone, please stay calm and stay seated!" Principal Arif commanded, as she trotted forward once more. "This is probably some kind of glitch with our new solar panels we just had installed. Everyone just go ahead and pull your cell phone lights out... the most dangerous thing that could happen right now is that somebody's toes get squished."

Several more phone lights began lighting up the auditorium with a dim glow. Val preferred the new ambiance; the lighting before was too harsh on her eyes. She rested her head back once more, letting out a long sigh.

A strong smell of spices wafted over Val's nose, reminding her of the Desi Grill — an old Indian restaurant she used to visit back home with her friends... except the auditorium smelled even more pungent, and not anywhere as pleasant. She covered her nose with her tank top and sank back into her chair. Her muscles twitched, as a minor tickling sensation journeyed up her arm. Val guessed it was a mosquito. Val *hated* mosquitos. She swatted her shoulder and pulled out her phone light; but to her surprise, there was no bug or bite mark at all, there was only water...

Principal Arif's voice echoed throughout the hall once more. "We are fortunate to use buildings as historical as these to educate our pupils;

but though we try our best to maintain them, every now and then our electrical wires trip and our pipes break. You guys probably have heard about the *March disast*— I mean the *March incident* of last year... when several of our students didn't dispose of their feminine sanitary products correctly."

The sound of police sirens grew closer, 'til several men in navy uniforms burst through the doors, heavily lit flashlights in tow. The leader, a tall, broad-shouldered man no older than thirty took a swift look around the perimeter, before marching straight up to Principal Arif.

"We received a frantic call from one of your teachers — is everything alright?" The Officer queried quickly, but steadily.

"Yes, Yes, Officer Khoo, everything's quite alright... just a bit of a power outage that's all. Our Janitor Ms. Mawar has already gone up to the roof to check on it. Do you know who dialed 999?"

The Police deputy shook his head. "We're not quite sure, it sounded like a woman in great distress..."

At that moment, a very shaken up, very embarrassed Ms. Nadar peaked her head out from a nearby chair storage compartment — cell phone in hand. Her face was as white as a ghost's. Fat tears streamed down her cheeks.

Principal Arif rolled her eyes. "Alright then... well, I guess if that's all, you guys can go ahead and go. We're good here."

"We're required to at least do an inspection before we go. Do you want me to send my officers up there to help Ms. Mawar? Officer Ashraf and Officer Zikri are trained to respond to blackouts as well."

"That should be alright... but make sure they listen to Ms. Mawar though. She was trained over the summer specifically on how to repair our panels."

"Okay." He turned towards his deputies, and spoke in what Val assumed to be Malay. Two officers marched back out the front doors, while he inspected the auditorium.

The Officer's heavy footsteps grew nearer and nearer... he flashed his light over her row. Val sat up a little taller in her seat. He was a *cutie*. She wanted him to think she was one too. Val tried to smile flirtatiously... but was caught off guard by his torch!

She shielded her face with her hands, grimacing at its blaze. The Officer leaned forward towards her, lingering only for a second longer before taking note of her discomfort and moving on to the very back of the building.

"Damnit!" Val swore under her breath. She grit her teeth and stamped the floor in frustration.

"Alright, everything looks good here." The Officer surmised. "We'll go ahead and head out then."

"Well thank you for coming, we are so sorry to bother you tonight..." Principal Arif apologized, as she stared daggers at Ms. Nadar, who winced. "Have a safe evening."

"You as well." With that, the officers meandered out of the building. Val listened, as their cars' engines rattled slowly away.

The rest of the program was very rushed. Ms. Dian spoke loudly on stage to overcome the absence of the microphone; droning over the importance of fully-charged cell phones and safety buddies. Concerned parents scribbled down the last of all the advice, before scrambling out of the auditorium for the evening. Val, remembering the way here, made her own way home. The evening was just slightly cooler than the day, and a soft breeze brushed the sandy brown hair off her shoulders. Despite the nice night, Val couldn't shake the jumpiness. It was like it radiated off everyone in that auditorium... Val understood that parents always worried about their kids, but there was some other nervous energy that she couldn't quite shake... something that was enough to cause stone-faced Ms. Nadar to embarrass herself like that.

A smile crept over the corner of her mouth at the thought of it. *"Dumb bitch!"*

CHAPTER TWO

Her alarm went off promptly at six o'clock Monday morning.

Val wiped the sleet from her eyes, finding it hard to push herself up from the surprisingly soft mattress. She donned an outfit that would shut Ms. Nadar up, put on a full face of makeup, and set off down the dark, breezy street. Dragging two cases filled with classwork and decorations behind her.

Her set of clunky, ancient keys rattled against the lock as the door to her classroom swung open. Val hurriedly threw up several posters before setting out to organize the class booklets and worksheet. So far so good. She hadn't forgotten anything at home at least. That was a win. By the time seven thirty rolled around, Val noticed from the back windows of her classroom that a hoard of students and teachers had gathered in the courtyard. She quickly hurried outside, just in time for the Malaysian pledge of allegiance:

"We, her people, pledge our united efforts to attain these ends guided by these principles: belief in God, loyalty to king and country, the supremacy of the constitution, the rule of law, courtesy and morality."

Val giggled, as the younger primary students searched the crowd in vain hoping to find the words; while the older kids yawned and poked fun at one another. Val had begun to head back upstairs to her classroom, when a chorus of young girls singing stopped her in her tracks.

"*Saya melihat ke kiri saya, saya melihat kakak saya, dan tersenyum. Saya melihat ke kanan saya, saya melihat kakak saya dan tersenyum. Saya melihat di belakang saya, dan bukan kakak saya saya lihat. Tetapi bersama-sama, lengan dan lengan, kakak saya melindungi saya...*"

"*I look to my left, I see my sister and smile. I look to my right, I see my sister and smile. I look behind me, not my sister I see, but together, arm and arm, my sisters protect me...*"

An eerie chill ran down Val's neck, all the way to the base of her spine. It was as if the words floated like smoke, whispering wisps of warning into her ears... her trance was only broken by a frail hand grabbing her upper arm. Val flinched back reflexively!

"Oh dear! I didn't mean to startle you like that." A familiar voice apologized.

Val turned around, and to her horror her current boss — Principal Arif, stood looking slightly taken aback right in front of her.

"Oh my god—" Val swore. "I am so, so sorry... I didn't mean to—"

"It's alright." She assured her, while politely patting Val on the arm. "I should be the one apologizing. I meant to introduce myself at the assembly yesterday, but given all the commotion... I couldn't find you after." She stuck out her hand to shake. "I'm Principal Arif."

"I'm Valentin — I'm Ms. Palaci — Ms. Val..." She stammered.

"Well, Ms. Val, it's nice to finally meet you." To Val's shock, Principal Arif seized her hand and leaned in, 'til her face was only inches away from Val's. "*I want you to know... if you need anything, or need anyone to talk to, my door is always open...*"

"Yeah, yeah... sure." Val muttered uncertainty. "Absolutely... thanks."

"No problem." Principal Arif said softly. She squeezed her hand tightly, before letting go and strolling off in the opposite direction.

Val was caught in a sea of white headscarves and dark ponytails, as she made her way back to her class. Instinctively she shook her head in confusion, and sneered at whatever that just was...

Val reached her classroom. She took attendance, introduced herself, and set off officially teaching the day's classwork. It was weird now being on the other side of things, but Val took to it naturally. By the third period, she had the routine locked down. It wasn't until her fourth and final school period that Val found herself in a bit of trouble...

At 12:30 sharp, the bell rang for the second to last time. Val went through the motions once more. Everything seemed normal, natural even by now. The girls were humming away in their little work groups... until a group of three chatty girls beckoned her over to them. Val shuffled over to their desks.

"Yes, ladies?"

The girls giggled. *Why are they giggling?* The Tamil girl in the center spoke up first. "So... you're from America, right?"

Val scowled at the girl. "Is there a problem on your packet you need help with?"

BAM. Interrogation.

"Have you met any celebrities?"
"What's Ms. Val short for?"
"Why are you here?"
"I heard you say to Principal Arif that your name was Valentina Palacio... how do you spell that exactly?"
"Have you met Obama?"
"I heard there's a lot of guns in America?"
"Do you have a gun? Are you gonna shoot the bad kids?"
"Is your Instagram private? Never mind, just found it!"

Before Val realized it, the girl to the right of her had her phone pulled out, and Val's Instagram profile pulled up on its screen. Val tried to snatch the phone away, but missed.

"Excuse me — no phones in class!"

The girl's face froze. Her eyes narrowed in shock, as the phone nearly slipped through her slackened fingers. *"Oh my god..."*

"What? What is Eng Ki?"

Val struggled to seize the phone in vain, as each of them took turns passing it around, then gasping. She already knew what they had found...

"*You dated Killer Wiz Akeem?*" The littlest amongst the three whispered in awe.

By now the whole class was clamoring to get a look at Val's Instagram. It was true. She had met the infamous rapper Killer Wiz Akeem; or as she knew him — Samual, at a club in downtown Phoenix one night, and had gone out with him a few days later. Val only managed to get through one date though; the man's ego had no bounds. He was even more insufferable sober somehow. Though it was just one date, her tagged photos were now filled with TMZ and daily mail paparazzi clippings.

Val finally snatched it from one of their grimy hands. "You guys have thirty minutes to finish your packets and hand them in for me to grade!" She seethed, waving the phone in the air for its original owner, Eng Ki to see. "You can have this back at the end of class!"

The girls sat together in huddled masses, trying to conceal their excited whispers. By the time the bell rang for the last time each group hurriedly turned in their packets, packed up their bags, and rushed out the door. The sound of cars, buses, and bikes whizzing by slowly died away, and Semua Tangan fell into an eerie quiet. Val shook her head as she graded, noticing that her last class basically failed everything.

Hours passed. Val scurried around her classroom, hanging up the last of her decorations. She was right, they were cooler than Ms. Nadar's. They had to be. A *perra* like that probably didn't even hang up real decorations anyways — just whooping paddles and jars full of students' tears.

She had just tacked on her final posters, when a soft, giggling coo echoed into her room, followed by the pitter-patter of tiny, wobbly feet. Val craned her neck to take a look outside. To her surprise, a toddler, no more than a year old, was slowly waddling down the hallway.

"Awe..." Val cooed to herself, as she watched the naked baby pass by her classroom. She turned back around, waiting for his mother to pass next. But there was no one... in fact, there was no sound in this building at all. Except for the gurgling infant, and his soft, little steps.

Her instincts got the best of her. She stepped out into the hall and searched in the direction from which he came.

It was empty.

"That's strange..." Val mouthed to no one. An unnerving, flighty sensation began fluttering deep within her gut. One that traveled up her chest, causing it to tighten. *This feels weird...* she thought to herself... *this feels really, really weird...*

Val tried brushing these thoughts aside, hoping to regain control of her heightened nerves. She spun the other way, readying her body for the sweet relief of everything being alright. The child tucked away... sleeping... snuggled deep in his mother's arms... but boy was Val wrong.

Her eyes reached the other end of the corridor, and her butterflies exploded like a grenade — to her horror, the baby was lying limp on the floor... his eyes empty and soulless!

Val didn't feel her legs move as they bolted down the hall, and didn't hear her voice scream as it cried out in horror. Her knees hit the floor as she reached the child and tried to shake him awake as gently as possible. Her fingers reached for his neck to check his pulse, but a door slammed somewhere in the building. She turned her head for just a second, before returning to the child...

but he was different...

No — he was dead! Not just recently dead, long dead! His flesh was grey... and rotten!

Val shrieked. She scrambled backward on her hands and knees. Out of the corner of her eye, a gray mass growled softly, but threateningly in front of her. She dared a glimpse in its direction...

Though most of it was shrouded in shadow, she could just make out its faded silhouette; which prowled back and forth on skinny legs that seemed adapted to anything... walking, climbing, *hunting*... More feral human than deranged beast, yet neither description fit quite right. It seemed to be something altogether entirely distinct, as if it came from another world... The only part of it that cut through the darkness were its two ruby eyes, each the size of pool balls. They burned like embers, as they stalked Val maliciously...

"Holy shit!" Val swore. "Oh... oh my god! Umm..." Val wished beyond anything that some instinct would kick in, but nothing. Literally. Nothing. She just froze.

But something did kick in. Val felt the presence of someone rushing up behind her. It was equally as frightening, but something felt different... she dared a glimpse over her shoulder... it was an Imam, dawning a familiar robe and cap... he opened his mouth. His words echoed louder than any megaphone.

"BISMILLAH!"

The man was still shouting as Val passed out onto the floor...

CHAPTER THREE

"*Walao Eh!* Oh dear — are you alright? Wake up!"

Val's eyes flickered open. Her body lay flat on the floor, except for her chest and torso, which was being cradled by a hearty woman. Something lurched in her stomach. Val spun around and threw up all over the floor.

"Oh no!" The woman cooed. She patted Val on the back softly. "It's okay dear — just let it out. It happens to the best of us!"

Val hurled until all that was left was a terrible taste in her mouth. Enough of Val's strength returned for her to open her eyes, and identify her rescuer as Ms. Mawar, the janitor. "The baby…" Val groaned.

"Ahh — so that's what *she* got you with. My first hallucination was a wounded dog… scared me for months after. Oh you poor thing… most of the time *she* waits at least a couple weeks to pull something like this!"

"Who's *she*? What do you mean? *She?*"

Ms. Mawar paused. A *weird* pause. One of those pauses where you're trying to figure out how to explain something that's really different. "That's a very good question… no one really knows… Some say *she's* a demon. Others say a million other types of vengeful spirits. The only thing we know is a very old, indigenous Malaysian, Orang Asli folk tale…

Legend has it that several thousands of years ago, a woman ate a mango so delicious, that she cried bitterly when she finished it. The woman planted it's seed in her groove under a full moon, using her own tears to water it. At the same time, a volcano far, far away erupted, causing the winds to carry ash to her plot of land. For some reasons lost to us, what emerged from the ground was not a mango tree, but a dangerous creature... The villagers tried to kill it, but the monster proved too powerful! It was too late... the land was cursed! The Orang Asli got together and decided it was best to leave her alone, so they packed up and left. Millenia later, as new people started arriving, they ignored the Orang Asli, and cut down the surrounding trees — building mosques, temples, hospitals, city halls, and churches. Eventually these groups of buildings became Semua Tangan Primary and Secondary School."

Val tried to push herself up, but her arms were too wobbly. "The... the man... there was a man here... an Imam? Where is he? Where'd he go?"

"Ahhh — You saw Imam Haruun. He's over there, well, his body's over there to be specific, buried in the graveyard along with all the other Holy men who used to serve here. You're really lucky he reached you in time — *she* could have really ruffed you up."

"But I just saw him! What do you mean he's *buried?*"

"Well, you know... you probably just saw his spirit. All the Holymen's spirits roam these halls, they're kind of like this school's protectors. If you stay late enough around here like me and Ms. Dian, you see them all from time to time. It's interesting he was all the way over here, I normally see him in the school canteen." She pointed towards where the kids gathered for lunch. "It used to be the mosque he presided over. They've done a lot of renovations since then, but you can still see the remains of the minaret in the corner over there."

Val didn't even bother to glance toward where Ms. Mawar was pointing. "Does everyone here know about... *all this?*"

"Oh sure — why do you think everyone was so quick to leave today? Even the teachers? If there're student groups that stick around after class, we make sure they leave before dark. The only people who will stay are me, Ms. Dian, and Principal Arif, and we never travel around here at night by ourselves. Did Ms. Nadar give you any sort of warning the other day?"

"No, she didn't..." Val seethed as she reflected back on the tour, remembering just how much of a little bitch Ms. Nadar had been. It all made sense. Val peered up at the sky, which was turning pink by now. "What time is it?"

"It's almost six o'clock dear." She grabbed under Val's arm. "Come on... let's get you home. You're staying with Yeo A'i right? She's not too far from here. You can ride on the back of my bike. I should make it back in time to help Ms. Dian before dark. Some of the first years thought it would be funny to throw their suckers down the toilet, and now... let's just get going."

Ms. Mawar flung Val's arm over her shoulder, and dragged her outside to the school parking lot. Val mounted the back of Ms. Mawar's motorbike, and less than two minutes later they were pulling up in front of Val's home. By that time Val managed to gather the rest of her strength, unlock the front door, and make it upstairs to her room. She stripped her clothes off, grabbed her pajamas lying on the floor from the night before, and crawled into her comfy bed, hoping for nothing more than a dreamless sleep.

...

The next few days Val felt as if she were experiencing an extended hangover. One even worse than the night after she had gone out with Killer Wiz Akeem. Her head throbbed, bright lights burned her eyes, and her stomach wanted nothing to do with food. She made it through the school days by taking as many aspirins as the bottle would allow, and by keeping a small trash can under her desk. Her classroom might be decorated better than Ms. Nadar's, but Ms. Nadar's definitely smelled better.

Most people assumed she had the tourist bug, but several seemed to recognize her symptoms as if they personally knew her horrific panic. One of her students, the shy, Malay girl, from the gang of three that gave her a hard time her first day offered to help pass out her classwork. The cafeteria ladies gave her an extra helping of Laksa, and a kind religious teacher from a few classrooms down offered to pay for a can of diet cola at the vending machine.

Val considered going back home to Arizona, but ultimately landed on the side of staying. She committed to teaching for a year, and Val hated nothing more than going back on her word. It was one of her most important personal vexations. But more than that, with each passing day her symptoms waned, while the memories of her desperation to get out and leave her old life behind grew stronger. Nightmares of the monster were soon replaced by waking terrors of her old bitchy boss and terrible commute, and soon her health returned in full. But every day after the final bell tolled, Val never stuck around.

One sunny Saturday afternoon, a cheery Yeo A'i poked her head into Val's room, insisting that Val accompany her to a grocery store. Val found herself mindlessly roaming the supermarket shelves, as Yeo A'i chatted away.

"You know, if you ever get bored, Penang Island is only an hour bus ride away from our village. I could even give you a ride if you'd like. There's so much to do — there's the beach, hiking in the rainforest-covered hills, trying all the food and cafes... shopping!"

"Mhm," Val mumbled, as she observed a block of cheese intently. "Oh — yeah, that sounds nice."

"It's wonderful really, my daughter and I used to take trips there every weekend." Yeo A'i recalled while peering around the store shelves wistfully; as if she were hoping a young version of her daughter would round one of them. "Oh, over there—" She thumped Val hard on the shoulder, then pointed towards a man a few meters away, who was inspecting a carton of milk like he had never seen one before. "That's Mr. Elmsworth, you've probably seen him around Semua Tangan." She waved her arm around in the air emphatically. "Mr. Elmsworth — *Mr. Elmsworth!*"

Mr. Elmsworth peered up from the milk towards their direction. By now Yeo A'i was dragging Val over towards the middle-aged, plump man, who appeared nothing short of *very* annoyed. "Yes?" He drawled.

"Mr. Elmsworth — Hi — Hello!" Yeo A'i stuck out her hand to shake. "I'm not sure if you remember me, but I'm one of your former students' moms. Do you remember a young lady by the name of Yeo Seng? She was one of your students around ten years ago. You'll probably remember she won the Borgory creative writing award for her ess—"

"No, I don't remember." The man replied curtly.

"Well..." Yeo A'i chuffed, "anyways, I just wanted to come by and introduce one Semua Tangan teacher to another." She pushed Val forward gruffly. "This Is Ms. Val, she's teaching the lower secondary form one students." Yeo A'i giggled to herself. "You teach the form two English classes, correct? The grade above Val? I'm so silly for assuming that you two haven't met yet, surely you have."

Val had actually seen this man around school. He'd stuck out to her since he was the only other American teaching at Semua Tangan. He had also stuck out because she had caught him getting into a full-on brawl with the vending machine the other day.

"It's nice to meet you sir, where in the States are you from?"

"Pennsylvania." He replied abruptly, not even bothering to ask her state. By now a short, plump, Malay woman, along with a pre-teen-aged boy had arrived. Both scowled, looking equally put-off by the exchange taking place in front of them.

Yeo A'i stuck her hand out for the young boy to shake. "Hello young man, you guys must run into the parents of your father's students all the time. Nice to meet you, your dad taught my daughter in school when she was about your age."

The preteen gazed up at Yeo A'i aimlessly. Val had never seen a boy so closely resemble his father.

"Well... we best be going." Yeo A'i rushed. "Right Val? It was nice to see you sir." Val felt a push from behind her back, and the two of them hurried forward together towards the check out aisles.

The remainder of the weekend was spent going on long walks with Yeo A'i around town, as she mulled over several midlife crises. Of starting an athleisure fashion line for middle-aged women — taking scuba diving lessons — selling her house and convincing her husband to retire, so they could move to the UK to be with their daughter. Val didn't mind listening to her go on and on one bit. She just appreciated having so much free time again, and spending so much of it outdoors, walking with a friend. Back in Arizona at the bank there was never any free time. Everyone would get to work as the sun came up, eat their meals quietly in their cubicles, and then leave. No goodbyes. No adios. No see-you-tomorrows. There was a *"fuck you Shannon, I quit"* once. But besides that, nothing.

Val got to walk to and from school every day now, with plenty of daylight remaining. Her classroom was always nice and sunny, and she more than relished her fifty-minute lunch break in the courtyard. Though the bench she sat at was not an ideal place for grading class-work; or for streaming TV shows.

"For god's sake!" Val swore under her breath, damning the glare that kept getting in the way of her: *"twelve facts you didn't know about ducks"* youtube video. Val pulled the AirPods out of her ears in frustration and shoved them into her skirt pocket, huffing as she took in the view from her spot. There was a soccer game, some cartwheels, a group of gossips... typical kid stuff. Out of the corner of her eye, Val noticed the religious teacher sitting on a bench not too far away; fanning away beads of sweat that were dripping down her cheeks.

"Do you want to sit over here?" Val suggested, while motioning towards her own bench. "Some of the AC from inside is leaking out?"

A look of relief swept over the young woman's face. "Yes — sure!" Val scooted over to accommodate her. "It's just way too hot, I was dying over there."

"Thanks again for the soda the other day. It helped my stomach settle."

"No problem, we've all been there..." Her eyes drifted out to a group of girls trying to choreograph some sort of dance, then dropped to her lap. "*She* seems to latch onto the newest faculty members. I remember my first few months here were not my best..."

Val was both startled and relieved by the girl's forwardness. "What... what happened? If you don't mind me asking..."

"No, no, it's okay." She sighed. "We should be sharing our stories with each other... It was two years ago. I had just started here, and for some reason I kept feeling like I was being watched or something... I thought it was my mind playing tricks on me, since I wasn't used to getting up and giving lectures to my students... but the feeling just stuck with me... A few weeks later, I was walking out to my motorbike after school one day, when for some reason I just started running as fast as I could! I don't know why, but I just felt like I had to for the life of me!" She paused to take another shaky breath. "Then I felt something tackle me to the ground, and there *she* was, on top of me!" The woman pulled back her sleeve, revealing several deep, jagged scars that ran all the way up her arm. "But lucky for me one of the Holy men drove *her* off."

"Which holy man helped you?"

"I'm pretty sure it was Granthi Balnoor. What about you?"

"I got Imam Haruun"

"I see... after that, I just try to keep an eye out around this place... anyways, besides what happened, how has Semua Tangan been overall? Who have you met so far?"

"I've met Principal Arif, Ms. Mawar, Ms. Dian, Mr. Elmsworth..."

"A true genius, that man."

Val chuckled. "I also met Ms. Nadar—"

The young woman gagged. "Ugh, she keeps lecturing me on the dress code. Something about my hijab not being a *'neutral color.'*"

"She gave me my first tour of Semua Tangan."

"That's ruff... I'm Amina by the way."

"Valentina — but everybody just calls me Val."

"Nice to meet you... You know, in secondary school, there really aren't very many teachers our age. Normally during lunch I just sit out here and play games on my phone. How old are you?"

"Me? I'm twenty-four."

"Really? Me too! What's your number? Do you have plans for Saturday night? My husband's having a birthday party — if you're free please come!"

Val's heart fluttered in her chest. She was starting to worry if she'd ever make friends here. "Yeah, yeah I'm free... thanks."

The two exchanged numbers and chatted for a bit longer until the bell rang, forcing them back to their jobs. It'd been a while since Val had found someone she'd naturally clicked with so well. It felt like a weight had been lifted, as she realized people here weren't all that different from those back home...

The weekend rolled around, and the whole of Saturday Val fretted over what exactly she should wear. Crop top with mini skirt? To clubish. Heels? Definitely not. Val hated heels. Especially *these* heels. She should donate them — or burn them, fuck it, right? New country, New Val... denim dress? Why'd she even pack that... Amina swore up and down that it'd be a super casual event, but Val overthought every little detail regardless. Around 7:30, Yeo A'i offered to drop her off at the address Amina had sent her.

"Message me when you wanna be picked up." Yeo A'i called from the window of her car.

She drove away, leaving Val in front of a very cute, single-storied home; with a well-manicured front garden. Several cop cars and bikes with sirens littered the driveway and edges of the street, while lively music from inside wafted out through the open windows.

Val took a deep, shaky breath. No matter how old she was, walking into a party full of strangers by herself would always be terrifying. Her legs were beginning to feel weak. Val made her way inside before her body completely gave out.

Was there a doorbell? Should she knock? Should she just walk in like she saw a few other people do before her? Would that be rude? Or weird since she didn't really know them all that well yet? There were shoes everywhere, littering the front porch. *Should she go ahead and start taking her shoes off now?*

Before Val had a chance to decide, the door swung open. A tall, dark, thirty-ish-year-old Tamil man answered, dawning a children's party hat. The man looked nothing short of utterly confused.

"Ummm... can I help you?"

"Hi, um — I'm Val, uhhh, Valentina! I work with Amina at Semua Tangan? I don't know if she told you or not, but she invited me to—"

"She's never mentioned you?" He growled suspiciously. His face grew more stern. "This is the first time I've heard about this? I'm sorry, but what was your name again? Valentine... Valentino? Is that what you said?"

Each of Val's cheeks were now hot enough to set a tea kettle on. There was no stopping her voice from cracking now.

"It's um — Valentina — Valentina Palacio? Val—

"Jano stop that!" A familiar voice nagged. Amina appeared behind the door, and thumped the man hard on the chest as he chuckled to himself. "I'm so sorry about my husband's rude manners, I told him ten times that you were coming!" Amina slapped his arm again. "What were you thinking?"

Jano had doubled over in laughter at this point. He tried to catch his breath, but failed. "Hey, hey look, I'm sorry." He placed his hand to his heart and bowed. "I couldn't help myself... by the way I'm Jano—"

"It's too late for that — Just go!" She ordered, pushing him down the hall. Jano scattered, giggling to himself the whole way.

Amina grabbed Val by the shoulders. "I'm so sorry, are you alright? You poor thing, I can't believe he would do that. What am I saying... he's such an idiot... of course I can believe it. Let's get inside before the mosquitoes find us."

Val barely had enough time to remove her shoes before Amina dragged her through the front door. She caught brief glances of the wedding photos lining the hall walls, but that was about all she could make out. Amina was lugging her down the corridor like a three year old would a naked barbie; only stopping when they reached the kitchen. Several groups of twenty and thirty-year-olds clustered together in small groups all around the house, stretching into the backyard.

"Everyone — everyone please!" Amina announced. Val knew what was coming next. She tried to compose herself as quickly as possible, but—

"This is my friend Valentina, the new English teacher from the US at Semua Tangan. She just got here a few weeks ago, and doesn't really know anybody yet, so please... don't be a *jerk* — like my *clown* of a *husband* — and make her feel welcome!"

Amina pulled Val over to an area of the kitchen where several snacks had been arranged. "We have a halal and non-halal food section." She gestured over towards two pitchers. "The left is virgin, while the right has a bit of rum mixed in — would you like a cup? Feel free to go ahead and serve yourself."

"Thank you." Val rushed, feeling relieved to have something to calm her nerves, even if just a little.

Amina and Val made the rounds. Val learned quickly that Jano was the town Chief of Police, and many of the party attendees were his policemen and women along with their spouses. Val listened politely to what seemed like a million different embellished cop stories. One man single-handedly stopped a bank robbery. Another saved a whole family from drowning. After an hour of constant bragging and exaggerating, Val and Amina took a seat a little ways from the TV.

"Valentina — right?" A Chinese woman to the right of her asked.

"Yup — and you?"

"Tan Soan." she replied.

The pregnant lady to the left of Val stuck out her hand as well. "I'm Parani."

"Nice to meet you." Val said for the thousandth time that night. "How far along are you?"

"Twenty-seven weeks." The lady groaned, while learning her head back on the shoulder of a girl sitting on her other side. "But I'm ready to get this baby out now. I keep begging and begging my OB to go ahead and induce me, but she's being such a stubborn bitch about it."

"For the last time — would you rather have a bit of temporary incontinence for a few more months, or *not* have your baby's lungs develop all the way?" The girl who had Parnini's head on her shoulder scoffed.

"And how many times do I have to tell YOU I would rather not have my baby's lungs develop all the way — now let's do this!" She commanded while grabbing a pillow and slapping her arm — signaling for an IV to be put in. "The cream you gave me for my diaper rash is not strong enough — I'm tired of this!"

Val turned to the OB. She looked young... maybe even younger than herself.

"So you're an OB? How old are you? If you don't mind me asking."

"I'm twenty-seven." The girl replied quietly. "I just graduated six months ago — Parani is one of my first patients."

"That's really cool... um... your skin is amazing, do you have a routine? I didn't catch your name by the way."

"Oh sorry... I'm Nur." She squeaked, while performing the smallest, most timid wave Val had ever seen. Pulling her hand back so quickly afterwards Val wasn't even sure if she had really waved at all. "No, I don't do any sort of skincare routine. Just put on sunscreen in the mornings and use a face mask sometimes."

"That's a routine!" Tan Soan snapped.

"Technically... but it's not like she's doing a fifty-step process every night or something!" Amina sassed. She pointed back at Nur. "We're actually sisters."

Val flinched back in her seat, somewhat shocked. She examined Nur up and down, and then Amina; reasoning that on closer inspection if it weren't for their vastly different auras, this might not have been such a surprise. They shared a few features. Both had similar noses, brows, and skin tones, but Amina was much more similar to herself; being on the more slender side of five-foot-five. Nur was a fair bit shorter, and rounder, but she did have very nice skin. If Val would have guessed, she would have pinned Nur as the younger sibling.

Val heard the front door swing open, then close. A curious Jano went to go inspect who'd just arrived. He peered down the hall, and a wide grin swept across his face. A few seconds later the officers in the kitchen began squinting over his shoulder, chanting in unison: *"Khoo Hun Chhiau! Khoo Hun Chhiau!"*

The ladies around her shared disbelieving looks. They swirled around in their own seats to get a better look at what was going on.

"There's no way..."

A collective awe was spreading through the party attendees.

"What is it?" Val pressed.

"He never shows up to stuff like this." Nur whispered.

"His cousin works with me at city hall, and she said he didn't even show up to her baby's Cekur Rambat hair shaving ceremony last summer." Tan Soan gripped, as she turned to Val. "It's a big deal here — I didn't hear the end of it."

Val craned her neck to see who exactly everyone was making a fuss about. To her surprise, it was the deputy who had responded to the school that very first night; still dressed in his uniform. He scanned the room slowly — his eyes shifting from person to person — 'till they found her. They lingered for a moment, then moved on when he realized she was staring back at him. Val felt her cheeks grow hot once more.

Amina pushed herself up from her seat and headed over towards the crowded kitchen. She returned a few moments later, dragging a very cheery Jano and Khoo Hun Chhiau behind her.

"Give him a second to catch up with the boys." Jano protested.

"Khoo Hun Chhaiu already spends too much time with *"the boys"* every day — in and out." She turned sternly to Khoo Hun Chhiau. "You need to meet some *new* people."

Khoo Hun Chhiau and Jano shared a look, which Val guessed meant that protesting was futile. Khoo Hun Chhiau sighed, before greeting the confused women sitting around him.

"Um, hello, I'm Khoo Hun Chhiau." He mumbled.

"We know." Parini sassed. "Your name was just chanted for like a minute straight."

"Also you went to school with my twin brother. I've already met you a thousand times." Tan Soan sassed.

"Err, right..." Khoo Hun Chhiau grumbled.

"Anyways," Amina cut in, "this is my sister Nur, and this is my fellow teacher Val."

"I think I saw you the other day at Semua Tangan, during the assembly blackout." Val added.

"You were there when it happened?" Jano asked, looking surprised. "Tell me, did anything *spooky* happen?" He mocked, while wiggling his fingers in front of his face.

Amina nudged him in the side, hard enough to make him double over.

Val recalled that night. That strange, strange night... it was too strange. Strange enough to dampen the mood. "Mmm nope... not really."

"Really?" Jano replied. "My officers must be a bunch of babies then. They were shaking in their boots by the time they made it back to the station."

Amina elbowed him in his ribs a second time, then turned back towards the rest of the group. "So — Khoo Hun Chhiau, Val here is from the United States. Jano tells me you've been all over the world nearly. Have you ever been there before?"

Khoo Hun Chhiau shook his head. "No, I haven't."

"Which state?" Tan Soan pried.

"Arizona. Phoenix, Arizona."

"Is that close to New Mexico?" Khoo Hun Chhiau chimed in.

"Yeah... it is. It's the state next to mine. How'd you—"

But before she had the chance to finish her question two officers started fighting in the kitchen. Something about who *actually* dug the mayor out of a landslide. Whatever it was they knocked a bunch of food over. Amina jumped up to attend to the situation, and the conversation amongst the group shifted. They all chatted for several more hours 'till the party started to thin. Her group casually moved into the front lawn.

Val was saying her goodbyes for the night to Amina and Jano, when Nur pulled her aside.

"So, umm..." she started quietly, forcing Val to lean in closer just to hear her. "We all meet at six thirty every Wednesday night here at Amina's — just us girls." She nodded towards the group they had been chatting with. "You should join us sometime."

Val nodded her head. "Yeah, sure — Sounds good."

"Cool — well... have a nice rest of your night."

"Yeah, you too." Val said brightly as she waved and turned around towards the road. It was a calm evening. Val had already GPS'ed the way back to Yeo A'i's home and decided that since she wasn't wearing her devil heels, she could just enjoy the nice breeze and walk back. If the roads got too dark, she figured her phone light should be enough...

"Hey — *Hey!*" A deep voice called from behind. Val ignored it — until the presence of someone running up behind took her by surprise. She turned around, to find Khoo Hun Chhiau jogging towards her.

"What're you doing?" He demanded.

A prickle of nerves jabbed her neck. Val realized she felt a little intimidated. His stature was imposing as is, but even more so now that he was talking down to her, like she were a child.

"I'm going home." Val said shortly. "What're *you* doing?"

He ignored her question and peered over her shoulder. "Is your car parked over there?"

"I don't have one." Val said matter of factly.

"Is someone giving you a ride?"

"No."

"Then how are you getting home?"

"I was gonna walk..."

"Right now?" Khoo Hun Chhiau pried. "You're staying at Yeo A'i's right? That's over two kilometers away! You need to ride with someone."

"What's the worst that can happen? Is a monitor lizard gonna steal my purse?" She joked nervously. "I think I'll be fine." Val turned on her heel, but Khoo Hun Chhiau caught her by the arm.

"There are tigers in these hills who hunt at night... I'll walk you home."

Val scoffed at the finality in his voice. It's the twenty-first century — he should know better than to talk to her like *that*. Who was this guy anyways? Could she even trust him? Val peered him over once more, taking note of his navy police uniform that blended in with the darkness. The last thing she wanted was to become tiger food...

"Fine." Val agreed. She took the lead, strutting off into the night.

They walked together silently for several minutes, occasionally ducking and weaving through rogue trees or overgrown roots. The stars twinkled clearly, while the wind blew softly through the low hanging branches. The only complaint Val had was the growing number of mosquitoes she could feel buzzing around her.

Val slapped her arm. "Damn — *seriously!*"

"Do you have any bug spray with you?"

She did not, and she didn't put any on earlier either. It would've clashed with her perfume. "No..."

Khoo Hun Chhiau frowned. "It's important you wear bug spray here, especially at night. The mosquitoes could be carrying dengue — or malaria."

Val didn't know what to make of this stony-faced, monotone man. He had barely spoken to anyone, let alone herself all night... but now he had somehow found the nerve to be telling her what to do? Where to walk?

Val changed the subject. "So... how'd you know about New Mexico? That's not a state most people would be able to recognize outside the US?"

"The TV show. *Breaking Bad.*"

"You watch Breaking Bad?"

Even through the darkness, Val could see Khoo Hun Chhiau's face turning red. "Ya." He mumbled, like this was the most embarrassing secret in the world. "A while ago."

Val kicked a rock down the street. She was never able to get too into the show, since it was too sexual and violent for her tastes; but to say Val's Abuela was hooked would be a *gross* understatement. Every day, when Val would return home from college, she'd find her grandma watching obsessively. The sly old woman would always end up convincing Val to view along though, by threatening to take the car they shared at the worst times.

"So... a cop who watches Breaking Bad... who's your favorite character?"

He paused. For a moment, Val considered that maybe he hadn't heard the question. But after several drawn-out seconds, Khoo Hun Chhiau made up his mind.

"Walter White... and Gus."

"Why's that?"

He took several more moments to respond. Val was starting to pick up on the trend.

"The other characters, Jessie, Saul, Tico — police officers catch guys like that all the time... they brag to anyone who cares to listen, and more than a few who don't. Even the ones who want to be known, the ones who think that their dangerous reputations will scare the community into not messing with them, end up behind bars in the end... but we don't catch the guys who don't brag. The guys who are smart enough to put their wits before their pride. Walter White had a lot of pride, but he had more common sense than ego. The same goes for Gus. When guys like that make mistakes, they aren't even on our radar, so we don't notice." He peered up towards the black sky. "They're only caught by us once in a blue moon..."

Val's jaw hung open – until a mosquito flew inside. She spit it out, hawking all over the sidewalk. Val had asked that question to several men over the past few years, and had never gotten such a layered response. Most of the time, they would just say Heisenberg was a badass.

"Ahhh, I see..." Val replied casually. She glanced down at his hand, noticing none of his fingers contained rings. "So... ummm, does your girlfriend? boyfriend? Like breaking bad as well?"

"No." He said bluntly. "We do things very differently here than in the west. I come from a *very* traditional Peranakan family. Our marriages are still arranged by our parents." He surveyed his surroundings once more, and his tone grew even more serious. "As a police officer, I am held to an even higher moral standard. It would be... frowned upon... if I were seen out with a woman who was not a family member."

"Ah... so if someone saw you walking me home right now, it'd be pretty scandalous." Val joked.

Khoo Hun Chhiau glared down at her, stone-faced.

The two continued in silence, 'til they rounded Yeo A'i's street corner. Val pulled her keys out as they reached the front door, and peered up at her escort once more.

"Well, thanks for walking me home." Val said cheerfully. "I think Yeo A'i might be asleep, but let me see if I can grab her car keys and drop you back off at your car or something—"

"There's no need." He cut her off. "I'll be fine. Just go ahead and get inside."

"Okay..." With that, she unlocked the door and entered, closing it softly behind her. Val ran to the window; watching as Khoo Hun Chhiau walked back down the street, until the darkness swallowed him whole.

CHAPTER FOUR

The next school week was busier than the ones before. Val regretted assigning book reports.

"Can we *please* work in groups of three?" The Tamil girl that sat in the center of the gang of three cried; who Val now knew as Wani. The girls grabbed onto each other's arms, and scooted their chairs and desks together.

Val had anticipated these three putting up a fight. "This is a project for two people, and—"

"But there are nineteen people in this class, and everyone else has a partner – look!" Wani begged.

Val rolled her eyes, and peered around her classroom. Sure enough, everybody else had already paired up. The three girls were the only ones left.

"You don't want to single *one* of us out — do you? Wouldn't it be cruel... so, so cruel, to make *one* of us do the *whole* project by ourselves — while everyone else only has to do *half* the work — for the same grade? Wouldn't it be—"

"Fine!" Val conceded. "Just... make sure you actually focus."

"Yes!" Eng Ki cheered, while trading high fives. The girls had worn Val down. That was victory enough.

"Don't worry, we'll do so, *so* good on this project. This — um... um..." Wani turned to whisper towards her friends. "What's this again?"

"It's a book report." Eng Ki whispered. *"Charlotte's Web."*

"For our book report on *Charles Webb!*" Wani boasted "The man, the myth, the hero among the weak!"

Both girls elbowed her to shut up, but by that time Val had already made her way back to her desk — the one with all the scratches. So many scratches... that *was* weird... why would a desk be this scratched up? Val racked her brain for some reason... any reason that would explain why, but was interrupted by a soft *"Ehm."*

Val peered up, it was the quietest girl from the gang of three, Zara. The poor girl was shaking, consumed by a fit of nerves. Val couldn't help but recall a chihuahua.

"I'm sorry..." She sniffled softly, with her head bowed. Val noticed a few tears peeking out from the edges of her eyes. "I forgot my book... I'm really — really — really — *sorry!*"

"It's okay — you can use mine for today." Val cooed. It was little Zara who had helped Val out in class when she was recovering from the monster's attack. Ever since then, Val had grown a soft spot for the shy, timid girl. Her other two friends were much more outgoing and obnoxious, but Val could tell the anxieties of pre-teendom affected Zara more deeply. "Just bring my book back when the bell rings."

The book fumbled in her trembling hands. *"Thank-k you!"*

After an hour class was dismissed for the day. Val packed up her belongings, and scurried out the door. The parking lot was a circus — one of the buses had a flat tire. Figures. Too many potholes in these roads. Val brushed up against several idling teachers and students as she made her way through the packed front entrance hall.

Val had walked half way across to the front doors, when something stopped her... almost as if someone had grabbed her from behind. The sensation sent a chill down her spine. She spun around on the balls of her feet, 'til she found herself facing the six statues...

Val shifted her eyes across the room. Everyone was acting normal... students and teachers were chatting, laughing, even playing children's hand clapping games. It was as if only Val was experiencing any weird sensation...

What the fuck is going on... Val thought to herself...

The statues stood there, together, towering over her. The longer she stared, the larger they grew... her head felt more and more tension —

almost like a firm hand was pushing it down — she tried to fight it, tried to move, tried to *scream*... but her body was beginning to fold. Her eyes were now staring at the floor.

"Ms. Palacio?" Principal Arif's voice pried...

Whatever seized her let go. Val unfolded her back, and stood up straight.

"Is everything alright?" Principal Arif pried again...

Val tried to steady her nerves. "Um — yeah, yeah... everything's fine... why do you ask?"

Principal Arif didn't look convinced. "I heard you had a little run in, with..." she glanced around, making sure none of the students were eavesdropping, before whispering, "with *her*, a few weeks ago..."

Val was caught off guard. "Oh — uh, yeah, I did."

"I'm sorry about that." She cooed, as she glanced around once more. "I'm guessing you wish someone would have warned you sooner... as an administration, we really haven't figured out yet how to prepare our new teachers for it."

"Really..." Val pressed.

"Yes really. Trust me, when I started here, I went through the same thing you did... it was terrifying. I couldn't sleep for weeks." She turned around, and pulled up her shirt; revealing a single, jagged scar, that ran all the way down her back. *"She* gave me this as I was exiting the bathroom."

Val nearly fainted on the spot. Scars were not her thing, any kind of wound or cut made her instantly squeamish. She'd make a terrible nurse. "I'm — I'm so sorry..."

Principal Arif lowered her shirt, and turned back around. "It's alright... if you would have asked me back then though, I'd have disagreed. I was furious that no one had warned me beforehand. I vowed to make sure every new teacher arrived, informed and prepared to—"

"Then why didn't you warn me?" Val seethed. "I met you the very first day of school, before any classes had even started! Why didn't you warn me then? Why didn't Ms. Nadar, or Ms. Mawar, or Ms. Dian warn me?"

"Because there was no point!" Principal Arif squealed. "After my accident, I warned every teacher who came after me for years! Do you know how many of them took me seriously? Zero — none of them — it changed nothing. They all laughed at me, or assumed I was crazy. Then *she* attacked them all, and they all suffered the same fate. It changed *nothing*. It did *nothing* to help!"

Val was too stunned to speak. "I — I..."

"After I became Principal, I decided it was no use to warn anyone. I figured it would be better instead to have us all keep an eye on the new teachers. Ms. Mawar, Ms. Dian and I have helped as many of our new faculty members afterwards as we possibly could." She gazed off to the side, in deep thought. "Unfortunately, *she's* always a few steps ahead of us..."

Val nodded her head, a wave of guilt flooded through her chest. "I — I'm so sorry..."

Principal Arif's sad, large eyes gazed back into Val's. "Don't be... I've had this identical conversation countless times." She turned to face the statues. "So tell me, who came to your rescue?"

Val peered up at the copper men once more. "Imam Haruun."

Principal Arif nodded. "Me too. I ask every single one of my teachers that question, always expecting their rescuers to be the one whose faith they share. Imam Haruum would save the Muslims, Monk Ho Kla the Buddhists, Father Kit the Christians... but yet there never really is any correlation..." She gazed up at the men admiringly. "It's nice to know that even in the afterlife, our spirits help one another not based on shared beliefs, but on who's most in need."

A small smile curled at the side of Val's mouth. "That is nice."

"I do want to ask you a favor though."

"What's that?"

Principal Arif darted her eyes around the room once more. "While I've been here at Semua Tangan, *she* has only targeted a select few of our students. For some reason, *she* has a history of going after our teachers more so... but lately there have been some signs that *she's* been tormenting a few of our girls now as well."

"Really?" Val gawked. "Like what signs?"

Principal Arif gazed over at a few of the students in the corner. "They've been more keen on traveling in groups, more than usual... I know it sounds silly. Girls tend to do that naturally... but lately I've gotten more reports of girls who are afraid to go to the bathrooms by themselves, or run errands for teachers without a partner. There's been talk that kids just seem more anxious this year..." She gazed down at the floor. "Most schools would just chalk it up to bullying, but we really do a good job keeping an eye on that stuff."

Val recalled back to before she had arrived — to all those hours spent doing the required reading on bullying. She'd found it morbidly fascinating, the psyches of troubled kids. "Uh-hu."

"We can never rule bullying out — it amazes me just how imaginative kids can be in their cruelty towards one another... especially now that they're online at younger and younger ages... we must stay vigilant! But, I've been doing this a long, long, time, and this seems different..."

Val nodded her head. She tried to think through which students could be showing the signs that Principal Arif had just described. There was one nervous and timid chihuahua that came to mind...

"I'll keep an eye out." Val assured her.

"Good." She checked her watch. "I really need to be going — I have an appointment with a contractor. Hopefully he'll update some of these *damn* pipes! Ms. Dian and Ms. Mawar have been working overtime keeping them under control."

"Ah — well good luck." Val called after her.

"Thanks." Principal Arif waved, as she hurried off. Leaving Val all alone.

Val kept alert the rest of the week, trying to detect any signs of odd behavior in her students; but only learned that all kids have *odd* behavior. Extremely *odd*.

Val never really paid much attention to her students; she paid attention to their classwork of course, but not her students themselves. It wasn't a conscious choice, she wasn't necessarily choosing *not* to notice them. It was a very, very, subconscious choice indeed, but now Val knew why. They *irked* her. Like, really really *irked* her. They were *weird*.

It was as if there was no pattern, rhyme, or reason for their behavior... on Friday afternoon, two students put a full face of makeup on each other. Eye liner, eye shadow, lipstick... using only white board markers. They didn't even have a white board. Val used a chalkboard. The day before, at least six of her students held a *"who could handle being slapped in the face the hardest"* contest; resulting in several tears being shed, and more than one detention. Val had to accept defeat, when she caught one of her students trying to *eat* her desk — with a knife *and* fork.

By the end of the week she had had enough. She needed a break from the unusual tweens, so when Amina invited Val out to see a movie with her friends, she was more than happy to zone out.

"That movie was so dumb." Jano griped as they left the theater. *"The Possession of Adeliah?'* Like they just gave away the entire plot in the title."

"What more did you expect?" Amina shot back. "The title was *'The Possession of Adeliah',* and we watched Adeliah's possession. What did you think was gonna happen?"

"Tsss — I don't know — maybe a plot twist or something? Maybe someone else gets possessed too?" He checked his watch. "Is it already one thirty? Damn — I'm tired. Who knows... maybe Adelia's demon will possess me in my sleep tonight. That would be a plot twist."

By now everyone had reached their respective cars and motor bikes, and had started to depart. Amina turned to Val. "Do you want Jano and I to give you a ride?"

Val was about to answer, when Jano cut in. "Amina, Amina... our house is in the opposite direction."

"No it's not." Amina argued.

"Tsss — yes it is. Beside's... I'm tired. Why can't Khoo Hun Chhiau take her home?" He grabbed Khoo Hun Chhiau by the shoulder. "From what I've heard, it's not like he doesn't know where she lives anyways..."

Khoo Hun Chhiau's cheeks flushed. He shoved a snickering Jano away forcefully. Everyone had been giving him a hard time the entire night. Most wouldn't stop staring at him, in awe of the fact that he'd made it to two social outings in a row.

"Would that be alright?" Amina asked. "If not, I will totally take you home myself," she glared daggers at her husband, "and leave this man child here for the night!"

"No, no, it's okay. I'll see you Monday."

The empty road back to Yeo A'i's was frighteningly black. Val feared that at any moment, their car would hit one of those tigers that could've supposedly eaten her.

"It's so dark... and foggy." Val yawned.

Khoo Hun Chhiau remained silent.

"I guess as a cop, you drive in the dark like this all the time."

Khoo Hun Chhiau glared at her, but didn't say a word. Val snuggled deeper into her seat. *Guess he's too tired to talk.* Val thought. *I can't be that annoying... long week maybe? He slept through the movie.* They drove together in silence; that was until Khoo Hun Chhiau's phone rang.

"Lu ho bo?" He answered. Val watched his already serious face grow even more solemn. *"Hamisu?"* It was all indecipherable to Val, but after a few heated words, Khoo Hun Chhiau stopped the car, and turned it around in the opposite direction.

"Is everything alright?"

"Yeah... we just need to make a detour. I'll get you home soon."

Val wanted to ask more questions, but she also didn't wanna be any more annoying, especially right now. Something *serious* was going on. What exactly? Who knew. But Val didn't wanna be even more bothersome by asking. She sat there, without answers, until they arrived at a modest house; nearly engulfed by rainforest.

"Stay here!" He demanded.

"What?" She called after him, but by the time her words had left her lips, he was already inside. Val grimaced, as he disappeared through the front door.

"Pshh stay here!" She mocked, as the trees rattled around her in the wind. She adjusted the seat, until it was all the way down, kicking her feet up on the dash. Val tried reading the news on her phone to distract herself, but it didn't work. The fear from *"The Possession of Adeliah"* was starting to set in, and everything she was dealing with at Semua Tangan was not helping...

"You're okay Val, just relax." She whispered to herself. "Ghosts aren't real... demons aren't real..."

But how could she be so sure? The Holymen sure were real. What was *she*? Could *she* be a demon? As scary and paranormal as *she* was, it made Val wonder..."

The wind blew a tree branch into the driver's side window, causing a loud THUMP. It was enough to scare Val into unbuckling her seat belt, and sprinting inside.

Val ran without thinking, not stopping until she had slammed the front door behind her. Once inside, she heard grunting, and someone complaining loudly in another language. Val followed the sound, until she was outside again. Through the dim patio light she spotted an elderly Chinese man lying on his back, while a disgruntled Khoo Hun Chhiau helped him up gently. He spun around at the sight of Val.

"I told you to stay in the car!"

"Sorry, sorry... it was just... is everything alright?"

"Yes, everything's fine." He grumbled.

"Do you need any help?" Val offered timidly.

"No!" He grunted, as he finished helping the man back on his wobbly feet. "Just — go inside and wait for me!"

"Okay." With that, Val retreated back inside. She plopped down on a sofa.

"Oof!"

This sofa was *not* comfortable... better to just stay standing... Val wandered around, until she stumbled across an ajar door. She nudged it open, revealing a cramped bedroom with a low hanging ceiling. Val poked her head through, and soon enough her feet followed.

The smell of must lingered in the air. A lone twin bed sat in one corner, an ajar laptop perched on a desk in the other. The floor was covered in piles of books and laundry, that blended into one another.

"Sad..." Val mouthed to herself. When a woman lived by herself, even if she was messy, at least there would be an air of coziness that made her space bearable. This room had no soul, Val found that often to be the case with bachelor pads.

Something glittered in the corner. She stepped over clothes and overstuffed trash cans, 'til she was close enough to remove the dirty boxers that hid half of it; revealing a large trophy, stacked on top of other plaques and medals.

Val picked it up. A little gold man stood on top of a marble square, dawning a speedo and swim cap. She tried to decipher the inscription at the bottom, but it was written in a language she couldn't identify... it wasn't English, or Spanish, but it wasn't any other east asian language either...

"What're you doing?" Khoo Hun Chhiau snapped from behind her. Val spun around, nearly fumbling the trophy in her hands.

"Sorry — *Sorry!*" she squealed, peering her intruder up and down. It was strange seeing him stand up right in this room, like seeing a child wearing clothes they've outgrown. Tips of his hair scraped the ceiling.

"I just didn't exactly know where you wanted me to go..." Val faltered. "Is everything alright out there?"

"Yeah, everything's alright." He sighed. "My dad fell off a ladder in our back yard. There was a branch on our roof... he should've waited for me to come home. Luckily he just fell off the first step. He's icing his back now." His eyes found the trophy in her hands. "Why are you holding that?"

Val's cheeks flushed. "Oh — uhh, I was just trying to figure out what language this was written in. I've never seen it before."

Khoo Hun Chhiau walked over next to her, grabbing the trophy from her hands. "This is Russian."

"Why do you have a Russian swimming trophy?"

"It's from when I was at university in Russia. I was on the swim team."

"You went to college in Russia?"

"I did my masters there." He placed the trophy back down on the floor. "I did my undergrad in Japan, and my Phd in Singapore."

Val remembered Amina mentioning something about him traveling the world. Her eyes lingered over framed diplomas in various languages that hung around her.

"You have a Phd? In what?"

Khoo Hun Chhiau tried to tidy his surroundings unassumingly, but it wasn't going well. More laundry toppled over, and a half eaten protein bar fell off his desk onto a statue of the Buddah's lap.

"Criminology. Right now I'm working on my second thesis from the National University of Singapore."

"You're a Professor at a University?" Val sputtered.

Khoo Hun Chhiau nodded. "I fly back one Wednesday a month, and in return I take one of the Saturday night shifts at the station for whoever covers me." He gestured over towards his laptop. "I teach remotely all the other Wednesday nights, just one class though. It's pretty easy. All their tests are graded by the website they take them on, so all I really do is lecture."

Val glided around the room, staring up at each framed diploma. "So, do you speak Russian or something?"

"And Japanese, and Hokkien, Mandarin, Malay, Baba and English." He said matter of factly. "I spent a summer in Denmark as well, but I can only say a few words."

Val sneered when he wasn't looking. In America, she felt special for speaking English *and* Spanish. It seemed like everyone here had her beat at languages, but not normally to the degree of this guy.

"What's the thesis you're working on now about?"

"Cyber forensic psychology — how different types of criminals' use social media. What platforms they're most likely to use, at what age. Who they're likely to communicate with, on what... the patterns between different types of criminals — *murderers, pedophiles, petty thieves, bank robbers, terrorists, arsonists...* Most governments are lagging *far* behind in their own research."

It was no wonder nobody had seen him outside of work. Her eyes glanced around the room once more. A photo of Khoo Hun Chhiau next to an older Chinese woman rested gently on the Buddah's lap as well. Right under that protein bar.

"Who's that?" Val pried, picking it up.

Khoo Hun Chhiau's eyes shifted to the photograph, then fell to the floor. "That's my mother." He said gently, as he took the photo from her hands.

"Is she here? Did she sleep through your dad falling?" She glanced around the room, then back down at the photo. Val couldn't help but admire the woman's bright, floral dress; which was nothing like she'd ever seen before. She should get one of these foreign dresses for her own mom. "Will she be mad that I'm in here?"

Khoo Hun Chhiau let out a sad chuckle. "She would be... but she's gone."

Val's heart sunk into her stomach, and her breath caught itself in her throat. "I'm... I'm sorry."

"It's fine." Khoo Hun Chhiau said softly; his eyes watering up a bit, as he placed the picture back on his desk. The beautiful woman in the beautiful dress smiling up at both of them; with wide, animated eyes that shined like the sun. It panged Val's chest seeing her there. How could someone so obviously full of life ever really die?

"That was one of the last pictures we took before she passed."

"How'd she die? If you don't mind me asking..."

"Alzheimer's, three years ago." He said stoically, though Val noticed his voice choked up a bit. "She'd struggled with it for years, but taking care of her eventually became too difficult for my dad alone. That's why I moved back here." He gazed down at the photo again. "I'm very lucky the university understood, as long as I stay on top of things, they really don't mind."

It was Val's turn to pause. She really didn't know what to say after all that. "So... you're thesis... do you write it in English or Mandarin?"

"The last one was Mandarin, but the one I'm doing now has to be in English." He scoffed. "It's killing me — all the grammar, the weird spelling, I can't ever get it right!"

"I can help!" Val sputtered. "I'm really good at all that." She really was. When Val had been in middle school, she'd made the national spelling bee. Val was eliminated after the first round; but it was good enough to win her family a mini-fridge, and herself some scholarships. "I am an English teacher, after all."

"What time does school end on Monday?"

"Two thirty."

He considered this proposal for such a long time, she almost felt embarrassed for even asking. Val bit her cheek in regret. She *should've* known better in a conservative culture like this one—

"I get off at five. Do you wanna meet me here?"

"No... that's okay." She said quickly. "We can meet at Yeo A'i's, that way you won't have to pick me up. My room has a desk you can use. Don't worry about it, really."

"Okay then."

The pair made their way outside the room. Val noticed the elderly gentleman trying to stand up from the rock-hard couch as she walked by. Val didn't blame him. She would need an ice-pack just to sit on that thing again; but Khoo Hun Chhiau immediately told him to sit back down regardless; or so Val guessed, as he was speaking Hokkien. To Val's surprise, the old man turned to her, and said something she couldn't understand.

"What's he trying to say?" Val pried.

"Nothing—" He groaned as he rolled his eyes, and pushed her out the door.

Val spent the next day tidying up her room, making especially sure none of her own dirty underwear would be left out. That Monday, she was downright itching to tell Amina all about helping Khoo Hun Chhiau, so Val seized her opportunity on the lunch bench.

"Wait—wait—wait... back up. So, he just agreed to meet up with you tonight, at your place?"

"Yeah — I mean back home that's not really a weird thing, you know? But is that strange here?"

"Well... yeah. But men are men, you know..."

"I don't know if it's like that." Val pushed back. "We're just working on his thesis, and this whole time I haven't felt like he's made any sort of move on me... actually maybe the opposite... he was very firm about being a cop and all the first night."

"You never know..."

The bell rang, and the two went their separate ways. Val spent the next several hours pondering over her conversation with Amina. *Could she be right? Was this his version of making a move? No? Nah... don't be ridiculous...* She tried forcing away some of the nervous butterflies that were fluttering in her stomach, but her efforts were in vain.

Val killed the time between school and her meeting with Khoo Hun Chhiau by flunking Wani for her book report on Charles Webb. Val was almost impressed. She had never seen a Grade F paper with so much Grade A bullshit. Regardless, by five-thirty Val was showered, dressed, and mindlessly scrolling through social media at the kitchen table, waiting to see if he would actually show.

There was a knock at the door. Val sprang up, but before she could reach it, Yeo A'i beat her there. She cracked the door open, and popped her head out.

"Officer Khoo — What a surprise! Is everything alright? Did Laina's dog get loose in the neighborhood again? Did she bite another child? I'll take a look in my backyard real quick to see if she got in through the fence—"

"It's alright... I'm actually not here on any police business. I'm just here to see Val—" He cleared his throat. "I mean, Ms. Palacio."

"Is she in trouble? Cause if so... I'm so sorry, I haven't seen her all day." She ducked her head back inside towards Val — mouthing the word: *"Hide!"*

"No—no, she's not in any trouble. She... um, she's actually helping me edit my thesis, since it's in English."

"Oh — well, um, give me a minute, let me see — ah-ha — she's just now walked down the stairs — must have been napping up in her room — Val, Come here! There's someone here to see you."

Yeo A'i opened the door all the way; revealing an obviously flustered Khoo Hun Chhiau, sporting an overstuffed backpack. They nodded awkwardly to each other.

"Well come on in then," Yeo A'i insisted, "before you get a heat stroke. It's too hot outside today."

Khoo Hun Chhiau shuffled inside. Val couldn't help but feel a little bit childish, like she was back in high school, asking her mom if it was okay for a boy to come over and study.

Yeo A'i tried to clean some of the table of her most recent project; where a mess of sewing needles and fabric had taken over. She cleared a small section with her arm.

"You guys can sit here, I guess... I'm so sorry for the mess. If I knew there would be company I'd have tidied up a bit."

"It's fine, we can just use the desk in my room."

"Really, would that be alright?" Val could see the relief on her face. "I could move this, but it might be risky, with all the needles I've lost so far... if you guys need anything, let me know. Tea — anything — I'll just be down here, working on my quilt."

"Thanks." Val called back from the top of the stairs. The pair made it into Val's room. Val nodded towards the desk, and Khoo Hun Chhiau unpacked his bag.

"So, you can use this laptop to go through and correct my past mistakes. Do you know about APA citations? Can you help me at the end with the proper format?"

"Yeah... sure."

The two worked quietly for hours. Khoo Hun Chhiau at the antique wooden desk, and Val sprawled out on her rug on the floor. She cuddled a plush pillow, peering up curiously at this man. This strange, strange man... for weeks after they shared a routine. He would come over around six, stay until ten, and then retreat back to his own house.

"So he just does that, everyday?" Amina pried. "He just comes over, works on his... whatever it is, and then leaves?"

"Yup. Well, not on Wednesdays. That's when he teaches his online class."

"Well, he has a lot more self control than I figured any man had. Jano would've exploded if we were in a room together for weeks at a time, with no physical contact..." She grabbed her stomach, and grimaced. "I swear, that man needs to find another hobby."

"Are you alright—" But before the words were out of her mouth, Amina's lunch was outside of her stomach. Val flinched, as chunks of regurgitated meat and vegetables littered the grass in front of her.

"Jesus!"

"I'm sorry!" Amina whimpered, wiping her mouth with a tissue. "I should've known that was gonna happen — I've been vomiting all morning. I had a little garbage can under my desk, but I forgot to bring it out here."

"It's okay." Val cooed, while feeling Amina's forehead. "Are you hot? Cold? Is your food bad? Is someone trying to poison you? Did you flunk the *wrong* student?"

"No, no, and no... just nauseous, and tired. I'm gonna swing by Nur's tonight. I mean, she's not *just* a baby doctor, you know, she can do other things too. I really hope it's not dengue... anyways, so you said Wednesday nights he doesn't come over? Is that right?"

"Yeah, it's just me and whatever Yeo A'i's working on."

"My friends come over on Wednesday's to watch whichever country's version of The Bachelor is on. Right now it's Romania. You're invited if you want, we meet around six at my place."

Val remembered Nur saying something about this before. "Yeah — I'll be there."

"No problem." Amina grumbled as she doubled over, and threw up once more.

Wednesday night rolled around, and instead of a joking Jano at the door, Val was greeted by Amina's kind face. They made their way into the living room, where a familiar group of girls were arguing.

"I think that's the *stupidest* idea in the world – letting a baby name itself!" Tan Soan griped. "What's it gonna choose? Babies only know what — maybe twenty words max. Purple? Triangle? Triceratops? Just name it after your richest aunt. When she kicks it, maybe she'll leave you a little extra something in her will. That's what my mom did with me."

"I'm not saying I'm gonna do it... but don't you think it makes *some* sense?" Parini protested. "Shouldn't people have the right to choose something as permanent as their own name?"

"*No* — the only people I've ever heard of changing their names were *fucking* weirdos. I met a guy back in college who changed his name from *'Mark'* to *'Death's Glory.'* Do you know how stupid that is? Besides — we, as responsible adults, should not be encouraging the youths to change their names to whatever's trendy on a whim."

Parini turned towards the kitchen, where Val was fixing herself a plate. "What do you think Val? I read online that it's common in America now-a-days. Is it? Do the kids choose stupid names like Tan Soan says?"

"I've never heard of anyone doing that before."

"HA!" Tan Soan boasted, nearly knocking her wine glass over. "See — even the American's think it's a stupid idea!"

Parini rolled her eyes. "Anyways Val, how are you adjusting now that it's nearly been two months? Any pros — cons?"

Val pondered this question, while shuffling over to the thankfully soft couch.

"Mhmm... well, I like how I'm not stuck in a cubical anymore."

"Go on..."

"Mhmm, my students aren't too bad most days. At least some of them..."

"Some of them have been getting on my damn nerves lately." Amina grumbled.

"I mean most are okay..." Val backtracked, "but then I do have these three girls... It's like their favorite hobby is to see how much they can get away with."

"Same — you know yesterday, my last class decided that every time my back was turned, they'd inch their desks forward just a little bit... I didn't catch on 'til I couldn't even move! They *trapped* me! Do you know how hard it is to get a bunch of thirteen year olds to do anything — and they just execute something like that perfectly on their own?"

"It's always those last classes—"

"They can't contain their bullshit any longer."

"My mom used to teach at the boys' school — to this day she never shuts up about how annoying her students were. Jano alone could take up a whole afternoon." Tan Soan added. "Speaking of boys — I heard a certain police officer has been stopping by your house lately..."

Val blushed. *Damnit.* Now everyone was looking at her. With *that* look. The one that calls out your bullshit without saying a word. "It's not like that... really. I'm just helping Khoo Hun Chhiau with his thesis."

"On his what?" Parini pried. "What kind of Policeman has to write a thesis?"

"The kind that's also a Phd student, that's why he's always so busy."

"Well, it seems like he's been making time for someone lately." Parini taunted.

"Like I said... there's literally nothing going on between us, all he does is work. I swear some days he doesn't even say hi, or bye..."

"That is weird." Nur whispered.

"Well, if that's the case, I have a brother who's living in Penang. I'll set you up next time we all take a day trip there. He's an *actual* doctor — a cardiologist — and as you probably already guessed, good looks do run in the family." Tan Soan sassed, as she flipped her black hair behind her shoulder. "Alright — shall we get started with *The Bachelor* ladies?"

"Well, actually..." Amina interrupted. "I have a little announcement... she patted her lap with her hands excitedly, and a large grin swept across her face. *"I'm Pregnant!"*

The room completely erupted.

"Congratulations!"

"Amazing!"

"Wow!"

"When did you find out?"

"I've been feeling sick lately..." Amina said shyly, "so I went to Nur for a check up, and she confirmed it."

Nur ducked her head, and grinned.

"Oh my god — is it a girl?" Parini pried. "What month will it be born? Will your baby be in the same grade in school as my baby?"

"I don't know the gender yet. I'm barely a month along, so you guys can't go around telling anyone yet. I just told Jano last night."

"He's not gonna keep something like that a secret." Parini scoffed. "You should've told us before you told him, we can actually keep our mouth's shut. That man is physically unable to close his mouth for more than five seconds."

"I made him promise — and I let him know the consequences would be absolutely brutal if he told anyone. I can't exactly hold the same kind of threat over you guys if you say anything... but I trust you girls."

Everyone nodded in unison. A slew of *"I promise"*'s and *"You don't have to worry"*'s echoed around the room, until someone decided to get to the task at hand. "Alright let's go ahead and start it already..."

CHAPTER FIVE

"Hey — You!" Ms. Dian hollered down the crowded hall, a little passed Val. "You there, Ms. Nadar!"

Ms. Nadar whirled around. "Me?"

"Yeah, you. Ms. Mawar and I are gonna need a third pair of hands, too—"

But before she had finished her sentence, Ms. Nadar had scurried away, down the staircase, out onto the lawn.

"Rotten bitch." Ms. Dian mumbled under her breath. Her eyes searched for another victim. They met Val's. "You there — come help us with something real quick."

Val wanted nothing more than to protest, since she didn't want to start her afternoon trek home too late; but before any words could leave her mouth, Ms. Dian had dumped several heavy cables into her arms.

"Follow me."

Val obeyed. Ms. Dian had an authoritative presence about her, and Val didn't feel it wise to object to such a stout, husky woman. Val watched, as Ms. Dian's generously padded, slumped shoulders, led the way down the hall; towards a ladder on the side of the building Val had never noticed before.

"Okay, I'm gonna stay down here and run this line to the battery storage units. You two head up to the roof." She held up her walkie-talkie. "Ms. Mawar will hook these wires up to the panels, while you just do whatever she says. If you need anything, call me over the walkie — got it?"

"Yeah! Yes — Yes mam!"

"Good." With that, Ms. Dian spun on her heels and started back down from whence she came.

Val held on to the cables, as Ms. Mawar climbed up the ladder, then tossed them up to her as she climbed up herself. It felt exciting being up on the rooftop — almost a little naughty, and freeing, as if she were breaking the rules somehow. The breeze flowed through her hair. Val breathed in the fresh, warm air.

"Alright." Ms. Mawar sighed. "Can you hand me that cable over there?"

"What? Oh, yeah, sure." Val glanced around. "So, uhh — what exactly needs fixing up here?"

"This."

Val bent over to get a better look — several tied-together wires had been completely slashed through.

"Was it a tiger... or a bear?" Val asked curiously. "This looks like a bear took a swipe at it. Is there some type of Malaysian brown bear I should be on the lookout for?"

"No bear." Ms. Mawar said shortly, in between going back and forth from the wires, to the small tools. "There's only one thing around these parts that can do something like that... and I think you had an unfortunate meeting with *her* the first day of school..."

"Oh..." Val stuttered.

They sat quietly, working at a peaceful pace. Val stooped next to a crouching Ms. Mawar, who occasionally called for Val to hand her a specific tool, or wiring. Val reasoned this would've made for a great tanning spot, if it weren't for the hazards...

"Sorry about Ms. Dian by the way, she can be a little rude sometimes."

"Oh... it's no big deal."

"She can come off quite bossy at first, but it's just her take-charge personality. We're roommates... you know? We share that scooter that I took you home on that first day." She looked back down at the panel she was repairing. "It put me off initially too when I first met her, but she really is a deeply protective person. She sees herself — well... me, her, and Principal Arif, as the physical protectors of this school."

Val spotted something out of the corner of her eye. "Yeah, I get it." She muttered, before turning around, and letting her jaw drop at the sight before her.

An old, Anglican priest stood facing away from them on the edge of the roofing... his long, black robes billowing behind him in the wind...

"It took me a while to come around to liking her, but now you could say she's my very best friend. Well, one of my best friends, we also have a few... how do you say it in English? Sausage dogs? Yes, I think that's right — sausage dogs. We rescued them a few years ago. They're like my own chil—"

"Ms. Mawar..."

"Is that not what you call them? The dog's shaped like hotdogs? What do you call those types of dogs, with little legs, and a long body? They're so cute. I swear when they run it's the cutest thing—"

"Ms... Ms. Mawar!" Val hissed. *"Look!"*

"What? Why? What's... Oh—" Her mouth gaped, causing her to look hollow. "Oh... my..."

They sat there silently, in awe, until Ms. Dian's voice crackled from Ms. Mawar's hip.

"Hey — come in... did you guys get the line going?"

Val sat up, until she was in a crouching position. Slowly she inched herself forward towards the man.

"Is everything alright? Come in — NOW!"

Ms. Mawar seized the walkie-talkie from her hip. "Hey," she whispered shakily, "it's — it's happening again..."

The jingling of keys wafted through the walkie-talkie. *"Okay, stay calm... I'm on my way now — don't do anything!"*

Val continued inching towards him. She was halfway there...

"Ms. Val!" Ms. Mawar whisper-called. "Ms. Val — come back here!"

She was only a meter away. Val was about to reach out to him when the sun caught her eye. She rubbed them and opened them once more.

The priest was facing her now. He extended his arms; as if he were about to be nailed to a cross — Val stumbled back towards Ms. Mawar, but it was too late — his arms wrapped around her. Val couldn't remember ever being held so tightly, and then they fell backwards over the ledge...

Val could hear Ms. Mawar's panicked scream, and sensed the wind rushing through her hair, as she fell... down... down... down...

...

An obnoxiously chirpy bird stirred Val. Her eyes fluttered open...

She found herself lying on the ground, prostrate, with the light glaring directly in her eyes again.

"VAL — VAL — VAL!" Ms. Mawar screamed as she jogged to Val's side from her right. "Ms. Val, can you hear me?"

Val grunted.

She picked up Val's hand. "Oh dear — Oh dear — *Oh dear!* Can you feel this? Can you move this?"

Val gingerly nodded her head and made a thumbs-up sign.

Ms. Mawar crawled over on her hands and knees toward Val's feet. "How about this?" She pinched Val's toes — hard.

"Ouch!" Val yelped. She flinched her foot back. "Yeah, yeah, I feel that."

Ms. Dian was at her side now. "Okay, I got the backboard. Don't move, you could have a spinal injury."

Val shook her head and sat up. "I—"

Ms. Dian and Ms. Mawar waited in anticipation. "I — I what?"

"I feel... *fine?*"

"You're not fine — there's no way. You just fell off a building."

"No, really." Val flexed her hands. "I feel fine... great... nothing."

Ms. Dian pulled Val's head back and shone her flashlight in her eye. "What're you doin—"

"What's your grandmother's full name?"

"My what?"

"What's your grandmother's full name? Just tell me!"

"Okay — Okay. Um, it's *Señora Maria Luciana Palacio Herrado Gomez Maestro De las Osa—*"

"We need to take her to the hospital right away!"

"You didn't let me finish!" Val protested. "Where was I... *Maestro De las Osas Marrón*. Some Colombians have long names."

Ms. Dian and Ms. Mawar shared a look, before examining her once more.

"Well — you don't have any scrapes, or bruises, or broken bones." Ms. Mawar felt the back of her head. "There aren't lumps, or bloody wounds, or scabs..."

"Her pupils are fine too." Ms. Dian sighed, as she peered up at the roof. "This place, I'll tell you what... alright, we're gonna help you up now, but easy, okay?"

They helped her stand up. Besides being a little shaky, Val felt perfectly fine; and surprisingly normal. They insisted on inspecting her from head to toe, before Ms. Mawar gave her another ride home; just to be *"on the safe side."*

"Man," Val groaned, as she handed her helmet back to Ms. Mawar. "I thought those holy men were supposed to be our... I don't know... *silent protectors?* Why would he do something like that?"

"You didn't see *her*, standing behind you? *She* was about to jump, or something. *She* looked murderous..."

A chill shivered down Val's spine. "No... no I didn't."

"Well, the good thing is that we're all okay... I'm okay, you're okay, Ms. Dian's okay... the cables will have to be finished another day I guess." Ms. Mawar sighed. She offered one last wave, spun her scooter around, and drove off back down the quiet road.

Val shook her head, turned around, then proceeded inside.

She'd barely entered the house when a small hand grabbed her wrist.

"It's about time you've got home!" Yeo A'i sputtered. "I've been waiting for you for the last hour — I almost left without you!"

It had slipped Val's mind to text Yeo A'i and let her know she'd be late for their afternoon walk. "I'm sorry, it was just that—"

"Oh — we aren't walking today." She said certainly, as she slung her purse over her shoulder, and dragged Val back through the front door. "We're on a mission..."

"What? Wait? Where are we going?" Val sputtered, while Yeo A'i continued to drag Val behind her.

"Don't worry." Yeo A'i sang happily, as she unlocked her car door. "You're gonna love what we're doing. You're not allergic to dogs now, are you?"

"No?"

"Good." With that, Yeo A'i shoved Val into the passenger seat, rushed around to the driver's side, and sped off down the road.

Val messaged Khoo Hun Chhiau, letting him know she'd been kidnaped, and a moment later, a dry *"okay"* was all she got in response. Val huffed, tossing her phone down into the closest cup holder.

"Okay — now, can you please tell me where exactly we're going?"

A sly, excited grin crept across Yeo A'i's face. "Okay, okay, well, you know how we go walking every day after you get back from school?"

"Yes."

"Well, I was thinking... something's missing... you know? I mean, I couldn't put my finger on exactly what, but then I was out gardening today, and it hit me — dogs — we need a dog to walk — it'd be perfect! I haven't had a dog in years, not since my daughter was little..."

"What does your husband think of this idea?"

"Oh who knows, I didn't ask him. Anyways – I called my friend who's the managing director of a shelter nearby, and she said we can come by anytime today until seven." Yeo A'i held up her bag. "I stopped by the pet store earlier and bought some treats. The dogs are gonna love us!"

Val wasn't sure if it was a good idea to adopt a dog on a whim like this, but she also really wasn't sure of anything anymore. And this sounded like *fun*. And she needed some *fun*. Especially after everything that'd just happened... They chatted the whole way. *What breed should they get? Should it be a boy or girl? What size?*

"I think it should be a dog with short hair since it's so hot — we don't want it to overheat on our walks. I read online that they can overheat easier than humans can." The pair pulled up next to a mid-size building, with a sign out front reading: *'Eng Lee's Happy Animal Shelter, Established 1992'* "Ah — I'm so happy we're here — I can barely park — look at me — I'm shaking!"

Yeo A'i was right, she nearly took the side mirror off the car next to her as she pulled in. Val climbed out. Yeo A'i was already ten feet ahead of her, skipping through the double glass doors. The ice-cold A/C that hit them in the face did nothing to temper her mood.

"Hello there–" Yeo A'i heartily greeted the woman at the front desk. "We're looking for a nice, sweet, baby angel to take home with us today!"

The woman turned around, and the animated, light, childish energy extinguished itself from Val's body at once.

"Christ!" Val swore.

"Actually... it's our policy that you submit an official application... then once we do a home inspection, you must wait two to four weeks before you can come and pick up one of our dogs... if, that is, you're even accepted!" Ms. Nadar sneered, as she peered down her nose at Yeo A'i. "We don't want just anyone taking one of our dogs!"

"Yes, yes, Ms. Nadar... is that it? Is that how to pronounce your name miss? or might I say..." She peered down at her name tag. "Thuya — can I call you Thuya? Well actually, I was told by Ms. Eng Lee that I can bypass the formal application system. She's a good friend of mine, our daughters were pals at school so she's been to my house several times. She knows that I have a proper gate and everything." Yeo A'i sifted through her phone. "Ah, yes — here it is — she told me to show whoever was at the front desk this email." Yeo A'i handed her phone over to Ms. Nadar, who barely glanced at it.

"I'm gonna have to make a phone call to confirm."

"But, that's her email address? Isn't that confirmation enough?" Yeo A'i asked indignantly.

Ms. Nadar held up her finger, as if to *shush* Yeo A'i. She dialed something into her phone. The call was brief, and Ms. Nadar looked even more agitated after it ended.

"Well," she scoffed, "it appears a *severe* lapse in judgment has been made... follow me please."

Val and Yeo A'i shared appalled glances, before following in line behind Ms. Nadar.

"So," Val spoke up, "you volunteer here?"

"Yes." Ms. Nadar responded, without bothering to look back at her. "For several years now. They've practically begged me to come on full time... I've always had a special connection with animals..."

At that moment, a dog larger than Val herself rounded the corner, yanking at its leash. It bounded towards Ms. Nadar — barking, snarling, and growling in her direction. Ms. Nadar leaped into Val's arms.

"Some connection..." Yeo A'i sassed under her breath.

"Anyways." Ms. Nadar sneered, as she gathered her wits about her once more. "Since they couldn't hire me, they *insisted* upon promoting me to a brand new position that they created just for me." She pointed towards her volunteer badge again. "I'm the head managing volunteer of: *"Sanitation, health, and intestinal transitions."*

Val's chest lurched. She got it. She understood... how did Ms. Nadar miss that? "Wait... so, if you abbreviated that title, you're the head managing volunteer of... *shit?* Am I right?"

Ms. Nadar stopped in her tracks. Her eyes widened, her nostril flared. Wow. She really had missed it... "No, no, you're mistaken—"

"Really? Then what exactly does the Head Managing Volunteer of *Shit*— I mean, excuse me... *Sanitation, health, and intestinal transitions* do exactly?"

"I clean the pens, and make sure when other people clean them they do a good enough job! None of them do by the way, I'm the only one around here who actually gets down on my hands and knees to make sure they're spotless."

"And what exactly do you have to clean in these pens? What's the main reason they get dirty in the first place? Could it possibly be, um — how do you say — *Intestinal transitions?*"

Ms. Nadar shook her head and glared in the opposite direction. Val could have sworn she saw a tiny, minuscule tear glistening in one of her eyes. She actually felt a little bit guilty. Maybe she should have kept her mouth shut, even if it was Ms. Nadar.

They made it to the first row of pens, where several mid-sized dogs barked emphatically at their presence. The three of them walked past five boisterous kennels until Yeo A'i stopped in front of a large, quiet, white, fluffy pooch.

"Awe!" Yeo A'i cooed. "Hello there — what a cutie!"

Val peered over his information sheet. "This one is heartworm negative, is good with small dogs and kids, and his favorite treat is peanut butter."

"Can we have a look? Wouldn't this one be perfect in family pictures? Such a good temperament, I haven't heard a peep so far."

"He's a long-haired breed, so his hair will matt the second you don't brush it out!" Ms. Nadar snapped. "I see this dog with more of a young family, you know... with maybe an owner who is a bit more *active*, and *youthful*... who's less likely to have joint problems... maybe you'd prefer a *senior* dog — like yourself."

Yeo A'i glared daggers at the foul woman. "Excuse me? I don't know who you think you're talking to, but I'm active." She shot back. "I ran a marathon in four hours and thirty minutes just last year. I can probably outlast this dog several times over. Besides, we could always trim his hair. I bet this one would like a little spa day every now and then... let's take him out!"

Ms. Nadar groused a bit more, but ultimately realized she was overpowered. It only took a moment of frolicking along with the dog for Yeo A'i to make up her mind. She signed the final paperwork a few minutes later.

"What should I put as her new name on this form?" Yeo A'i wondered out loud, to anyone who was in earshot. "I'm gonna go with *"Princess Diana!"*

"He's a male."

"Mhmm... well then *Prince* Diana it is!"

"You can't be serious?" Ms. Nadar gasped.

"Oh, I'm dead serious."

She finalized her signature, and Val, Yeo A'i, and a leashed Prince Diana sashayed out the door; just as the sun was setting.

"That's strange." Yeo A'i noted.

"What? What's strange?"

"It's just that, I've never been to an animal shelter, where the biggest bitch wasn't a dog."

CHAPTER SIX

Yeo A'i was right, the thing they were missing on their daily walks was a dog. Prince Diana pranced along happily beside them every day; occasionally tugging lightly at his leash, to bark at a sunning lizard, or a menacing leaf. It didn't take long for his accommodations to live up to his name. The living room was littered with tennis balls, tug-of-war ropes, stuffed animals, and chewing bones. Several large, posturepedic dog beds were strategically placed around the house. Yeo A'i had even bought a children's hard plastic pool for the back garden; that way he could lounge around in the water when temperatures rose above his majesty's comfort zone. There was only one frequent house guest who didn't seem too keen on the new arrival...

"He got what now?" Khoo Hun Chhiau gasped.

"A Pawdicure — you know, like a pedicure for humans, except for dogs since they have paws. Isn't that so cute?" Val trilled, as she sat on the floor, sprawled out, scratching Prince's belly.

"Tsss." Khoo Hun Chhiau mocked. He shook his head, and hunched further over his laptop. "What a waste of money."

"He's an active boy, and his poor paws have to walk on a lot of rough surfaces."

"I meant getting the dog in the first place." Khoo Hun Chhiau scoffed.

Val gasped. "Khoo Hun Chhiau... are you telling me, that you don't like any dogs whatsoever?"

He rolled his eyes.

"I didn't know you were a dog bigot!"

Khoo Hun Chhiau whirled around in his chair. "That's not — that's not it! I just don't see the point of having a dog as a pet, is all. They're animals — they should be kept outside, in nature, with *other* animals!"

"Sounds like a dog hater to me. Tell me... did a dog bite you as a kid, is that it? Is this some kind of repressed childhood trauma?"

Khoo Hun Chhiau's cheeks turned pink. He slowly turned around to face his computer again. "They're a hazard to children..." He muttered.

Val pushed herself up from the floor, and walked over to Khoo Hun Chhiau's cluttered desk, slamming his laptop shut.

"What're you doing?"

"I'm not checking your thesis today?"

"You're not?"

"And you're not writing it."

"I'm not?"

Val nodded resolutely. "We're gonna bond with Prince Diana!"

Khoo Hun Chhiau groaned as he fought to loosen her grip over the laptop.

"Stop it! Hey — *Hey* — give it back!"

Val seized the shiny silver MacBook and hid it behind her back. "We're gonna walk him until your doggy racism goes away!"

Khoo Hun Chhiau tried grabbing it from behind her back. "Stop it — seriously! It's already four-thirty, it's gonna get dark soon."

"No it's not — and besides, doesn't the soccer field at the boys' school stay lit until nine at night? We can take Prince there. You can play fetch with him!"

Khoo Hun Chhiau conceded defeat, since Val had victoriously sandwiched the computer in between herself and the wall. He gestured towards his police uniform. "It's gonna be too hot out."

Val glanced around the room, trying to think through suitable items in her wardrobe. She searched her suitcases until she found an old pair of basketball shorts from high school. Val untied the strings around the waist, and loosened them as much as possible; then grabbed her largest sleeping shirt, a men's XXL, from an old charity drive that had run out of smaller sizes. Val tossed both over toward him.

"Here, these should work."

Khoo Hun Chhiau kicked towards her with his feet. "What about my boots?"

"Yeo Ai's husband has a ton of flip-flops lying around that he never uses. I'm sure he won't notice if a pair goes missing for a few hours."

Khoo Hun Chhiau didn't look too thrilled with her idea but didn't press it. He unbuttoned his shirt, Val couldn't even pretend to not watch. She'd never gotten a proper look at his biceps, his chest, his broad shoulders, and defined abs...

"Are you looking at me?" Khoo Hun Chhiau scolded.

Val snapped back into the moment. "What? No — stop it — just hurry up already!"

The very last thing she wanted him to do right now was hurry up. She caught a few more sneak peeks before he slid on the new outfit, and opened his arms wide. "So, what do you think?"

Val took a look. The shirt was a little too baggy, and the shorts went well above his knees; but still he managed to look *very* good. It was a bit unfair... he'd probably look good even wearing a trash bag.

"Good." She said quickly, before seizing him by the hand, and dragging him out the door. "Come on, let's not waste any more of that precious daylight you're so worried about!"

Val grabbed Prince Diana's leash, while Khoo Hun Chhiau tried on a plethora of sandals. The three of them walked to the boys' school; catching the tail end of a children's soccer game, before having the entire empty field to themselves.

Khoo Hun Chhiau leaned over from his crossed-legged position; grabbing the slobbery tennis ball Prince Diana had dropped at his feet. He shook some of the drool off, before throwing it impressively far.

"So," Khoo Hun Chhiau sighed, "you've been spending your Wednesday nights with Jano's wife?"

Val nodded. "Yup, well, and her friends too. We watch the Bachelor."

Khoo Hun Chhiau cracked a rare smile and shook his head. "Ah."

"It's pretty fun, I used to watch the American version in the states with my family. It kind of makes me feel like I'm not so far away from home, you know?"

Khoo Hun Chhiau nodded his head. "I get it." He said softly, as he hurled the ball once more for a heavily panting Prince.

Val remembered back to what she had learned a few weeks ago, how he had lived abroad for years.

"How'd you deal with homesickness when you went away?"

Khoo Hun Chhiau let out a long, remembering sigh. He stretched his arms, and leaned back on his palms. "It was really hard the first year, mostly I just studied. My Japanese wasn't very good at first, so I could only make friends with the other international students." He recalled, with a lonely look in his eyes.

"Then you just moved to Russia? That's pretty random?"

"It was, but I ended up loving it. I have a lot of good memories there."

"Really? Like what?"

"Well, I had the same roommates for two years in a row, we grew really close as a group. One of them was an Australian, who was obsessed with Breaking Bad..."

"Ah." Val grunted.

"Yup." Khoo Hun Chhiau sighed. "We all joined the Intramural swim team, and we just didn't take any of it too seriously."

Not taking things seriously didn't seem to be Khoo Hun Chhiau's strong suit. "You must have been pretty good though, you have a trophy in your room."

Khoo Hun Chhiau shrugged his shoulders lazily. "I was alright..."

The two threw the ball for Prince what seemed an endless amount of times. To his royal highness it didn't matter that their arms might be getting tired; his legs sure weren't yet. They kept at it, as the pair watched the sun set slowly over the never-ending stretch of trees, and listened to the final call to prayer reverberating around town.

"So... you went here as a kid?" Val pried. "What was it like at an all-boys school?"

"It was fine, I met Jano on this soccer field our first year. He liked to get me into trouble every now and then..."

"I bet." Val scoffed. She took a deep breath, and asked the question that had been on her mind since they'd arrived. "Is it... is it haunted here?"

"No." Khoo Hun Chhiau said sternly. "There wasn't anything like that here. That's only a Semau Tangan problem..."

"Ah, you know about that..."

"Everybody knows about that." Khoo Hun Chhiau explained as he wrestled a stick Prince Diana had found out of his mouth. "The officers have a formal protocol with Principal Arif, in case the worst were to happen." He turned to Val, looking concerned. "You haven't been attacked, have you?"

Val nodded her head. "Twice, actually. Well, two and a half times... maybe three depending on what you count... I don't know."

Val described the first day of class, where *she* had lured Val out of her classroom with the hallucinated dead baby. Then the time in front of the statues, and climaxed with the falling off the roof fiasco. Val watched, as his face contorted in concern.

"You need to be more careful!" Khoo Hun Chhiau pleaded, while grabbing his head and pulling his buzz cut. "You've only been here for what — less than three months? And you're averaging an attack a month at this rate!"

"Hey!" Val snapped. "It's not like I was warned about any of this beforehand! What am I supposed to do? Put eyes in the back of my head?"

"Just be more... *observant!*"

"I am *observant!*"

"No, you're not!" Khoo Hun Chhiau scowled. "The other day, I saw you mistake a dog treat for a granola bar — and you still finished it!"

He had her there. Truth be told, Val had made this mistake several times. Yeo A'i always bought gourmet treats for Prince that very closely resembled human food, and stored them in the pantry next to Val's snacks. Some tasted better than Val's snacks. Especially the peanut butter ones.

"Well, even if I become observant, this... *thing*, can be invisible. I don't exactly have infrared vision or whatever!"

"Just—" Khoo Hun Chhiau stuttered, "just try not to be alone, at least. I know it can attack in groups too, but it would still be safer for you in general. And for Pete's sake, don't go on the roof again, even if someone asks you to."

Val rolled her eyes. On the one hand, she didn't appreciate how he was talking to her; like he had any authority over her behavior. It went against every feminist principle she held dearly. On the other hand, Val could see the grave concern in his eyes, and hear the anxiety in his wavering voice. Maybe it wouldn't be such a bad idea to heed his advice...

"Okay — okay, I promise."

They chatted and sat together a while longer until the lights on the field went out, and the mosquitos started attacking. The three comrades made their way back to Yeo A'i's house, and were almost halfway home, when Khoo Hun Chhiau stopped in his tracks, and abruptly changed the subject.

"So... you do know that the emergency number here is 999. Not 911... right?"

"*Yeees* — that was like the first thing my mom made me learn when she found out I was moving here."

"Well, call them whenever you feel in trouble again, with you know, *her*... but message me too... you have my number. Just let me know next time something happens."

This took Val by surprise. A happy one, one that made her feel safe again. She let out a breath that she'd been holding ever since she got here. Hell — ever since she'd stepped onto those flights.

"Yeah, sure, okay, I will..."

CHAPTER SEVEN

The next week everyone seemed to be in high spirits around Semua Tangan, as Friday drew closer. Her student's hands trembled in anticipation, as they delicately handed in their parental permission slips for the field trip. Treating the flimsy paper with more importance than a one hundred Ringgit bill.

"Careful!" Zara chided Wani, who accidentally backed into her while she was handing Val her slip. The line for the bus was growing obnoxiously rowdy. Students were becoming unable to contain their excitement any longer.

Val grabbed the paper tendered by Zara, took a cursory look, and waved her onto the bus. "Are you excited for today?" Val asked.

Zara bowed her head, and an absolutely massive grin spread across her face. She boarded the bus as quietly as a mouse.

"Save us seats with enough room for our backpacks!" Eng Ki hollered.

"In the back!" Wani added.

Val snatched the slips from the two girls. "I trust that you two will be on your best behavior today... you guys won't be pressuring Zara into any shenanigans."

"Who, us? Trouble?" Wani asked sarcastically.

"We never pressure anybody into trouble. Well, not on purpose at least..."

"We've matured... like... like cheese! We're as mature as cheese!" Echoed Wani. "In fact, we don't get Zara *into* trouble, we get her *out* of trouble. We protect her *from* the trouble... *Ouch!*"

Eng Ki had elbowed Wani in the ribs, hard.

Val gazed down at them suspiciously. "What exactly is that supposed to mean?"

The two girls shared a wary look. "Nothing, *nothing* — don't worry about it." They rushed, while dashing past her onto the bus. Val listened, as the heavy clunking of their feet found their friend, and claimed their seats.

It took another half hour to get the remaining students boarded and settled. Val took a seat at the very front of the bus next to Amina, and to her surprise; Nur.

"You're coming!" Val squealed. "How?"

Nur smiled shyly, before fogging up the cabin with bug spray. "Principal Arif asked some of the teachers if they knew anyone else who could supervise today, and Amina volunteered me. I cleared my patient schedule so that I could have the day off."

Nur's soft voice was being drowned out by what Val assumed was some kind of scream-off. Val tried several times to quiet the bus down, but it was all in vain. The cheese-heads didn't know the meaning of quiet.

After nearly two hours, the bus finally pulled in front of their destination; lining up behind the other buses that had caravanned along with them. Students nearly toppled over themselves trying to disembark. Val followed the hoard, as it hurried towards a large, open, wooden landing.

"*Everybody — Everybody, please —* If you would gather around me!" A blond-haired Kiwi, wearing tan cargo shorts, a white fishing shirt, and a straw hat pleaded. "I said around me, not on me! Alright, do I have everyone's attention? We can't start unless you-lot chill out a bit. Can everyone hear me in the back?"

The herd of tweens quieted immediately.

"Welcome–" she bellowed, before peering down at a clipboard in her hands, *"Semua Tangan Secondary"*, to the Eastman Elephant Sanctuary!"

The girls squealed and wooed in delight, a few even let out scattered claps.

"As you have probably guessed, today we'll be learning about the wonderful creatures that are the Asian Elephant. I hope everybody brought something to swim in, cause today you'll be getting a little more up close and personal with them than you might expect..."

There was no secret about what was coming next. It was all her students could talk about...

"You lot, at the end of the day, will become junior elephant keepers — hu — how about that! And elephants, especially ours, need a lot of help. Alright, everyone follow me!"

The crowd trudged behind eagerly; tripping over one another as the keeper rambled on.

"Here at Eastman's sanctuary, we have three hundred elephants on seven-thousand acres of land. Most of the big boys and girls you'll meet today are rescues from Thailand and Indonesia. Sadly they've been mistreated by the locals in their area. Some were forced into giving rides to tourists twelve hours a day — really fat ones; others were attacked by village farmers. For that reason, many of them require a lot of tender love and care. However, cupid has a special, extra thick arrow that he's pierced some of our big guys with, so you'll spot quite a few babies who've been born here at Eastman's sanctuary. Can anyone here tell me how long an elephant's gestation period lasts? Anyone? Anyone at all?"

Several eager hands poked out around the crowd, but Val was distracted by the sight of something else. She could have sworn, out of the corner of her eye, a shadow was following along behind the crowd. But this wasn't like any shadow she'd seen before; it had a greyness about it, a sinister greyness...

They reached a high, wooden landing. Students rushed to the ledge, leaning over as their eyes drank in the view. Grey and orange spotted elephants as far as the eye could see roamed about lazily; walking in herds scattered here and there. A few were itching their backsides on trees; while some seemed much more interested in each other's backsides... Val caught a glimpse of a baby, running underneath his mother's legs. Her heart warmed in her chest.

"Alrighty then, yes — yes, a lovely view isn't it. If I can just have you look to your left, we have a special guest making an appearance."

Loud gasps reverberated in Val's ear. She maneuvered her head to catch a better look at the largest elephant she had ever seen in her life, a leviathan that was being led on a rope by a keeper only a short distance from the students.

"This senior here is named Captain Pumpernickel." The keeper proudly proclaimed while slapping the side of his leg. "Now, normally we never put our elephants on a lead — we prefer the carrot, not the stick — but this big guy has a host of old man problems. Show them Jack."

The keeper frowned, then sighed. For a man who had one of the coolest jobs in the world, he looked surprisingly apprehensive. He gestured towards the elephant's one eye nonetheless.

"As you can see," The first keeper lectured, "Captain only has one eye, since he lost the other in a very scary, very intense accident... when he poked himself with a stick! Not his fault of course... it was a rowdy game whatever it was. His other eye will need cataract surgery soon, that's why it's looking a bit cloudy. Many of the babies here are his grandbabies or even great-grandbabies, quite the ladies' man he was back in the day. He's also quite constipated right now, as you can tell from his *very* large tummy. That's been a frequent problem with him lately, hence the scheduled enema, and the need for a lead..."

Val grimaced.

"Okay, well, on you go then."

The second keeper frowned again, but still trudged along. Like a soldier going to war.

The students were escorted from one spot in the sanctuary to the next over the following few hours, learning interesting, if not gross facts about the giants that surrounded them. After feeding at least a hundred pounds of sugar cane to several over-eager elephants, who approached her as if they were enthusiastic lap dogs, and not absolutely massive beasts; the tour broke for a late lunch. Whereafter Val found herself being ushered off, to change into her swimsuit.

"I don't see the need for this?" Amina grumbled as she tucked the last strands of hair under her swimming cap. "Can't elephants bathe themselves?"

"Yes, but I think they like getting scrubbed down. It's like a spa day for them!"

The teachers and students scurried back outside in front of a large spring; where several elephants were already starting to line up, readying for what was coming next.

The keeper clapped her hands in front of her theatrically and rubbed them together.

"Alrighty — are you guys ready for this? You're all gonna be giving these big guys a scrub down! But first, I'm gonna need one volunteer from each group."

Hands had never shot up faster. Girls were practically begging their friends; some offering as much as their own parents' houses to be the volunteer.

"Alright — *you — you — you — you — you — you — you — and you!*"

The chosen ones sprinted up to her, seized the clipboards she held in her hands, and returned to their slightly deflated friends.

"As you can see, on the sheet of paper in front of you is a diagram of an elephant. As y'all are bathing your big guys, I want you all to keep an eye out for any abnormal scrapes, bumps, sores, or bruises... a bit of an *elephant inspection*, if you will. This information is very important to our vets here on our staff. Those of you who volunteered will mark down on the diagram where the vet should look at each elephant."

The tables had turned. The girls who were once so eager to volunteer themselves were now deflated. The last thing they wanted to do right now was any sort of *"work".*

"Alright, ladies — let's line them up!"

One by one, the elephants walked across the beach of the spring, until only one faced the front of each group. Their heavy paws shook the earth, as they turned around, and frolicked gayly into the water. Once they were submerged the girls followed after them, nervously holding their buckets, soap, and soft sponges.

"They're so... *rubbery...*" One of the girls in Val's group grimaced, as she scrubbed some dirt out from behind the elephant's ear.

"Well, what did you expect?" Principal Arif, who was working on a baby elephant next to them, shot back. "Did they look soft? Look at their skin, it's more droopy and saggy than my 99-year-old grandmother's."

"Mine has a pimple near its butt!" One of the other girls screamed. "Should I pop it?"

"Absolutely *not* Ms. Putri! If you touch anywhere near that thing, I'll put you down for a year's worth of detention — do you understand? But do mark it down on your clipboard."

The girl quietly sneered, before getting back to work scrubbing the elephant's backside. Principal Arif turned to Val, lowering her voice considerably so that the other students wouldn't hear.

"Hey, so, I've been meaning to ask you a question..."

"Oh, yeah?" Val responded mindlessly. "Sure, anything."

Principal Arif gave one more quick look around, to make sure the girls were focused on the elephants, before continuing. "I've been noticing a lot of... interesting behaviors... from Ms. Amina lately. She's been sick to her stomach quite a bit."

Val felt her face grow hot. "Mhm, is that right?"

"Yeah, and well, I know you two have become quite good friends, and well, she seems to have gained a few pounds, but only in her belly... what I'm trying to ask is if there's anything I should know about her yet? Is she expecting... something... in the coming months?"

Val tried to look somewhere else, but her face always gave her away. She was never good at keeping secrets, honestly she was terrible at it, but *this* time Val had actually kept her mouth shut.

"I really think you should be asking Amina that question. It's really not my place—"

Principal Arif grabbed her arm, and squeezed down hard. *Really* fucking hard.

"What're you d—" Val gasped!

"Please!" Principal Arif begged, in a hushed, urgent whisper. "This is something I need to know about *now!* There will be no time to waste once we get back!"

"It's just a baby!" Val protested. "You gotta have teachers getting pregnant all the time? Isn't there some protocol for her maternity leave?"

"It's not just that—" Principal Arif hissed, her dark eyes nearly bulging out of their sockets. "The moment *She* knows a pregnant woman is in her midst, the second *SHE* senses a mother with child — it'll be very dangerous for Amina at Semua Tangan. We must know ahead of time so that we can be prepared."

"Who's we? What're you talking about?" Val whispered frantically, as she snatched her arm away from Principal Arif's now deathly grip.

"Us!" Principal Arif seethed. "You, me, Janitor Mawar, Groundskeeper Dian — we all need to come together and form a plan to make sure Amina doesn't leave our sights!"

Val paused. This was a problem. A predicament. One her brain wasn't ready for.

"Listen, I get it... *she* will target Amina... but I don't want to break her trust! I just started making friends here, and I really like them. You're gonna have to ask her on your own before I get involved."

"You don't understand the urgency of this! I need to know—"

But something had caught Val's eye... she could have sworn a student had just flown into the bushes right before the woods. They still jostled slightly in the breeze. Val peered over at the rest of the students, none of whom seemed to notice anything out of the ordinary. Except for two, familiar young faces... who were now frantically racing towards the trees themselves...

It was Val's turn to seize Principal Arif's arm.

"Ouch! Hey — what're you—"

Before she could finish, Val was dragging her out of the water. The crunchy pebbles beneath her feet stung from the sunlight, but Val didn't care.

"It's *her!"* Val hissed. *"She's* here!"

"What're you talking about? Who's here?"

"*HER!*" Val snarled back. "The *HER* we were just talking about! I think she's got a student in the forest — we need to go now!"

Val watched the sudden realization hit Principal Arif. All color drained from her face, and her mouth dropped open. "We need to go now!"

The two scrambled to reach the forest thicket, where Val had just witnessed Eng Ki and Wani disappear. Before Val climbed into the brush, she heard loud gasps from behind, echoing from several of her students."

"Ah—" The keeper squealed. "Well, glad to see poor Captain's enema finally kick in. Don't be shy — It's just a bit of *raw* nature for you."

Val ignored the commotion, and dashed off behind Principal Arif into the thicket. They followed the hurried footsteps of the two girls ahead of them until they hit a clearing.

For a brief moment, Val just assumed she must be dreaming... there was no way what she was seeing right now, right in front of her, at this very instance, could be real, it couldn't be... but there *she* was none-the-less. A gray figure, crouching on a large rock just in front of them. *She* twirled a long wretched finger, while Zara thrashed violently underneath.

"HEY!" A high-pitched, shaky voice to the left of her bellowed. "*LET HER GO!*"

The gray figure gazed up at Eng Ki curiously; making a face Val could only describe as unbothered, amused, and malicious at the same time, but it didn't last long. Wani picked up a rock and lugged it, hitting *her* square on the cheek. The creature stumbled back and grabbed the side of *her* face; whimpering just momentarily, before turning back to face the young girls. *Her* ruby eyes blazed like fire... *she* began to crawl towards them...

Val panicked — she picked up a rock from the ground and mimicked Wani. Principal Arif joined in by hurling another stone. The creature swirled its head to look at them. *Her* large, malevolent eyes piercing Val's soul... *she* changed directions, and lunged at the women now!

Wani and Eng Ki took their chance. They sprinted towards Zara, who was lying on the ground, foaming at the mouth. The creature noticed this too. *She* stopped in her tracks, and for a moment it seemed Wani and Eng Ki would reach her. They were almost there, just fingertips away...

The gray creature lifted her arms into the air... Val felt an unknown force seize her, then throw her up... she hit a tree twenty feet above the ground. Val was held there, gasping for air as if she was pinned by her throat. She kicked wildly around the empty space underneath. Her hands grasped desperately at her own neck, but it was no use.

Val peered around at the rest of the group, who were all in the same predicament as she; being invisibly tethered to surrounding trees. The four of them formed an awkward square around the creature, as Zara began thrashing again. Val tried to scream, but she could barely force down enough air to even breathe.

The creature sneered a horrible smile. A smile that *irked* Val. The biggest smile she had ever seen, yet it still didn't reach the creature's eyes. *She* crawled over Zara until she was on top of her stomach, and their foreheads were touching. Val imagined being in Zara's position; being so close, face to face with that... thing... demon... monster... It made her stomach flip.

She watched, as its face began to change; from a snarl, that would frighten the most ambitious predator, to a wide, ominous, laugh. *She* laughed, and laughed, and laughed — as her howls and wails echoed around the forest. It was such a deep, uneasy, petrifying sound, that Val even felt as if the ancient, towering tree she was pinned to shook, deep within its trunk.

The creature stopped abruptly, climbing up onto the elevated rock that *she* had perched on earlier. *She* raised her arms once more, but this time, it wasn't Val, or Wani, feeling her terrifying power, but only Zara. Her limp, frail body started rising up into the air. Five feet... then ten feet... passing the creature, then Val and the others, rising ever higher, and higher, and higher... Val's heart sank, as she imagined the horrible fright the last wisps of Zara's poor consciousness must be feeling right about now.

The creature commenced laughing again; more loudly, and maniacally than before. The sound filled Vals' ears with dread. This was it... she was about to witness the murder of her favorite student... Val shut her eyes.

But then, something happened... something, *unexpected*... another rock hit the creature dead in the face. Zara dropped thirty feet or so, before being caught in the air again by the creature's force. *She* swirled her head around wildly, before her plum-sized, ruby eyes found the source...

Nur was standing where Val had just been, scooping down to retrieve another rock.

The creature lunged towards her — seizing Nur's throat in *her* hands — then pinning her to another tree. *She* snarled and growled, clawing her ten-inch stiletto claws at Nur's face. Nur struggled to throw *her* hands off her. *She* had nearly worn Nur down, when a thunderous quaking shook the ground...

A large, grey mass broke through the trees... a familiar elephant stampeded towards the creature and Nur. *She* dropped Nur to the ground, and Nur managed to scramble away just in time, as Captain rammed his head straight into her attacker! The creature wailed, and dropped to the ground, before a gust of fierce rage seemed to reinvigorate *her*. *She* snarled at the beast, before jumping onto its head, and attempting to claw at Captain's remaining eye. He threw *her* to the ground, cushing *her* under his massive feet.

Val felt the force holding her lift. She dropped to the forest floor, there was no time to waste, even though her ankle was *very* sprained. She, as well as Principal Arif, Eng Ki, and Wani sprinted to catch Zara before she hit the ground...

They caught her just in time.

Val felt something in her shoulder snap, but there was no pain. The adrenaline rushing through her veins would've been enough to arouse even the elephant who was now moving towards them in his battle against the creature.

The fight was not going as well for Captain. Several messy claw incisions down his back oozed blood. He grabbed the creature with his trunk, and threw *her* against trees, and down on the ground, before sounding out a loud, trumpeting wail...

The forest was quiet for a moment... before a slow, steady, rumbling began to shake the ground again... leaves and branches tumbled from trees like rain. They scrambled for cover, as the dust around them shook into the air...

A stampede of elephants from all directions descended upon them one by one, until at least thirty elephants surrounded the creature. *She* attacked each animal as enthusiastically as she had fought Captain; going from one to the next with the tenacity and rage of nothing Val had ever seen in her life.

It was a battle like none had ever witnessed, which Val watched crouched underneath a small, but steady rock formation, along with the six other humans. Eventually though, it was no use prolonging the inevitable. There were too many elephants — even the babies were coming now. Cuts, scrapes, and bruises littered the evil creature's body, as *she* retreated away into the forest; with a fury in *her* eyes that Val guessed would never subside...

The six of them hustled back out of the trees, towards the spring as quickly as their limping bodies would allow. The pain of Val's sprained ankles made her knees buckle, but they had to keep going...

"I'll have to come up with some story..." Principal Arif huffed. "I got it — we're gonna tell them that a tiger dragged Zara away — do you understand me? I need us all to stick to the same version of events!"

Everyone nodded. They finally made it back out of the trees. Zara's consciousness slowly returning, as she was lugged back through the sanctuary, and onto the nearest bus.

"I'm a doctor!" Nur squealed. "I can take care of your injuries." She turned towards Eng Ki and Wani, who besides a few minor scrapes and bruises appeared perfectly fine. "You two — go get me a bottle of water and several cold rags!"

The two girls sprinted off. Nur reached for her emergency kit, and pulled out tools Val couldn't recognize.

"Blood pressure 110 over 60 — oxygen 93 — pulse 65—" She listened through the scope for her breathing. "Shaky, but there." Nur picked up the neck brace and fastened it around Zara's neck. "Sweety, can you hear me." She called in Zara's ear.

Zara nodded her little head.

"Can you feel this?" Nur grabbed her arms, then legs, and squeezed.

Zara let out a soft: "Mhhm."

"Do you have any pain here, or here?" Nur asked firmly, as she pressed down on different parts of her stomach.

"No." She cooed.

Nur grabbed a tiny silver flashlight from her bag. "I'm gonna need you to open your eyes for me." Nur commanded. Val watched Nur pry Zara's almond-shaped, black eyes open; then beam her blaze into Zara's pupils, which recoiled as the light hit them.

Nur had Zara recite her name, where they were, the name of her school, and her birthdate. After the world's easiest interrogation Nur let out a long, winded sigh, and wiped the sweat from her brow.

"She's gonna be okay!"

Val felt her own body go limp in relief. They barely had enough time to catch their own breath, when Wani, Eng Ki, and a stuttering Amina clamored onto the bus.

"What's going on exactly? Wani and Eng Ki say someone was attacked by a tiger?"

Principal Arif scowled at the two girls. "Why did you tell her that?"

"You said to tell people she was dragged off by a tiger!" Wani cried. "We were just following your orders."

"You can tell the faculty the truth." She sighed, her eyes rolling. "No Ms. Amina, it was *her*... our *her*. Zara here is fine, but she was attacked!"

"Here?" Amina gasped. "But *she's* never left the grounds before! How'd *she*—"

"Something must have enticed her enough to leave." Principal Arif growled. "What's going on outside right now?"

"Well, the rest of the students were finishing up bathing their elephants, when all of a sudden they stampeded off somewhere. It was quite scary. I think some of the elephants got injured somehow. They ushered us away so I'm not really sure what happened. Thankfully no one was hurt, a few of us are a bit shaken up, but that's it. The students are headed towards the buses now."

"Go tell everyone to grab their things, and to board all the buses but this one. It will be a bit cramped but it'll have to do — three to a seat should hold them all. And let them know that everyone's okay and that there's no need to panic. I'll inform the faculty of today's events once we get back."

Amina turned to leave, but before she had taken the last step off, Principal Arif called to her once more. "And when you get done with that, grab the remaining bags from the locker room, since they are probably everyone on board this bus's stuff, and come back here to ride with us."

Amina nodded, before hobbling off the bus, and doing as she was instructed. She returned a few minutes later with help from the bus driver; who came to her aid since the two of them were tripping over themselves carrying everyone's belongings. The driver dumped everything onto the seats behind her, then took off behind their caravan.

Principal Arif turned to Nur, who was now checking Zara for any trace of a temperature. "Thank you for coming today... we're so lucky to have a doctor in our midst at such a crisis."

Nur gave one of her now signature shy smiles; the confidence and authority she boasted just moments ago having since melted away. "Oh, it's nothing really... just doing my job."

Wani turned to Zara, who by now was in slightly better spirits. She could sit up with the help of Eng Ki on her other side.

"Are you okay?"

Zara nodded her head softly. "Yeah." she cooed. "I'll be okay, just need to rest..."

Val turned to Amina, lowering her voice. "She knows." Val whispered.

Amina shot her a bewildered look. "Who? Knows what?"

Val nudged her head towards Principal Arif. "She knows you're pregnant. I didn't tell her I swear — she guessed it."

Amina's jaw dropped. She grabbed her stomach, and turned around to face Principal Arif. "How'd you—"

Principal Arif rolled her eyes once more. "That's not the point here — we need to focus on your safety. *She* might've followed us here because *she* sensed your pregnancy."

Amina gasped once more. "I — I..." She stuttered. "But *she* didn't even attack me today — *she* attacked little Zara."

"That doesn't matter, for all we know, *she* could have been following you. In all my years at Semua Tangan, I have never seen *her* more riled up than when there are pregnancies on campus; and most of her anger is directed at those who are pregnant. However, as we saw today, *her* rage can and does spill over to other targets..." she peered over to Zara again, who was now being fed yogurt from Wani's lunch box. "We need to make sure you're not alone at all times at the school."

Amina was about to protest, but instead let her jaw hand. She nodded her head in uneasy acceptance. They drove along for several minutes before Wani asked what was on everybody else's mind.

"How'd *she* get there?"

"Isn't it obvious?" Principal Arif replied. "*She* rode the bus with the rest of us."

"I think I saw *her* following us around the sanctuary." Val added.

"Well then, how's *she* gonna get back?"

No one said a word; having already known the answer. They exchanged silent, nervous glances amongst one another...

CHAPTER EIGHT

"You did what?" Khoo Hun Chhiau fumed, while pacing back and forth the length of Val's room.

"I followed *her* in there." Val bickered back. "What was I supposed to do? Let my students die?"

"You could have called the police! You could have taken more people with you! Instead you drag Principal Arif along? She weighs what — Fifty kilos max — and is nearly in her seventies!"

"I didn't exactly have any options... and besides, *she* was able to take on a whole herd of elephants by herself. I doubt a few police officers would have changed things much." Val sassed. She swung her arms up in the air in exasperation, before feeling as if a rubber band in her shoulder had just snapped.

Yesterday, after the bus had made it back to Semua Tangan, Principal Arif had a quick staff meeting; informing everyone of the actual events that took place, and of what everyone's stories should be if asked. Nur did a quick checkup of Val, quickly finding the rotator cuff injury in her left shoulder; most likely from catching Zara. Surprisingly, Principal Arif had come out of everything with just a few scratches and bruises.

Val remembered what she had promised to Khoo Hun Chhiau, but decided to wait on messaging him until the next day. After a nice, pleasant breakfast, at which Yeo A'i and her had made plans to get a dual pedicure/pawdicure with Prince Diana, Val had picked up her phone and sent him a quick message — just saying something with *"her"* had happened, but she was okay. Twenty minutes later, he was now sitting on her bed, dressed in a dark navy suit; looking as dashing, and as gripey as ever. Val could've sworn she smelled aftershave.

"What do you mean *she* took on a whole herd of elephants?" Khoo Hun Chhiau pried angrily.

Val rolled her eyes and finished her story. She watched, as Khoo Hun Chhiau's lips pursed tighter and tighter, until they disappeared into his mouth. By the end of it, he was rubbing his face stressfully.

"She's tougher than she looks, you know... and out of anyone alive, Principal Arif has the most experience dealing with *her.*" Val reassured him. "Where are you going anyways, all dressed up like that?"

Khoo Hun Chhiau shook his head and peered up at her with heavy eyes. "I'm catching a flight in a few hours to Singapore. I took next week off at the station so I could catch up on some stuff at the university."

Wasting a vacation week to go do even more work sounded utterly appalling to Val. "And you have to wear a suit on the plane?" She pried.

He shook his head, and his voice grew louder. "No, I have a presentation I'm giving in front of some people."

Val raised an eyebrow. "Some people? Who? You hadn't mentioned anything about this before?"

"That's because it's none of your business!" He bellowed, as his black, fiery eyes scowled at her. "None of this, here, should be any of your business!"

"I — what do you mean none of this is my business? I'm the teacher — this is *MY* business—"

"You shouldn't even be here — none of this should be your problem! You're not prepared to deal with half the stuff that goes on at that school!"

Val felt a rush of blood reach her head all at once. "Excuse me? What're you trying to—"

"You should be at home — you never should have come here!"

"Who are *YOU* to tell *ME* what I should and shouldn't d—"

But he cut her off once more. "You need to leave — *now!*"

"Who are you to tell me to leave? You're in MY ROOM!"

"That's not what I meant..." Khoo Hun Chhiau growled.

"I—" But the wind had been knocked out of her. Someone could have roundhouse kicked Val in the stomach, and the sensation would've been the same. She tried to summon the words she would say next, but her lungs, and her spirits, had deflated.

"If you don't have the money for a ticket home, I'll loan you some... actually, I'll buy you a ticket myself." He pulled out his phone and started furiously typing.

Val couldn't believe the absolute selfish nerve of him. A part of her wanted nothing more than to take a seat, and try to emotionally recover from whatever he'd put her through just now. Another wanted to throw him out the window.

"You need to leave..." She growled.

It took a moment for Khoo Hun Chhiau to recognize she'd said something. "What?"

"Get out!" She seethed, pointing to her door. "Get out now — and don't come back!"

Khoo Hun Chhiau flinched, like he'd just been bitten by a dog, or stung by a bee. For a moment she nearly relented, but then the pain she'd felt came cascading back.

"Val... I"

"Leave!" She yelled as tears started to prick the corners of her eyes. "Leave — Get out — Move!" She cried, pulling him up from the bed, and pushing him out through her door; down the stairs, through the dining area, and past a thoroughly confused Yeo A'i; who was sipping a cup of tea curiously observing them.

"Val... I was... it's just not safe! You need to—"

They reached the front door. Val thrust it open and shoved Khoo Hun Chhiau outside. "Just go!" Val blubbered, while trying to keep her voice from cracking. It didn't work. "Seriously just... go..."

Val watched, as Khoo Hun Chhiau's emotions wavered; from anger, to remorse, to reflection... then finally back to anger.

"When I get back here this time next Saturday... I want you gone..."

Val slammed the door in his face, then turned around, and collapsed onto the living room sofa, sobbing. She had no idea where all this emotion was coming from, but it was becoming harder and harder for her to control. Yeo A'i and Prince Diana had reached her within mere seconds. Yeo A'i cradling her body, and Prince Diana licking the tears off her face.

"I'm really glad I made that appointment for us now." Yeo A'i demurred.

They sat curled up together until Val finally wiped her last tear away. She changed out of her pajamas, before heading out; embarrassed by the scene she'd just caused.

"Well, that wasn't very nice of him." Yeo A'i griped as the nail tech began scrubbing the bottom of her feet. "You know, he may not have handled his emotions very well just now, but I don't blame him for being a bit worried about you working at Semua Tangan."

Val winced, as the middle-aged woman in front of her pushed back her nail cuticles. It was her least favorite part of the pedicure. She much preferred just letting her feet soak in the warm water. It calmed her, siphoning the stress away from her body like very few other things could.

"What do you mean you don't blame him?"

"Well, you know…" she faltered. "Now don't get me wrong, I love Semua Tangan. Always have, always will. The staff is great, the teachers are excellent, the administrators have their shit together, and the whole community is like one big family. My daughter's time there was some of my most precious years of motherhood… but there's definitely a danger lurking…" her tone shifted to a more solemn countenance. "Everybody knows to always keep their eyes out, just in case something grave happens… word travels fast here. We all already know that was no tiger attack that happened yesterday."

Val gasped, nearly kicking her very upset nail tech in the face in her shock. "You guys already know about that?"

Yeo A'i nodded. "A tiger attack? I'm shocked Principal Arif couldn't come up with a more convincing lie. There are only around three hundred and fifty wild tigers left in Malaysia, and that breed is the smallest type of tiger there is. What would a Malayan tiger be doing prowling around an elephant sanctuary?"

"She really didn't have time to make up a better one." Val mumbled as a question popped into her mind. "Did your daughter ever have any run-ins... with *her?*"

Yeo A'i let out a long, remembering sigh. She glanced down at the nail tech, who was now massaging her calves. "She did... once."

"What happened?"

Yeo A'i's mind seemed to wander again. Far away, back into a distant memory... "She was only about ten at the time. I remember her crawling into the passenger seat of my car after school, a bit shaken up. I tried to get her to talk to me... I tried to get her to explain what was wrong... I assumed that she'd gotten a bad grade, or maybe someone had said something mean to her that day. There was a particularly nasty girl I remember, Farah, with an even nastier mother." Yeo A'i scowled. "One time she spit gum into my baby's hair, then got off by saying that she "accidentally sneezed" cause she was allergic to my daughter; but that's a story for another day. Anyways, I just assumed Farah had pulled another stunt or something; but she seemed a bit more troubled, a bit more disturbed... so, after several hours of prying, and more than fifty pinky promises and swears that I wouldn't call her crazy, she finally opened up... the story she told still keeps me up at night if I dwell on it for too long..."

"What'd she say?" Val asked softly.

Yeo A'i let out another long sigh. "She said that she had gone to the bathroom one class by herself, and afterwards when she was washing her hands, she saw *her* in the reflection of the mirror!"

Val's heart flipped.

"She said that *she* — that creature — whatever it is, put her hands over my baby's eyes, and then she fell into a trance of some sort. She said that it was like she had woken up in the middle of a forest, at night, by herself... she said that she walked around aimlessly, for hours, or more like something led her for hours... some unseen force that she couldn't quite describe to me. Almost like she was being pulled by an invisible string!"

Val could relate to being coerced by invisible forces at this point.

"She said that after hours and hours, she finally crawled up a tree, and started watching a family... but not just *any* family, an indigenous Orang Asli family; in a partially completed house made of old woods. She said that she saw a father sleeping on a mat, a mother cooking, and a small toddler moseying around. Then, after a few minutes, the toddler seemed to notice her, and it made eye contact!"

Val braced for what was coming next. Any story with a toddler, and *her* in it was not one she was keen on rehearing. "And then what?"

"And then she woke up." Yeo A'i finished.

Val felt her muscles relax within her chest, and her breath steady. "That's it?"

Yeo A'i nodded. Well, she woke up with some scratches on her hand, three scratches to be exact. I had to bandage them up when we got home that day. I can still hear her screams as I washed them with rubbing alcohol. That whole day was very strange..."

"I bet... to have a daughter go through something like that, I mean, that's not gonna be covered in any parenting books. Well, maybe some pretty curious ones..."

Yeo A'i shook her head. "Not that... it's strange because the exact same thing happened to me when I was her age, twenty-five years before."

Val felt the blood leave her hands and feet, and rush to her chest — as if to restart her heart. "Are... are you serious?"

Yeo A'i nodded once more. She pulled up the frayed ends of her long sleeve shirt, and revealed three squiggly scars on the palm of her hand.

"I only ever attended Semua Tangan for one year, when I lived with my grandmother when I was ten. My father had suddenly been promoted in his company, so he had to move to London; and my mother had gone ahead with him. For that one year, I was all by myself here, that's when I had that encounter with... *her.*" She looked away, her voice quivering. "*She* must have spotted me one day in the drop-off line and decided to pay my child a visit."

For the second time that day, Val was at a loss for words. "Yeo A'i... I'm so, so sorry!"

Yeo A'i wiped a minuscule tear from her own face, and turned back to face Val. "It's okay, it happened a long time ago, me and my girl are doing just fine now." She assured her as she forced a soft smile. "But that's why I don't want you to take Khoo Hun Chhiau's words to heart. It's obvious the boy really cares about you!"

"It is?" Val asked, with a doubtful expression on her face. "I don't know about that..."

"Oh, it is." Yeo A'i smiled. "I remember him as a teenager. He was the captain of the boys' soccer team; which is kind of a big deal in our town, but the pride never seemed to go to his head. He always remained so... so reserved, so modest."

Val never knew this about him. A sinful part of her regretted not snooping around his room sooner that night. "And?"

"Well, you don't see it... there's no way... but I see him fix his hair before you come to get him at the front door. I see him check his breath, and sneak on a bit more deodorant in his car before he gets out. I see the way he looks at you, and how he lets you drag him around the house like you do. That's *very* out of the ordinary for Khoo Hun Chhiau. I once saw him recoil his hand so quickly when he and another woman had grabbed the same soup can, that he smacked himself in the face!"

Val snorted. "Seriously?"

Yeo A'i nodded. "And if someone would have told me last year, that Khoo Hun Chhiau, the modest, polite, police officer; who according to his own late mother never broke curfew, not even once; would be coming over to my house every day to hang out with a single *American* woman late into the night, in her room alone — I would have laughed in their face!"

Val tried to conceal her deeply redding cheeks, but to no avail. The nail tech was now working on her right hand, which was pinned to the armrest. The other was still too painful to move. *Damn* rotator cuff!

"It's still no excuse though, the way he was acting today..."

"No, no it's not." Yeo A'i agreed. "He should know better than that. That was *very* rude of him, but still... all I'm saying is that I *sympathize with his feelings*. When that happened to my daughter, I nearly packed up all our things and moved as far away from here as I could."

"Why didn't you?" Val asked. "Why doesn't anybody do something about... *her*? Why don't they move the school — bulldoze it — or something?"

"Oh, you know... most of the time people just don't talk about their run-ins with *her*. Occasionally when they do happen and are brought up at our city council meetings, something more pressing *always* happens elsewhere. I swear his town has the attention span of a four year old... on crack..."

Val chucked.

"But then children grow into adults, move away. The parents who stay get numb to the news. We also haven't exactly had a string of good treasurers to say the least... like i said, a bunch of four year olds on crack. When all's said and done, nothing ever happens. Never has. Never will."

They finished their session. The pair paid, and thanked their nail techs for a job well done, before picking up Prince Diana from his appointment. Val could have sworn his nails were every bit as glamorous as her own.

Val went about the rest of her week as she normally would; teaching, attending Wednesday night bachelor viewing parties, and taking long walks with Yeo A'i and Prince. To her dismay however, she found that as much as it pained her to admit it, her nights felt much more lonely now, without Khoo Hun Chhiau's silent presence in the corner of her room; typing away on his old, rickety laptop. Every few days, Val would check her phone, finding a random *"hey"* or *"can we talk"* message from him, but Val never responded. He deserved to suffer for how he had made her feel that day; small, belittled, powerless.... when she had told him her story, she'd expected sympathy, some words of encouragement, maybe even a hug... instead all she'd gotten was his chastising wrath.

The next time Val ran into Khoo Hun Chhiau was the following Saturday. Amina had invited Val out to a roller rink, and had conveniently left out the fact that Jano had invited Khoo Hun Chhiau along as well. She ignored him, instead choosing to skate next to Nur, which wasn't the best idea. They kept falling, then trying to help each other up, then just falling some more. It didn't help that neither of their ankles had recovered from the week before.

By the end of the night, Val was covered in skid marks and bruises. She rubbed her numb feet, changed back into her sneakers, and headed outside after Nur; who had agreed to take her home. They were nearly to her motorbike when Val felt a tug at her arm... she turned around, not surprised at who was standing in front of her.

Khoo Hun Chhiau was glaring down at her, with wide eyes that needed something.

"Hey," he said softly, "can you ride home with me?"

Val pulled her arm back. "I already have a ride." She snapped. Val flipped her hair over her shoulder. *Maybe that was too much...*

But at that moment, they heard a painful scream echo across the parking lot. Val swirled around to find the source... Parini was leaning against the trunk of a nearby car, doubled over...

Water dripped down her jeans.

"She's gone into labor!" Nur called, springing into action. Nur ran over, put an arm around Parini, and helped her into the car. The shell-shocked husband was absolutely useless. Nur grabbed his keys from him, shouting instructions.

"Get in the passenger's seat — I'll drive — do you have your overnight bag packed — is it in this car?"

"Yes!" Panted Parini, as another, long, painful moan cascaded from her mouth. "It's — It's in the trunk."

They sped off, leaving Val and Khoo Hun Chhiau behind, by themselves. Val searched for Tan Soan, or Amina and Jano, but they must've left already. She peered back up at Khoo Hun Chhiau, who seemed a bit frightened by what just happened; like he hadn't quite recovered from the shock. To be honest, she hadn't either.

"Wanna go get some ice cream?" Val asked.

Khoo Hun Chhiau nodded. They crawled into his old, cluttered proton, and drove slowly down the highway; reaching *The Hippocalories* just a few minutes later. They quickly ordered, and took seats near the corner of the room. The pair sat together in awkward silence, until Val's heart dropped into her stomach. She ducked down under the table.

"What in the world are you doin—?" But before Khoo Hun Chhiau had finished, his question had been answered. Three familiar preteen girls had entered the ice cream shop; giggling like goblins.

Val popped up for just a second. They hadn't noticed her. *Good. Great.* She thought. *God I'm stealthy. I should've been a spy, not a teacher.* "Ouch!"

That last part was out loud... it was too late. Zara noticed Val bump her head. She slapped Eng Ki and Wani so they could see. Val had never seen the three of them grow such wide, mischievous smiles. Before Val had even enough time to stand up, they'd rushed over; surrounding all points of escape.

"So—" Wani smirked, as she rubbed her hands together menacingly. "What's going on here?"

"Did we interrupt your *DATE!*" Eng Ki screamed, as she slammed her hands down on their table, like a detective in a really unrealistic movie. Val really could *not* with these cheese heads right now...

"No!" Val seethed. "Don't you three have more important things to do? They're almost out of chocolate ice cream... probably enough for just one more person..."

Wani's eyes fluttered momentarily, but the sight of a teacher out and about in such a compromising position was just too strong of a catch. "I don't even like chocolate ice cream!" She lied. "The fact of the matter is, we need to get to the bottom of what's going on right *here*, right *now!* You never mentioned in class that you had a *boyfriend!* You better not — what did TMZ say again — *"Leave him on read"* — was it? Like you did your ex Killer Wiz Akeem!"

"That's sure what he said in his new song, *Desert Princess*... have you heard it yet Ms. Val?"

"Number one in the charts!"

"I wonder who he could be talking about... now who do we know that has been known to date Killer Wiz Akkem, who also lived in a desert?"

It was Khoo Hun Chhiau's turn to grimace now. He turned to Val, his face now beat red. "You dated who?" He mouthed.

Val nearly pulled her hair out from her scalp.

"Ohh!"

"He didn't know!" Zara whispered.

"You didn't tell your current boyfriend about who exactly your last one was? Tell me—" Wani went on, relishing this moment more than she probably had any other in her life, "is it just... too soon? Haven't worked out how you were gonna break the news? Aren't you so lucky then that you ran into us to do it for you?"

Val was sure one of her teeth might crack from grinding them.

"Listen—" She seethed, "if you three don't get out of my sight this second, I'll write you a detention cleaning toilets with Ms. Nadar — she'll make you get on your hands *and* knees!"

Eng Ki scoffed. One hand found her chest, the other, Wani's shoulder. Val huffed. Maybe this wasn't a strong enough threat. If any group could break a teacher's spirits, it would be these three. "Excuse us, your eager, and faithful pupils, for ruining your date!"

"Date? Did someone say date?"

The three girls composed themselves on the spot, as what appeared to be Zara's parents approached.

"Who's out on a date? Khoo Hun Chhiau? Is that you?"

Khoo Hun Chhiau lost all composure. "No, no, Mr. Tengku... well, it's me, but no one is out on a date here... I'm just taking this young lady home after one of our friends went into labor."

The adults scowled down at him, shifting their eyes from Khoo Hun Chhiau, to their ice creams, then finally to Val herself. Val avoided eye contact.

"Well," Zara's dad said sternly, "carry on... girls, stop bothering these two and go get yourselves some ice cream."

The girls scurried away with their tails between their legs. Khoo Hun Chhiau and Val sat in silence once more.

"So, uhhh... you dated Killer Wiz Ahkeem?"

"Shut it." Val snapped.

"Okay, okay.... uhh... I just wanted to apologize for the way I reacted the other day. That was wrong of me, but you have to understand—"

"You made me feel horrible!" Val sputtered, quietly though. The gang of three were not far off. "I'd just had a terrible, *terrible* experience, and all you did was shout at me like that — when you asked me to confide in you!"

"I know—" He groaned. "But you have to understand where I was coming from. I just wanted you to be safe! I just wanted to protect you from *her*... and I thought the only way to do that was to get you out of here!"

Val's cheeks grew red, with both anger and something else. "It's not your job to protect me! I'm a grown-up, I'm perfectly able to protect myself!"

"I know, it's just that after that story you told me, I... I don't know..." He grimaced, and looked off through the window, out into the pitch-black night.

Val reflected back to her conversation with Yeo A'i. *I sympathize with his feelings*, she had said...

"I'm sorry I scared you... but you had asked me to tell you if anything happened, and I did. Then you just went nuts on me like that."

"I know, I know." He confessed. "And I still want you to tell me when things like that happen again."

Val nearly scoffed, but the look in his eyes held her back. "Okay, but only if next time you promise to keep your cool, and actually comfort me if I'm scared, or something..."

"Okay." Khoo Hun Chhiau nodded cooly, though Val could read through his composed demeanor, seeing the eagerness underlying it.

Val stuck out her hand to shake, but quickly retreated it when she noticed Zara's parents glaring at her. They finished their ice cream, and Khoo Hun Chhiau dropped Val off in front of Yeo A'i's house.

CHAPTER NINE

Killer Wiz Akeem's new song had seemingly spread around to every student Val passed. She shrugged off the quiet, sporadic, snickering going on in her classes, but with each sideways glance and interrupted gossip session, her patience was pushed further to its limit. More than once she passed by a student, only to hear a cough that sounded conspicuously like *"Desert princess."* Students responded to questions regarding the spider Charlotte's devotion to Wilbur the pig, with answers that made as much sense as that he, Wilber, *"was a goddess amongst pigs";* or *"had skin as smooth as butter"* that *"any spider would be willing to shell out every last inch of webbing for; if only they could see his beautiful, piggy smile one more time..."* There were even a few very bold students who risked it all; incorporating the most provocative of lyrics, that made the hair on the back of Val's neck stand up.

By the time Val walked out of her last class of the day, she ended up giving the whole period detention. Someone had drawn a very graphic picture on her chalkboard. Presumably of a scantily clad Val, licking chocolate syrup off of a shirtless Killer Wiz Akeem. No one would fess up and admit who had done it.

"You should have made her fatter — add in a couple extra rolls around her stomach!" Wani whispered to a stout, sneaky girl after Val had handed her a detention slip. But before Val could catch up with them, they had scurried away.

"Damnit!" Val huffed, before giving up and stomping off towards the front entrance of the school. Val had just made it to the front doors, when her body rammed into another teacher, who was rushing out from behind.

Val clambered on the floor, picking up her things. "Excuse me — watch where you're going!"

Ms. Nadar kept forward as if nothing happened. Val seethed, as her palms clenched around a box of tampons.

"You just knocked me over! Aren't you even gonna help me gather my stuff?" Val fumed.

"Ms. Val — Ms. Nadar!" Principal Arif's voice echoed from behind them. "A word?"

This made Ms. Nadar stop in her tracks. She hesitated, before turning back around, looking rather annoyed by this last-minute request. She headed straight for Principal Arif, stepping on several of Val's things while trudging over to her.

Val swore under her breath, as her favorite pen snapped underneath Ms. Nadar's ugly green flats. But Val didn't dare gripe at her now, right under Principal Arif's nose. Grumbling, she gathered the rest of her things; stuffing them in her purse, while pushing herself up from her hands and knees. Then dragged her sore body over for what she was sure to be a stern word about how *"teachers shouldn't be bickering in the halls."*

"Look, I'm sorry." Val started. "But Ms. Nadar really needs to watch where she's going—"

"What?" Principal Arif mumbled. "Never mind that — I need to brainstorm some ideas with you two..."

Val scratched her head. "What about?"

"Is it about how we can better enforce the *'no selfies in the bathroom'* rule? Cause I have a million ideas on that one—"

"Ms. Nadar, that's not an official school rule... no matter how many times you *pester* me to make it one. We have a much more important matter to discuss. Someone has snuck into the sports closet with a pair of scissors... now none of the soccer team uniforms, or the scraps that are left, will be usable... I borrowed some money from another fund, but we'll have to replenish it as soon as possible. Any ideas on how we raise enough money to do that?"

"We could charge every student breaking the *'no selfies in the bathrooms'* rule a hundred ringgit each?"

Principal Arif rolled her eyes. "How about you, Val? Do you have any tricks?"

Val thought back to her teen days on her own school's sports team — specifically playing JV basketball. A JV team that never even made a basket, much less won a game against another team. No thanks to Val, she sucked. Spectacularly. She was the only senior left in JV, but she used to help them in another way.

"We could do a bake sale?"

"A what?" Ms. Nadar barked.

"A bake sale — basically, you bake a bunch of brownies, cookies, and other sweets, and then you sell them at lunch and at games. That's how we always raised money for our teams."

Principal Arif pursed her lips, and gazed off for a second. "This... *American Bake sale...* do you remember how to make everything?"

"Yeah, I used to bake with my grandma all the time."

"Right then — we'll do this starting the game on Friday night. I want you two to make as many of these American pastries as you possibly can."

"Oh, that won't be necessary... I can just make them myself. I'm sure Yeo A'i can help me if I need it—"

Principal Arif was already shaking her head. "Nope. I want both of you to work on this together. Do you understand me?"

Ms. Nadar and Val shot each other seething glances once more, before Ms. Nadar begged one last time. "If you would just let me charge the stu—"

"I said you two will work together on this and that's final!" She huffed as she strutted off in the opposite direction. Her head scarf blowing in the breeze as she went.

Ms. Nadar and Val exchanged cursory glances before Ms. Nadar started. "My place is being fumigated right now—"

"We can meet at my place Thursday afternoon." Val said shortly.

"You should've just kept your mouth shut!" Ms. Nadar snapped. "I could've raised enough money for a whole year's worth of sports equipment if you would've just let me explain my selfie idea!"

Val had had enough of this conversation. She stormed off, back to Yeo A'i's. On the morning of Thursday, Val mentally prepared herself as best she could, listening to as many meditation podcasts as her phone could download; and even springing for an extra tub of ibuprofen on her way to Semua Tangan.

"You can do this." Her meditation app drawled in her ear. "No one can make you feel any negative emotions if you don't allow them..."

"I can do this." She repeated. "No one can make me feel any negative emotions if I don't allow — *"Hey!"*

Val had reached her classroom door. There, tacked on outside, was a TMZ picture of her and Killer Wiz Akeem, sloppily making out outside that *stupid* nightclub. Someone had even kindly written *"good morning"* over her butt. Val tore the photo down and stomped inside.

It seemed that every student of her's had chosen this day to test her patience. In her first class, two girls fought so viciously they literally stabbed each other's arms with their pens. Glitter pens, so their blood was *glittery*. In her second period, a girl nearly lit her desk on fire. Her third period was suspiciously quiet, but by lunchtime she'd found out why. They had all drawn little pock marks on themselves, and had in mass gone to the nurse's office afterward; claiming they had a bad case of *"Flamingo Pox"* and needed to go home for the day. Apparently it was *very* contagious. They were all denied, but it didn't stop her fourth and final class from trying it out as well.

"But I'm so itchy!" Wani cried, as she scratched at a mark on her arm, which smeared glitter. "I feel feverish!"

"No—" Val barked, "and for god's sake at least use a marker! Why'd you guys even name this stupid disease after a flamingo?"

"Because our pox are pink!"

Val had finally had enough. By the end of the day, she'd assigned toilet cleaning duty to anyone who had claimed they had "Flamingo

Pox" or one of its many derivations that were starting to spring about. When the final bell rang for the day, Val knew she wasn't ready for whatever would soon come, but there was nothing she could do now.

They met at the front entrance hall and walked back together to Yeo A'i's in silence. Ms. Nadar dumped several grocery bags worth of baking supplies onto Yeo A'i's bare counter.

"So—" Ms. Nadar started, "I went online, and watched some youtube videos on how to bake *"American"* style pastries. Where's your spatula? I bought a measuring cup with both metric and imperial measurements."

Val ignored her and poured everything into a mixing bowl. "Yeah— yeah, just go ahead and put some butter in a pot and brown it."

Ms. Nadar stood there, gaping silently. Her eyes shifting from Val's powdered hands to the unused measuring cup. "Mmmm, I never read anything online about browning butter? I went ahead and printed out the instructions for chocolate chip cookies if you wanna take a look... also, it's better to get all the ingredients exactly measured beforehand..."

Val pressed her lips together, and let out a long, exasperated sigh. "Ms. Nadar — you know what... *Thuya!*"

Ms. Nadar let out a small grunt. Her eyes grew dark, and hard.

"That's right—" Val teased, "I know your first name's Thuya, and I'm not calling you Ms. Nadar anymore, since you're probably what — a year — two years older than me? It's just weird."

Ms. Nadar scowled. "As we are colleges, we should be referring to each other in a formal sense—"

"Oh stop it Thuya right now or I swear I'll set Prince Diana on you! I've been baking with my grandma since I was six — okay — I don't need any instructions or measuring cups. I just need you to shut up, and do what I tell you to do. Do you understand?"

Ms. Nadar was shaking in her ugly green flats. Her cheeks flushed with color. Val knew she was about to spit back some ugly, wretched retort... but at that moment, Khoo Hun Chhiau burst through the front door; holding a bag of take-away food in his hand. Val tried in vain to shush him away, but he didn't notice until it was too late. He stood in front of the kitchen, in full police uniform, drinking soda from a bag; looking utterly perplexed by the situation in front of him.

"Uhhh... did I interrupt something?" He asked.

Val slapped her forehead with her palm, then gestured frantically for him to go upstairs. Khoo Hun Chhiau eyes swerved from Val, to Ms. Nadar, to Val again. His face turned pink. "Are you still—"

"Yes yes I'll be up in a bit!" Val rushed. "Just go ahead and start without me!"

A look of slight disappointment furrowed his brow; but like a good police officer he followed orders. The sound of his creaking footsteps left an awkward silence between the two girls in his wake.

A large, malicious grin spread across Ms. Nadar's face. "So," she snickered, "the rumors between you two are true..."

Val felt her own face grow hot this time. She swirled back to furiously beating the ingredients in her mixing bowl. "I don't know what you're talking about."

"I'll admit, some of the rumors that've been swirling about you are a bit far-fetched. I just assumed this one belonged in the trash with the rest of them, but now I'm beginning to wonder... what are you two exactly?" She pried mockingly.

"He comes over so I can correct his English on his college papers." Val stuttered, holding back a retort of the rumors she'd heard spread about Ms. Nadar... that her father had been a *prolific* Bollywood adult film star, while her mother was just the pure essence of bitch. If it were any other teacher, Val would've surely given detentions to the students who spread such nonsense, but it wasn't. "I don't know why he's here so early today. Usually he comes by after he gets done with work."

"That's not what I asked." Ms. Nadar teased. "I asked what you two were, not what you two get up to..."

Val was happy that a bit of flour was covering her cheeks, because by this point they were sure to be glowing. To be honest, Val had been wondering that herself lately, and couldn't work out an answer. She remembered what Yeo A'i had told her, that Khoo Hun Chhiau had cared for her more than she'd realized... but he himself didn't seem to care much for her besides as a very valuable spell check. He had seemed oddly protective of her, but at the same time oddly cold. She mulled it over for a few more moments before turning back to Ms. Nadar.

"We're friends, Thuya. Very good friends."

Ms. Nadar scowled back at her, before returning to her list of instructions and measuring cups. A few grueling hours later Yeo A'i returned home after a very long vet appointment. His royal highness it seemed had swallowed that missing spatula.

Yeo A'i looked like she'd had an even longer day than Val, so when her eyes found Ms. Nadar they glared daggers. Val could nearly see the flashbacks from their afternoon at the animal shelter flare in her mind's eye. Val tried mouthing a very urgent *"I'm sorry"* to Yeo A'i, but she stormed out of the kitchen as quickly as her small feet could carry her.

They carried on silently for several hours. Every now and then shooting the other one an angry glance, as if to say, *"Hurry up with the blender."* Or, *"Your cookies are probably burning by now."* But neither of them broke the silence until Val started licking the empty brownie mixing bowl. Eating up the gooey layers that didn't make it into the baking sheet.

"That's absolutely disgusting!" Ms. Nadar snarled. "What in the world are you doing?"

Val rolled her eyes; before snatching up a spoonful of it, and reluctantly handing it over to Ms. Nadar.

"Look, I know it looks disgusting, but you need to try it before you judge me."

"I'm not eating that — it looks like runny poo!"

Val shoved the spoon into her hands. "Yes you are, it's the best-tasting thing in the world! Trust me, if you don't absolutely love it, I'll eat a spoonful of *actual* shit myself. How about that?"

Ms. Nadar glowered disgustingly at it once more. Val caught hints of a gag. She sniffed it, before taking the teeniest, tiniest lick Val had ever seen an adult human perform. Ms. Nadar instinctively jerked her head back, but doing so with a pleasant, surprised look on her face.

"See!" Val sassed happily, though the foul woman's face quickly soured again. Of course, only Ms. Nadar could manage to be miserable even after eating brownie batter. Ms. Nadar had both been proven wrong, and given one less thing to complain about; her favorite activity in the world apparently. "I told you, you want some more?"

"No!" Ms. Nadar seethed, as she simultaneously snatched the other spoonful out of Val's hand, and deep-throated the rest of the *runny poo*. "It's so oily!" She gripped. "Is all American food this oily? Is that why you guys are all so fat?"

"I'm not fat!" Val pushed back. "Have you ever even met an American person before you met me?"

"Mr. Elmsworth is American, and he's one of the fattest men I've ever seen in my life."

Ms. Nadar had her there. "Well... we Americans celebrate every body shape and size." Val lied. "And I happen to know that Mr. Elmsworth doesn't let his weight stop him from finding people who love him, he has a lovely wife and son. Where do you get off having such a bad attitude? You're literally the rudest, most unpleasant person I've ever met in my entire life! You come in here, judging my favorite things about my culture and my friendships. Can you just say one nice thing about someone, that isn't followed by a backhanded compliment? Do you have any friends anyways? Do you have a boyfriend? A girlfriend? A best friend? Any family you rely on and keep in touch with?"

Ms. Nadar remained silent; her jaw tight, and unmoving. Her eyes pierced Val's like knives. "For your information, I have plenty of friends and family... I may not have a boyfriend, but we don't do things here like you guys do in the west... we have morals!"

"There you go again!" Val seethed. "And do you really have friends? Please, just name one for me, who doesn't have four paws, and doesn't growl when you try to pet it! I know you don't have friends at Semua Tangan, and I know your fellow volunteers didn't put you in charge of the *"Shit"* brigade or whatever because they enjoy being around you!"

"It's *sanitation, health, and intestinal transitions!*" Ms. Nadar exploded back. "I took it up with my supervisor after you left, and she assured me that they missed that abbreviation just like I did!"

"Oh stop it — you know they meant the *SHIT* department!" Val enunciated. "And you know what? That was a shitty thing for them to do! I actually felt pity for about five whole seconds, then I remembered it was *you*." Val fumed. "What makes you want to always insult people? Why do you love fining people for the smallest things at school? What's your problem with children playing too loudly, or taking too many harmless selfies? Why are you even a teacher? Why was your first instinct to tell me the food I was clearly enjoying looked like diarrhea?"

Ms. Nadar's face twitched, and her eyes watered, as if she were on the verge of tears. For a moment it seemed she was about to crack... but instead she said nothing more. Choosing instead to silently turn back to her mixing bowls.

They finished baking, wrapped the baked goods in wax paper, and cleaned up the kitchen in silence. By the time Ms. Nadar had left, Val was drained. She crashed in a heap onto her daybed.

The treats sold well enough the following lunchtime and evening. Ms. Nadar had made an ugly bedazzled poster, with the words *"American Bake Sale"* written across the top; decorated by magazine cutouts of famous Americans. Val spotted the likes of Oprah, Obama, and Muhamed Ali; somewhere in the sea of hillbillies, obese men eating burgers, and greedy stockbrokers rolling in cash. When Ms. Nadar wasn't snapping at the clientele, reminding them that each bag contained three daily servings of added sugar per child; she was sneaking away bags from Val's batch, and throwing them into a small trash can underneath the table. Making weak excuses each time Val caught her.

The last week before mid-year break was nothing short of a whirlwind. Val scrambled to get back everyone's graded homework and projects, as well as assign a bit of light reading for her students. But no more Charlotte's Web. *Anything* but Charlotte's Web now and ever again. By the last day of classes, Val was very much looking forward to the two week break.

"What're you gonna do?" Amina whispered as the children in front of her chanted the Malaysian pledge. "Any plans?"

"I'm not sure?" Val responded, while wrapping a shawl around her shoulders; since a surprisingly chilly breeze picked up around her. She really hadn't arranged anything at all. "Probably just watch a lot of TV."

"Jano's taking me to Langkawi!" Amina trilled. "I hope I don't get sick on the ferry though. I'm so tired of vomiting..."

The girls had switched from chanting the pledge, to singing the school anthem.

"Have you tried thinking about cows when you're nauseous?" Principal Arif whispered next to them. "I know it's silly, but I swear it works. Or maybe that one's supposed to fix the hiccups..."

Val and Amina's giggles were cut short, by a loud shriek that rang out amongst one of the girls standing at attention. Val swirled her head around.

There in the middle of the pack, a lone girl was pointing up toward the rooftop in front of her. Val peered up, and to her horror, there was the Anglican priest, staring down at the children from the same ledge as the day Val had collapsed alongside him. His arms were out at his sides... several shrieks erupted from the student body, as teachers and students alike took notice.

Val chanced a glance at the other buildings encompassing the courtyard. On the edge of each, a different holy man was perched, in the same manner as the Priest. More and more howls of horror and wails of shock cried out amongst the student body. There was a moment of pause, before the men started chanting together in unison. Each in their own language.

"Om mani padme hum..."
"Hamree karo haath dai rachhaa..."
"Our father who art in heaven..."

The shrieking started once more. Val saw Principal Arif's mouth move, in what seemed to form the words *"Gather the student's inside,"* but the girls screaming and the holy man's chants filled Val's ears. There was no fighting the goosebumps that erupted across her body. *This* was panic. *This* was fear. Val wanted to run.

But no one else was running. Everyone was scared, but no one had abandoned their students. Not even Ms. Nadar.

Val needed this. She copied Amina's direction, and grabbed the students closest to her, shoving them towards the main entrance hall. This wasn't the most useful strategy though, everyone was a wreck. Screaming, crying, scream-crying...

After a few chaotic moments, where Val and the other teachers had at least formed some semblance of a queue to the doors, the chanting stopped. Everyone turned to face the holy men. The only sound was that of the trees shaking in the breeze, and of Principal Arif; who was vociferously yelling for the children to look away. No one was listening to her...

Val watched in horror, as the Holy men, with their arms spread out from their sides, fell in unison off the rooftops, towards the ground below. Val felt her stomach twist.

Another gasp from the crowd.

Val threw up a little in her mouth.

Just centimeters before they hit the dirt, the Holy men disappeared in a flurry of robes and bare feet.

Chaos... absolute chaos!

Girls wailed and cried, while grabbing their friends and tripping over one another. Val tried to navigate the sea of tears, but it was no use. The only shining beacons of hope were Ms. Dian, and Ms. Mawar; who were standing on tables, propping open doors, commanding orders, and with their hands forcing students into a single file line.

They ushered everyone out the front doors, across the street ahead of them, in what Val quickly surmised were the fire escape positions. When all were lined up and every head counted, Principal Arif sent out an alert to the news and police. Stay-at-home mom's jockeyed with school buses and police cars to pick up their children. When the last teary-eyed student was dismissed, Principal Arif gathered the teachers into the entrance hall and began giving orders.

"Is everyone alright?" She asked.

It was a silly question. No, no one was alright... everyone was on edge, but there was no point in saying so.

"Good." She said quickly, looking down in rapid, furious thought. "This was no coincidence... this was a *warning*. They're trying to warn us about something... but *what* exactly?

At that moment, Jano, followed by several policemen in bulletproof vests burst in through the doors behind Principal Arif. It was an odd sight, Jano in his police uniform; but the machine gun slung around his shoulder was what really shocked Val. He approached Principal Arif *seriously*. Jano, acting *seriously*. That irked Val more than the gun.

"We've secured the perimeter, and are keeping watch from all points of possible exit or entry. If any student or news person comes sniffing around we'll catch them before they're able to breach."

Principal Arif's eyes flickered from the machine gun Jano held, to the belt full of grenades on his counterpart, to some sort of flame thrower to his right.

"That's good, very good, very good... but if I recall correctly, I don't remember us discussing the use of such... heavy... artillery within our protocol. I have plenty of sage in my office that might be more useful..."

"I think it's sweet." Mr. Elmsworth mumbled under his breath. Val could have sworn he was drooling.

Principal Arif scowled. "The point is, I don't want any of these—" she waved her hands over the equipment, "things used, unless absolutely necessary! Do you understand me? Where did you get all this stuff anyways? Please don't tell me all your men are armed as such?"

"Everyone has varying weapons according to their skill level. Some may be more lethal than what we're carrying, but not all of them... Officer Yusuf here only has his pistol."

The small, younger man loitering awkwardly behind him scowled. "I accidentally drop one grenade, and now look at me!" He cried. "I'm completely useless!"

"Hush up!" Jano ordered. "And serves you right, you could've killed us all back there! I have half a mind to take that pistol from you!"

The small, eager man instinctively reached for his sidearm. A look of utter contempt etched itself across his pointed, snarling face.

"The point is—" Principal Arif interrupted, "all I need your men to do is keep a lookout for any curious school children, rope off the news agencies, and watch my teachers around the school as they burn the sage I've got stored in my office — understood?"

Jano nodded. "Yes mam." He turned towards his radio. "All units — please be advised to use the utmost caution." His voice lowered considerably. "And keep the gatling gun on the back burner... for now..."

"The what?" Principal Arif cried.

They bickered a while longer, before Principal Arif, as well as several other officers, went to retrieve boxes of large, gray lumps. The teachers divided up into pairs; with one designated *"Box Holder"*, and one *"Sage Burner"*. Amina and Val grabbed onto each other within milliseconds.

"Now I especially don't want the two of you to go alone." Principal Arif demanded as she eyed Amina's small, but present baby bump. She turned back to Jano. "Can you have one of your officers escort these two on their designated route?"

Before Jano could get a word in edgewise, the small, wiry man with the pistol from earlier was already waving his arms in the air.

"Oh!" He shouted, like a four-year-old. *"Me — Me — Me — Me — Me — Me — Pick me!"*

Principal Arif rolled her eyes, but ultimately gave in. "I suppose you will do..."

Jano was about to object, but the look on Principal Arif's face was so forceful that he simpered back and groaned. When Principal Arif's back was turned he pulled Val aside, and in a worried tone, pleaded, "please... *please* watch out for her!"

Val nodded. "Don't worry. I won't let her out of my sight."

Jano didn't look any less worried, but turned towards the rest of his officers all the same. A thought ran through Val's head.

"Hey—" She whispered before he would be out of earshot. "Where's Khoo Hun Chhiau?"

"He's leading the left flank." With that, he marched off, stomping down the brightly lit corridor.

Val and Amina were assigned to cleanse the graveyard, since Principal Arif surmised this would be the safest place, due to it being hallowed ground. The three of them trudged off, back through the *dreaded* courtyard, through the soccer field, and out to the back right corner — where the quiet patch of graves lay.

"So... your husband's Jano?" Officer Yusef pried slyly. "Tell me, what's the most embarrassing story you have on him?" He pulled out a notepad and pen, and peered up at Amina hungrily.

"Ugh — where do I begin!" Amina teased. She rested her back against the side of a headstone, and winked at Val. "For starters, he has a collection of pet slugs he likes to sew dresses for in his spare time..."

Officer Yusef scribbled Amina's pointless drawings eagerly. Val rolled her eyes.

She strolled carefully between the graves; waving the fat-burning lump of sage around like she might miss a spot of air. Val tried not to cough as the smoke wafted around her, but a gust of wind blew it directly into her face. Val's eyes watered, and her lungs filled with soot. She doubled over, and began coughing profusely.

"Whew!" Officer Yusef yelped, as he waved the smoke away, then pulled out a cigarette. "Go easy Ms — Ms — well, I actually don't know your name — Ms. American lady." He turned back around. "As I was saying — did Jano start drinking nail polish at the age of nine or ten exactly? Ms. Jano's wife? *Ms. Jano's wife!*"

Officer Yusef's cracked, high pitch yelp was more than enough for Val's heart to skip a beat. Her head swiveled around, her eyes searching

— they fell upon a limp hand sticking out from behind a headstone — laying in a pool of blood!

Val rushed over, her feet carrying her with a lightness and speed Val didn't know she had within her. A lightness that would extinguish forever when her eyes found the unconscious, sprawled Amina, with an ugly gray mass on top of her; tearing into her shoulder, with *her* pointed teeth!

There was no time to think. Val ran and tackled the creature, until both her and it were intertwined. The creature bit her shoulder, and scratched her arms, before pausing... Val heard gunshots... then came a hot, searing pain in her calf. Val cried out in agony.

The creature looked away from her, towards a quivering, pale-faced Officer Yusef. It only took the creature two predatory-like steps in his direction for him to squeal, drop his gun, and run off back toward the school. *She* turned back around to jump on Amina once more, but Val had reached *her* first, and they resumed their tussle.

Val had been in very few fights in her life; once with her cousin when she was a young girl, and once with a bully in middle school, but this brawl was much different... it wasn't as much a fight as a desperate attempt to hold on, as the creature clawed, bit, and snapped at her, trying to shake her off.

Val felt her nose crack, her wrist snap, and the sting of several, shark-like teeth sinking into her shoulder. The creature bashed her head into a nearby footstone over and over again. Val thrashed violently for what seemed an eternity... hoping it would be long enough for something, *anything*, to distract the creature away from a profusely bleeding Amina...

"Hey—" Someone yelled. "Hey you!"

The creature's large, bright red eyes paused... she glared up to see the source. A chorus of very loud, very nervous police officers erupted, throwing stones...

The creature growled — then roared — as they came nearer and nearer. *She* crawled on her hands and feet towards them, with the quickness of a slithering snake. Val seized her chance. She dragged her body across the ground until she reached Amina. Lugging her limp body as far as she could; 'til they were both behind the largest, sturdiest-looking tombstone in the whole graveyard. She pulled Amina closer in. Machine guns erupted across the courtyard, each like a dart to her eardrums. From the sound of the creature's growl, it wasn't more than a slight nuisance. They might as well have been mosquitos... Val poked her head out just barely from the tombstone to watch the war zone behind her; dodging as bullets chipped away at the smooth rock.

It was a full-on battle. Grenades were being thrown — the gatling gun was out in full force — even a few flames were reaching to lick the creature's skin — but all of this together was not enough to stop *her* advancing, it only slowed *her* down. *She* flung her arms in the air once more, and to the officers' horror, bullets and grenades froze in mid-air... before being flung back towards them. They ducked down just in time. Shards of glass, full and partial bullets, and pieces of grenades shattered whatever semblance of windows and doors were left.

It seemed *she* had won... the creature was advancing now, boastful enough to be on her two feet instead of her four. *She* walked upright, and for a moment Val's blurred, double vision would have described it as almost human-like...

The smoke was now clearing. Val caught a glimpse of several officers inside, who were trudging along the broken glass, shuffling something to the forefront. The creature leapt forward, fifty feet into the air... *her* wide, red eyes glimmering, in *her* thirst to pounce down on *her* foolish frontline prey. A long tube, propped up on the shoulders of the officers poked its nose out of the shattered window. Men shouted frantic, inaudible orders to each other while the creature's body cascaded closer and closer; as *she* descended on them from above.

The rocket launcher shot its projectile just when *she* was a mere arm's length away. Val's ears were pierced with such an overwhelming ringing, it made her vision shake. It hit the creature square in the chest — propelling *her* twenty, thirty, one hundred, one thousand feet into the air — until a long, drawn-out yowl, and a rustling could be heard within the thicket of the forest canopy.

Val took a deep, shaky breath. A slew of blood was running down her face into her mouth. She threw up onto herself, closed her eyes, and let her mind slip into darkness...

CHAPTER TEN

Val wasn't sure where she was when her eyes fluttered back open. They rested on a harsh light that flickered above her bed. Wherever she was it was somewhere unfamiliar, loud, and busy.

"She's awake!" A familiar high-pitched voice rang out across the room. The door to the hospital room flung open, a slew of people tripped over each other's heels just to get inside. The shaky outline of what Val was sure to be Jano raced to her bedside first. His eyes red and puffy.

"Thank you! Oh thank you — thank you — *thank you!*" He clung onto her freshly pressed bed sheets, and let large, sloppy tears soak into the linens. "You saved her — you saved my wife — she's gonna be okay!"

Val's memory started to return, but from how long ago she wasn't sure. Her face felt funny. Val pressed her hand to her nose and felt a bulky stint. "The baby—" she muttered softly, "and the baby?"

"The baby's fine. We got her to the hospital in time to do a blood transfusion. You're an angel — an American Angel!"

"Oh calm down!" A stout, hearty nurse, who so reminded her of Ms. Dian fussed. She dragged Jano several steps backwards. "Give the poor girl a rest, she just woke up and you're accosting her like this!"

Jano raised his hand over his face and took in a deep breath. "You're right — everyone's okay — everything's okay — my wife and baby are okay — I'm gonna kill Officer Yusef!"

Yeo A'i nudged her husband, carefully positioning a cushion underneath his sleeping head so he wouldn't notice her shoulders' absence. She stood up and tip-toed over to Val's side.

"Hey sweety." She cooed softly, pushing a bit of hair out from Val's face. "How're you feeling?"

"Not great." Val moaned. Her voice had a nasally rasp, and her wrist felt uncomfortably stiff, but damn did she feel... completely beat up.

"You need to rest." Yeo A'i prodded, as she tucked her further under the sheets. "Your head got pretty banged up. The doctor should be making the rounds soon enough. He'll definitely want a word."

Val had nearly closed her heavy eyelids, and slid back into a dreamless sleep... but just as her mind slipped away, something brought her back. The sound of heavy rushing footsteps stampeded down the hallway. Her door swung open again.

Khoo Hun Chhiau, still dressed in his dirty, soot-ridden police uniform, stood panting in the doorway. Their eyes met, and Val watched as a look of most relief melted away his hard, cold demeanor, for only the briefest of moments. His knuckles were nearly as white as his lips. The only part of him that didn't look pale and nervous were his eyes... Val could see traces of red through the dark, puffy circles. He stared with an intensity and fire that was nearly too much for Val to bear...

Yeo A'i sensed the tension. She silently pulled up a seat on Val's other side, and gestured for Khoo Hun Chhiau to sit. His eyes fell, as he marched across the room, plopped down on the chair, and cradled his head with his hands.

Val drifted in and out of sleep for the next few hours, until the doctor arrived; followed by Nur and a wheelchair-bound Amina. Val's heart leapt at the pale, frail sight of her, also at the IV sticking out of her arm. Before she could get any words out, Amina interrupted her.

"Yesss." she drawled. "I'm alright, I'm alright... just needed more than a few stitches and a few bags of blood. Other than that I'm feeling quite myself. It's you we need to worry about now."

"She's right." A lanky, confident-sounding young doctor butted-in. "Hi, I'm doctor Eugene Min. So, Ms. Val, how are you feeling right about now? A little banged up I suppose?"

"Uhh, a little." Val mumbled back. "What's wrong with my nose?"

"Oh, that? You just needed a minor manual realignment. You'll have to keep the gauze up there for the next three days, and the stint on for the rest of the week, but that was relatively minor compared to the rest of your injuries — by far the easiest fix."

Val caught a glimpse of her reflection in his shiny name badge. The stent was mirrored on either side by two, heavily blackened eyes. If this was the easiest fix, she dreaded what he would say next...

"You received a concussion due to the fractures in your skull. But your scans came back, I think that you're well on the way to improving in that department. Your wrist has been severely sprained, that will take at least six to eight weeks to heal, if not longer." He demurred. "You also needed several stitches to your chest, shoulder, and upper back. Those will need to stay dry and clean until we're able to take them out..." his tone changed, becoming much more solemn. "I don't know if you're aware of this or not... but it appears you've suffered a gunshot wound to your left calf. Don't worry, your leg will make a full recovery. You were lucky that it hit the muscle. We retrieved the bullet, and sewed that up as well."

"Yusef was less than useless." Jano swore as Amina clutched his hand in hers. "He'll be on probation and desk duty forever — I swear!"

Val had forgotten about being shot. To be honest, that injury was the one causing her the least amount of pain right about now.

"Yes well, I hope so as well... I'd like to keep you here one more night, just so we can monitor your head. If everything looks alright, I'll dismiss you home tomorrow." He clapped his hands together and peered around the room nervously. "Alright then, who here will be taking care of Ms. Palacio for the next few weeks?"

Val expected Yeo A'i to jump to her side, but to her surprise, she was quiet. Yeo A'i turned to her, with guilty, horribly sad, watery eyes.

"I... I guess I am."

Val didn't understand... usually, Yeo A'i would jump at the chance to help. Make it her new project even. But a long, faraway memory drifted back into her muddled mind...

"What day is your flight to see your daughter?" Val asked quietly.

Tears were dripping from the end of her nose. "In two days." Yeo A'i choked.

"We can take care of her!" Amina boasted. "We owe her nothing less than for saving my life, as well as our baby's."

Jano scowled at her. "Excuse me — did you forget about the *non-refundable* deposit I put down on our hotel room in Langkawi? How am I supposed to refund the ferry tickets? The night cruises? I won't get these two weeks' vacation back! Besides... It's not exactly like you're in the best state to be taking care of anyone else right now?"

"Oh, I'm sorry—" Amina mocked, "where's the crying, sobbing, *"Our hero — our American angel"* Jano I was just hearing a moment ago?"

The two bickered, while a downcast Nur mumbled something quietly between them. "I have so many deliveries in the next few weeks, and I'm supposed to visit my grandma."

"Well someone needs to take the poor girl in!" The doctor cried. "Honestly one of you needs to step up!"

"I'll cancel the flights." Yeo A'i whimpered, as she started sobbing quietly into her shirt.

"No!" Val cried, her hands grasping for Yeo A'i's, which felt cold, and bony. "Please—please—*please* go! I can take care of myself!" Val lied valiantly. "But whatever you do, go see your daughter, she'll need you much more than I ever could!" Val lied again.

Khoo Hun Chhiau made a grunting sound that reverberated across the room, which fell silent immediately. He glared up at everybody, before quietly demanding: "Can I see everyone outside for a second?"

The room exchanged cold, fearful glances, before following Khoo Hun Chhiau out into the hall. Val could hear nothing. She shared uncomfortable looks with the doctor; who, Val could tell, didn't appreciate having his authority undermined like this. The only sound Val could make out from behind the white, plain walls were a few hushed, pressing tones. After several minutes, Yeo A'i shuffled back into the room.

"So, we've had a discussion... and before I go on, you are well within your right to object, or stop me at any point in this conversation."

Val nodded curtly. "Um... okay? What is it?"

Yeo A'i let out a long, soulful sigh. "Khoo Hun Chhiau has offered to help you while my husband and I are away... he offered to sleep on our couch, and look after your health. He says he has enough vacation days saved up to take off... but if that makes you uncomfortable, we've decided that we'll stay."

"Oh..." Val simpered. "Um..." Truth be told, she didn't know what to think about this. Was this *okay?* Was this *safe?* She hoped so. It only took one more look into Yeo A'i's heavy, tearful eyes for Val to make up her mind. "Yeah, sure, that should be fine." She said cautiously.

Yeo A'i immediately perked up. Her skinny, pale fingers tightened around Val's once more. "Oh thank you — *thank you!*" She squealed. "You are such a sweet, selfless girl!" With that, she fixed Val's bed sheets, dimmed the lights, and stroked her hair. "You really should be getting some more rest. It'll be a long day tomorrow getting you moved back to the house."

Val felt relieved that she wouldn't have to stay up much longer. Her eyes were starting to feel very heavy again, and no sooner had the door closed behind Yeo A'i, Val fell fast asleep.

...

Val awoke early the next morning. After what seemed like a million tests, x-rays, and one *way* to invasive scan, she was finally discharged. Before Yeo A'i and Khoo Hun Chhiau had wheeled her outside though, it seemed the nurses wanted to go through the whole packet of treatment information, line by line.

"It's very important her stitches don't get wet." The nurse who looked so like Ms. Dian asserted. "We recommend all stitched areas be covered with saran wrap while bathing."

Val was relieved that the other two were listening. She herself was not.

"These pills are taken three times a day, these once a day, and this cream and iodine must be put on whenever you redo the gauze and wrappings. We want to see her back here in a few days. If anything with her memory changes, or she starts feeling a lot of pain, bring her back immediately."

Val woke with a start, as Khoo Hun Chhiau wheeled her chair to Yeo A'i's van. Val struggled to push herself up, but before she could straighten her wobbly, weak knees; Khoo Hun Chhiau had already bent over, and gently swooped her out of her chair, and into the back seat, as quickly and as easily as if she were a child. He buckled her seat belt, and the three of them were off to Yeo A'i's. She stared out the window the entire way, gazing mindlessly past the emerald-colored lushness surrounding her. Val wondered about *her*... was *she* okay? How badly hurt was *she*? Val had an inkling that *she* wouldn't be gone for good just yet..."

They made it home. Val was wheeled up the driveway, then all the way inside to the stairs, where Khoo Hun Chhiau resumed carrying her once more. Val had had several dreams where she'd been wrapped in Khoo Hun Chhiau's arms... but none of them involved two black eyes, and a grumbling Yeo A'i dragging along a wheelchair behind them in tow...

Khoo Hun Chhiau laid her down gently on her soft, pillow-top bed. Val felt her body once again become engulfed by pillows, blankets, and a stuffed animal or two. This feeling could pass as heaven. Val breathed out the longest sigh. For the first time in days, she checked her phone. There were missed calls and texts from her mom and abuela, but the last thing Val wanted was to upset anyone back home. She resigned to only messaging them for now. Val could only imagine the look in her mother's eyes if she were to see her face right now.

Val fell in and out of sleep. The next day Yeo A'i came into her room to say one final goodbye; running through the last hurried instructions of how to take care of Val, as well as Prince Diana, before rushing out to catch her flight. The crunching of gravel from her van pulling out of the driveway echoed around the house; one last reminder that it was just her and Khoo Hun Chhiau alone here.

The first few days passed by in a blur. When Val wasn't sleeping, she played on her phone; while Khoo Hun Chhiau sat at his desk, quietly tapping away on his keyboard. Occasionally Val would catch him asleep there, hunched over in place like some kind of working-class zombie. After a while though Val noticed he'd taken too frequent naps on the trundle bed that had been stored away, but now sat propped up, parallel to her own.

Three days passed. Val was starting to smell... It took her twenty minutes to get her swimsuit on in the bathroom by herself. The *damn* thing kept flipping inside out somehow. She finally managed to tie the last string around her neck, and Khoo Hun Chhiau was allowed in. He wrapped her injuries in saran wrap, ran the tap, and helped her lower herself into the shallow bathtub.

Val sat there, not exactly knowing what to do... her leg and arm hung awkwardly over the side; while Khoo Hun Chhiau's hands got to work. He pulled out a large rag, ran it through the soapy water, and lifted up Val's arms. Cleaning them underneath... it was kinda weird... but he was careful not to touch her stitches, so that was nice. He pulled a cup out from behind himself. This part was like she was at the hairdresser. He filled it with water, leaned her head back, and let the warm water run over her scalp. Massaging a dollop of shampoo through her hair. It was the best Val had felt in days.

"You're pretty good at this..." Val purred. "Is this how you seduce the *ladies?*"

"Not exactly... this was how I took care of my mother when she lost her memory."

Every pleasant, relaxed feeling left her at once. A wave of embarrassment cascaded over her like a tsunami. The bath water felt just a little too hot. *"Oh—"*

He wrung out the rag again and started washing her feet. She was a lot easier though — she wiggled less."

Val pulled her feet back from his hands. "It tickles!"

"And she smelled better too."

She scoffed.

"A lot better."

Val splashed him repeatedly, while Khoo Hun Chhiau chuckled and hid behind the curtain like the hero police officer he was, afraid of some bathwater. "Okay — okay, I'm sorry — do you want help out or not?"

Val side-eyed him once more, before letting him unplug the drain. He lifted her up quickly, wrapping a towel around her, and sitting her back down in her wheelchair. They watched *The Office* and ate Cheetos while she dried. Something she'd done so often back home, that she even caught herself instinctively guarding the remote from her Abulela. If it wasn't the most gruesomely violent TV show known to man, her Abulela wasn't interested.

Though the wounds on her body were still far away from being completely healed, with each passing day they felt less and less painful. After several good nights of sleep, Val was starting to enjoy sitting in bed, watching her favorite shows. For a while Khoo Hun Chhiau wouldn't relax, because *of course*. There was always more *work*. The man was probably born from a briefcase instead of a woman; but Val was undaunted.

She threw corn chips, she sang songs, she played her TV shows too loud so he couldn't focus. His work ethic was no match for her nonsense. Eventually he gave up, taking a seat down next to her with a blanket around himself. Bowls of cereal and soup piled up around them until none were left, and another load of dishes would restart the cycle all over again.

"Okay—okay!" Val trilled one day, as they waited for a movie to load up on the screen. "If you got to have one superpower, what would it be?"

Khoo Hun Chhiau scratched his head, taking only a few moments to answer. "Too read minds."

"Of course you would!" Val groaned.

"What?" He simpered, looking taken aback.

"You just wanna see which criminals are lying to you." Val teased. "You wanna read the minds of people who you're interrogating, so you can finally catch the Walter Whites' and the Guss' of the world. Am I right — Am I right?"

Khoo Hun Chhiau blushed and rolled his eyes. "It'd be very useful in those situations... and good for my research. What about you? What would your superpower be?"

"Well—" Val began, but then faltered. Now that she was thinking about it, there were so many to choose from, yet none that appealed to her somehow... but just as she was about to give up, a good one — in fact, a great one slipped into her mind.

"I want to be immortal — young and healthy forever!"

Khoo Hun Chhiau nodded. "That's not bad... but it'd be lonely? Wouldn't it?"

Val shrugged. "I guess, or you could make new friends when your old ones die out. Who knows what immortality would really be like... I guess there isn't a soul on this planet who'd know."

"I can think of one off the top of my head." Khoo Hun Chhiau shrugged.

Val scoffed, and nearly gave him a playful push when her eyes met his. She realized exactly what he'd meant. "Oh... you mean, *her*..."

He nodded again. This time, more slowly, without much gusto.

"Well, *she* can't be immortal now really." Val reasoned. "That old wise tale about *her* being thousands and thousands of years old... I mean, I've been up close and personal with *her* now twice, and *she* doesn't seem anywhere close to being old."

"How would you know what an old creature like *her* would look like compared to a young one?"

Val shrugged. "I don't know, I just know... I mean, *she* doesn't seem like a child or a teenager to me, but—" she inhaled a long, heavy breath, before continuing, "*She* seems young to me... like *she* isn't any older than me."

Khoo Hun Chhiau sighed. "Well, I remember my grandmother warning me about *her* when I was a child, and she told me she remembered her grandmother warning her about *her*..."

Val stared out her window, into the back garden, which was filled with palm and durian trees that swayed gently in the wind. Once in a blue moon, Val could see a pair of monkeys' eyes staring back at her... but the pair of eyes she thought about now were huge, and red, and angry... How lonely *she* must be, in those woods, all by herself, for thousands of years...

Khoo Hun Chhiau sensed her sadness, and gave her a rare, paternal pat on the back. The movie started, and they returned their gaze to the nonsense machine.

CHAPTER ELEVEN

The days slipped into weeks, and before Val knew it her prop was off her nose; which looked the same. *Thank God.* The black eyes were gone. Her leg healed enough so that she could graduate from a wheelchair to crutches, and soon her wrist was in a proper splint, and free from that itchy cast and sling.

As Val suspected, Semua Tangan was postponed for an extra week. Contractors were working overtime turning the war zone back into a school; all while Yeo A'i Facetimed Val at least every other day, checking in on her, and as equally important, on Prince Diana, who'd grown rather close to Khoo Hun Chhiau. Val had even caught him packing Prince's stuff up along with her own, for the trip to the Cameron Highlands Val had found herself roped into.

"Look, I can't leave you here alone to take care of him, so since you're coming he has to come too." Khoo Hun Chhiau explained for the thousandth time, as he stuffed several chew toys into Val's suitcase. "It's only for three days, and I already put the pet deposit down at the hotel — it won't be so bad."

Val groaned. She'd grown so accustomed to laying around that every time she stood up it made her head spin.

"Are you sure we can't just stay here? Why can't you get one of your TA's to go for you instead?" Every time he explained this *"security conference"* thing, it sounded less fun and more confusing.

"No – It's too important for me not to go." He rolled his eyes, scowling down at the now overstuffed suitcase that wouldn't close. "It's not like you have to watch or anything. You can stay up in the room with Prince, or do whatever you want while I'm busy."

Val moaned, and rolled over onto her bed, groaning into her pillow. Before long Khoo Hun Chhiau had packed their bags, stuffed them into his little grey Proton, and the three of them were off. Val's attitude quickly turned around, as they drove higher and higher through the misty mountains. Mountains with sloping fields of tea leaves on all sides.

Val pulled her jacket over herself, as a chill crept inside the car. She rolled the window up until only a small crack remained. They swerved right, a greenhouse appeared, with a sign reading: *"Strawberry farm — pick your own strawberries!"*

"Oh my goodness!" Val squealed. "We *have* to go!"

Khoo Hun Chhiau rolled his eyes. "I'm definitely gonna be too busy for that."

"Maybe you and I can go Prince, what do you say? You aren't deathly allergic to strawberries or something, right? Or are those grapes I'm thinking about?"

Khoo Hun Chhiau scoffed and shook his head, but Val was sure she caught the guise of a little smile.

They pulled into the courtyard of a majestic colonial hotel. A vast garden, full of exotic plants Val had never seen before sprawled around them, as they rounded the semi-circle driveway. Before they had come to a complete stop, a team of hotel workers had descended upon the tiny sedan. They'd already grabbed a majority of the luggage out of the trunk by the time Val had even opened her own door and stepped outside.

She fiddled with her crutches and Prince Diana's leash, until they were inside the lobby. Val plopped down on a wicker chair near a large fireplace; while Khoo Hun Chhiau checked in at the front desk. A squashed-nose girl with beady eyes and a pointed chin smiled flirtatiously as he approached. Val scowled, but there was barely any time for the girl to get a word in; a group of men approached Khoo Hun Chhiau heartily, as if they were old friends. He shrugged them off and returned to where Val was sitting, holding two room keys in his hands.

"Who were those guys?" Val pried.

Khoo Hun Chhiau shook his head in exasperation. "Who? Oh — them? They're just trying to convince me to join their firm in Mumbai. I've told them no a hundred times, but they never listen." He helped Val up onto her crutches. "We should get going."

The pair hurried to the elevators, dodging several groups of men and women who seemed to have the same ideas. Khoo Hun Chhiau hurried past each and every one of them as if they were carrying the plague; until they reached two rooms, side by side.

"Alright, here's the key to your room. I have a copy in case you lose this one."

"Oh—" Val stuttered, slightly taken aback. Her stomach knotted again, into a stiff, uncomfortable ball. This would be the first time she would sleep in her own room since the attack. The thought of being on her own, in such an unfamiliar place, troubled her immensely. "Can I keep Prince with me?"

Khoo Hun Chhiau frowned, before reluctantly handing over the leash. "Meet me downstairs at the bar for dinner in an hour." He gestured to his watch and promptly slid into his own room. The door clicked softly shut behind him.

Val turned to swipe her key against the teak door. The hotel workmen dropped her bags off beside a four-poster, wicker king bed, and shuffled outside, leaving her alone with Prince. Flowing white curtains caught her eye, as they blew in the breeze from an open window. A flat-screen TV faced a large, white sofa in the corner of the room; while a full jacuzzi peaked around the corner of the ensuite bathroom. As Val was now more than able to bathe herself, she turned the tap and poured herself a glass of complimentary white wine.

"This isn't so bad... right Prince?" Val sighed, but Prince Diana wasn't listening. He was too busy trying to *bite* the fan. It hit him in the mouth. He was bleeding now. Dog blood everywhere. It literally flew around the room. Still didn't stop him from trying again. *Useless guard dog...*

Val cleaned it all up. By the time she was done there was only ten minutes left till dinner. She rummaged through her suitcase, and to her delight found the only garment she had packed from home that would be considered nice enough for a place like this. A small, spaghetti-strapped black dress with a slit at the bottom. Val pulled it on, powdered on a fresh layer of makeup, and shuffled with her crutches out the door.

It definitely felt strange sitting at a hotel bar all by herself. The looks older men shot her were a little too eager for her liking, and it didn't help that Khoo Hun Chhiau was already late. After several frantic messages, and more than too many close calls, Val gave up. She drained her glass and was about to order another, when out of the corner of her eye, she spotted someone beelining it for the high chair next to her.

"So..." The younger man said casually, in a horribly thick Australian accent. "Are you a white or red girl?"

Val shuttered, not only at this pathetic excuse of a pickup line, but at the sound of his down-under English. It was like knives to her ears...

"*Lo siento?*" Val faked. "*No te entiendo... y tampoco quiero...*"

"Oh..." He purred, now more motivated than ever. "I didn't take you for a Spanish girl. Let's see here... blanco o rojo vino? Did I say that right? Now you look like a red girl if I were to guess... but... blanco o roj—"

"White is fine!" Val snapped. She checked her phone once more to see if Khoo Hun Chhiau had responded back; sending an urgent: "*Come here ASAP!*" before the nuisance hollering at the bar-tender next to her could see a thing.

"I'm Scott by the way." He drawled, as he sloppily handed Val another wine glass. She downed it in two big gulps. "So... what's a beauty like you doing all the way over *he-a* in the middle of Malaysia?"

Val wanted nothing more than to cover her hands with her ears. Or better yet, to go ahead and rip them off.

"Teaching." Val said curtly. "I'm an English teacher."

"Wooh... got any little rug-rats taking the mickey-out cha?"

"What? Um yeah, I guess…" Her mind darted to the gang of three, whose favorite pastime was *"taking the mickey"* out of her. "What about you?" Val replied, in as bored of a tone as she could muster.

"Oye — me? I'm a consultant for Match SPGA services, aye! I've been sent here on a bit of a recruiting mission…" he flashed his silver name tag, with the words: *"Scott Seller: Match Security, Police, and Government Agency Services",* written along the bottom. "We're out of Singapore, but we do business worldwide. We have locations in Mumbai, Seoul, Moscow, Addis Ababa, Rio—"

Val had zoned out. Just as she was about to make up some lame excuse to head back to her jacuzzi, Khoo Hun Chhiau entered the salon. The moment he walked in, it seemed all those men who'd had their eyes glued to Val immediately switched, and started jocky-ing for a conversation with Khoo Hun Chhiau.

He brushed them aside, and beelined it towards Val. Throwing his hands up in front of him apologetically.

"Sorry, sorry — I was held up — one of the front desk workers accidentally spilled coffee on my laptop — luckily everything was backed up." His eyes shifted from Val to Scott, and another semblance of a grin began creeping from the corner of his mouth. "What're you doing here?"

Scott pounded down another shot, smiling triumphantly. He spread his arms wide. "Aye, got recruited by Match don't ya know. You didn't think I wouldn't eventually end up tracking you down mate? How'd you like the room upgrade? Come here!"

His stocky arms encompassed Khoo Hun Chhiau, and squeezed with deathly force. Val eyed the other groups of men in the room; who were giving him a wide berth now, but still had their eyes on him…

"You're not here to pester me into joining your firm too? I could really use a break right now."

"Of course I am — but that can wait, let's get dinner! My treat, and I won't be taking no for an answer." He grabbed Khoo Hun Chhiau's shoulders, and led him over to one of the restaurant tables, winking as he passed Val. "And your little lady friend can join us as well…"

Khoo Hun Chhiau rolled his eyes, and scoffed loftily. "She's not my... she's injured, and I need her to correct my work."

"*Whew!*" Scott sighed, as Val scowled. "I'm glad about that. How horrible would it've been, if I was hitting on the guy I was supposed to be recruiting's girlfriend! In that case, she can be my dinner guest then..."

Val glowered at the both of them. She had half a mind to go back upstairs and order herself room service, but her stomach was growling ferociously. It'd probably take longer for her food to arrive there.

She plopped down begrudgingly; and listened as the two men chatted for hours; reminiscing about the good ole days in St. Petersburg. Val sat there, silently wishing she were back up in her jacuzzi; when a stray thought crossed her mind...

"Wait—" Val interjected, during a very disturbing story, involving Scott, two Russian sex workers, and a durian. "Are you the guy who introduced Khoo Hun Chhiau to Breaking Bad?"

"One and the same! I forgot how much we used to watch that show. Now that we're on the subject..." He scooted forward, as if to hunch off the men prowling around their table, like circling sharks. "You and Match would really accomplish a lot together if you were to say... come on board, and work on some of our new criminal detection algorithms. Your research could make you a very, *very*, rich man, if only you could find people who you trusted to effectively market and sell your stuff..."

Val took this as her cue to leave. She said a quick goodbye, before heading back upstairs. Khoo Hun Chhiau tried to say something to her before she left, but Val ignored him. She was still angry that he hadn't faked that he was her boyfriend. It would've at least given Scott some motivation to stop. She took Prince Diana out to use the bathroom one more time, before changing into her pajamas, snuggling into her soft silk sheets, and letting her mind wander away... far, far away...

She was walking over fallen sticks, in a thick, dark forest. A set of yellow eyes had been following her for the last few hours, but she ignored them. It'd be daylight soon — and she was watching a troubled-looking boy pace back and forth in front of a small thatched hut. She had followed him the whole night. Slowly creeping behind as his heavy footsteps stomped right through her patch of ground, which by now none of the humans dared to enter. Occasionally she felt he'd sensed her presence, but he walked on. Strange. Stupid. Intriguing. Impressive... nothing it seemed could get in the way of this young man's determination. Needless to say this had piqued her interest; so she stalked after him.

Another energy exuded behind her. This one a powerful, excited, predatory spirit... one that she was more than familiar with... the yellow eyes crouched low, before pouncing down on her from above... it only took one flick of her hand to freeze it, and another flick to break its neck! The Tiger lay there, unmoving, silent, still... dead... any lingering energy was eviscerated in a matter of milliseconds. She turned back to the man, who'd noticed a slight disturbance in the trees, but after a few moments he returned to worrying about his own troubles.

The sun began rising over the horizon, burning through the previous night's mist. A rainbow of spectral colors lingered near the cloud line, but she had the feeling that no matter how beautiful of a morning it might be, only bad omens were in store for this young man...

A ripped curtain covering the entrance of the hut trembled, and a fat elder gentleman emerged behind it; dawning nothing but a large bone piercing his septum, and a knee-length, brown cloth. At the sight of the young man, he looked puzzled.

"Hmm..." The man grunted, prompting the boy to jump at the sound. He took a deep breath, and clenched his fists, before finding the strength to confront him.

She watched. The conversation commenced in hushed whispers, before crescendoing into a full-on shouting match! A girl popped out from behind the curtain next. She squinted at the sun, and stumbled out onto the soft grass, holding her swollen belly. As soon as her eyesight adjusted, the young woman started wailing, and pleading with the young man. Begging him to do something away from her. She held up a shaking, bony finger into the direction from whence he came. The boy's face reddened, and his hands shook as he refused! He pointed at her belly, and then at himself, before slipping into a fit of sloppy, desperate tears. Bellowing every other word.

The older man had had enough! He slapped the boy's face and grabbed his waist, tossing him several feet into the air. He landed in a pile of mud nearby where she was hiding. The look on his face as he gritted his teeth of utter bitterness, of rage, of fiery torment; she could identify with nothing more purely than this... the boy wiped his mud and blood-soaked face, and pulled out a stone that had been sharpened to a point. Mud splashed in a swirl around him. He twirled around, sprung to his feet, and lunged back at the man — who collapsed in a bloody heap!

Through the cries, and screams, and howls of fear and agony, she sensed other energies... worried, shy, frightened ones behind her once more. She turned around... three tiger cubs had crawled out from the brush and were pawing at their mother's majestic, lifeless body. They gazed up at her without any hint of worry, or concern, or fear. Without any knowledge of why their protector was like that, or who had caused it. Her red eyes locked with one of their small, glowing, oval ones.

Val opened her eyes. She felt dizzy... not right somehow. Her whole body was suspended several feet above her bed. The shadow of an older Orang Asli woman dawning a fringed skirt, headband, and several bracelets stood menacingly at her feet. She pointed above Val's limp body...

Val peered up, into the large, red eyes she had grown to fear so much. *She* growled, and snarled in Val's face! *Her* mouth opened, as if to swallow her whole...

Val lurched out of her bed, gasping for air. Prince Diana was licking her face and whimpering. The sheets and comforters flew off them both, hanging like ghosts in the air.

Val grabbed Prince and hobbled out of the room, letting the door slam behind her. Her knuckles twinged with pain as she frantically knocked on Khoo Hun Chhiau's door, but she didn't care. Val continued knocking, through the sound of heavy, frantic footsteps on the other side; until the door swung open. A shirtless, drowsy-faced Khoo Hun Chhiau stood before her, rubbing his eyes.

"Wha — What is it? What's wrong?"

"C-c-can Prince and I sleep in here tonight?" Val asked shakily. "I can't sleep in my room... I... I need to sleep somewhere else."

Khoo Hun Chhiau peered down at her curiously. "What's wrong with your room? What happened?"

"I... I can't go back in there." Val croaked. Her lips began to tremble. "If you won't let me sleep in here, I'll go down to the bus station, and I'll take the airport shuttle so I can catch a plane back to Arizona."

Khoo Hun Chhiau's face turned white, and stony. "What're you talking about? Just get inside before you wake anyone up."

He stepped aside. Val's shoulder brushed his chest as she passed through the narrow hallway, into a room that perfectly reflected her own. She collapsed on the bed. Her body shaking violently as puddles of tears left beige stains on his linens. She felt the weight of Khoo Hun Chhiau sitting down next to her. He patted her back unconfidently; like he hadn't comforted someone in a really long time. Val let herself cry it out, until she could finally mutter a few, shaky words.

"This... this is crazy..." Val panted. "I didn't sign up for this."

Khoo Hun Chhiau peered down at her, looking quite unsure of what to do next. He grabbed the blanket from his bed and draped it over her shoulders and head.

"No you didn't... but you can get through this. A lot of teachers have taught at Semua Tangan, and I've never heard of one actually dying before... you'll be okay." He paused, before continuing on, quieter this time. "You're not really going back to Arizona... right?"

"Why do you even care?" Val snapped, her chest heaving in a chaotic mix of emotions. "You couldn't wait to get rid of me just a few months ago. Is it too much of a hassle to find someone new to check your spelling?"

Khoo Hun Chhiau rubbed his eyes and groaned. "I didn't... you know I didn't mean it like that! I just meant... look, can we drop it? I didn't mean to make you feel like I don't care about you, if that's what you're upset about... but you're not really leaving, right?"

Val chuckled. "Walter White called, he wants me to set up a meth headquarters there."

"Stop — I'm serious."

Val felt her breathing still, and her muscles relax. "I guess not... but how do I protect myself? How do I protect my students — or Amina?"

"I've talked to Jano about this already, the city council is gonna start stationing policemen around the school as patrol. They're figuring out ways to keep teachers in direct contact with the station this week. They're even talking about actually closing Semua Tangan down next year... for good."

Val's heart dropped. She'd grown very fond of Semua Tangan, regardless of *her* presence.

"No — I don't want it to close!"

"Okay Ms— *'I'm going back to Arizona!'*" Khoo Hun Chhiau mocked, using an imitation of a girl's high-pitched voice. A *bad* one.

"You know what I mean." Val retorted. She paused, to think over what she was about to say before she said it. "You know, you could've at least pretended to be my boyfriend tonight... your friend Scott was *not* taking my hints. It would've really helped."

"I'll talk to him tomorrow." Khoo Hun Chhiau sleepily reassured, as his eyelids drifted.

They laid there, curled up in silence on top of his four-poster king bed. Val noticed Khoo Hun Chhiau's heavy chest start to rise and fall rhythmically. Her eyes grew heavier and heavier. Before long, Val wafted into a peaceful, dreamless sleep.

...

Val awoke the next morning under the heavy white comforter she'd fallen asleep on top of. Her groggy eyes spotted Khoo Hun Chhiau at the foot of the bed, not quite done buttoning up a blue button-down.

"What — what time is it?" Val croaked.

"It's almost eight."

"Ughhh!" Val groaned as she fell backwards. "It's too early."

"Then go back to sleep." He chided, while fiddling with his tie; which had accidentally snagged on one of his shirt buttons. "You should probably get some more rest."

Val considered it, but the prospect of sleeping in a room by herself again if Khoo Hun Chhiau was leaving soon sent another chill up her spine.

"I'm up, I'm up... here, let me help you with that."

Val shuffled to the edge of the bed, carefully prying the tied knot out from underneath the pale button. She was so close, only centimeters from his face. The lingering hint of aftershave wafted up her nose. It took everything in her power not to lean just a little bit closer right then and there... Val spotted his leather belt a few feet away, and gulped back several sinful thoughts...

Khoo Hun Chhiau stepped towards the mirror, inspecting his tie. "Good — thanks." He said shortly, while rushing to put on the rest of his outfit. "So... what're you planning on doing today? Facetime your family now that your face has healed? Take Prince on a walk around the grounds?"

Val considered this, but figured it was best to wait till she was back at home. She recalled their drive here through the misty, mountainous plateaus, and remembered the sign they'd passed.

"I'm going strawberry picking."

Khoo Hun Chhiau stopped tying his shoe and peered up. "Really?"

"Yeah—" Val beamed, "why not? I've got the whole day to kill."

"How're you gonna hold the basket while you're on crutches?"

"It can't be that hard." Val trilled. "It's just a few small strawberries, it's not like they're gonna be that heavy or anything."

But Val realized exactly what Khoo Hun Chhiau meant just a few hours later; when she struggled to hold both crutches, a pair of scissors, and the basket underneath all at the same time.

"Damnit!" She swore as the scissors clanged to the floor of the greenhouse. Val scooped down to pick them up, but then one of her crutches fell over; nearly knocking over a row of strawberries.

"Son of a Bitch!" She screamed as several families scurried away in horror.

"Sorry — *Sorry!*" She called. Val sat there, feeling defeated on the concrete floor. She was about to give up when a familiar, small hand protruded in front of her.

"Nur—" Val yelped, "what're you doing here?"

"Oh—" Nur grunted as she helped Val to her feet. "Just checking in on my grandmom." She pointed over to an elderly woman sitting in a wheelchair down at the end of the lane. It's her birthday, so I thought I'd do something a little special for her today. What're you—"

"Long story." Val cut her off. Nur eyed her skeptically. "So... that's your grandma, she's cute. My grandmother would love this too. If she were here we could take them out on a little grandma date."

"Um yeah, I guess... are you here by yourself?"

"Well Khoo Hun Chhiau is at the hot—" Val stuttered, "physically speaking, I am here by myself."

Nur smiled cheekily. "Wanna join my grandma and I? We're going to her village after this to eat. I mean, if you don't have plans..."

"Yeah, sounds good." The two of them walked towards the end of the row, where Nur's grandmother was holding up a shaky, bony hand to one of the strawberry vines, about to slice through it.

"*Nenek, ini kawan saya Val...* Grandma, this is my friend Val."

Nur's grandmother looked up at Val, with large, black, ancient eyes, that recognized her immediately... eyes that she remembered from last night, at the foot of her bed... pointing up at *her!*

Val whimpered, but quickly composed herself before Nur noticed anything. They shuffled around row to row, Val keeping her eye on the strange, frail old woman. *How was she in her dream? What're the odds of all this happening?* Her thoughts grew nearly as heavy as her strawberry basket, which was beginning to tug at her arm like the small hand of a heavy child.

They weighed both baskets and paid. Val took the passenger seat of Nur's sedan.

"So... your grandparents are from the Cameron Highlands? That's cool — did you and Amina come here a lot as children?"

"All the time." Nur squealed. "I don't know if you've noticed yet, but my grandma is one of the Orang Asli. She converted when she married my grandfather. It's a really crazy love story if you ever hear it one day... we were actually raised here until our parents moved when we were teenagers. I still have the scar from the hairbrush Amina randomly threw at me when she found out." Nur rolled back her sleeve, revealing a jagged gash.

Val gritted her teeth. "Jesus!"

"Yup." Nur agreed. "I nearly bled out. They had to take me to the ER to perform emergency surgery. I saw a woman there give birth, and that's when I decided I wanted to be a doctor."

Val had seen a woman give birth once before, in the dreaded *miracle of life* video. Worst biology class *ever.*

"It must be a really interesting job you have."

"It's incredible." Nur went on. "Best job in the world."

"How's Parini by the way? How'd she do with all of it?"

Nur chuckled. "Panari was a bitch, but overall she did well. The only injury was a busted eardrum — and that was mine, so I guess it doesn't count."

Val giggled, as they pulled into a cozy orange cottage nestled amongst matching village houses. Nur got out and raced around to help her grandma back into her wheelchair. They hurried up the steps together, Val following after them inside. The living room was dark and cluttered. Several old ladies sat around drinking tea, while the Malaysian news played in the background.

"These are my grandmother's roommates. They all share a caregiver, but I gave her the day off. I'll be in the kitchen getting everything ready, don't mind me." Nur called.

Val turned to Nur's grandmother and company. She tried smiling and waving, but they did little more than nod and glare at her. Val hoped the food wouldn't take too long...

Val tried to follow along with the news, catching bits and pieces when they actually spoke a bit of English. From what she could make out, there had been some sort of streaker in Kuala Lumpur who'd been caught in the act. She watched as the lanky, unbothered man was led away in handcuffs; his backside only covered by a single white feather. She giggled quietly, while the grandmothers scowled in disapproval.

Nur finally arrived back in the room. Val felt relieved to have some company that didn't seem to hate her. After all the food was cleared, one of the older ladies with a birthmark on her left cheek pointed a finger at Val, then turned to look at Nur.

"British?"

Nur shook her head. "American."

The old woman looked pleasantly delighted. She said something back to Nur in Malay that Val couldn't make out.

"She says she loves KFC." Nur translated.

"Oh—" Val squealed, as the woman mimed a bucket of chicken. "I love it too — very good — very much like home." Val flashed two thumbs up, and the woman beamed.

"Berapa banyak senjata yang dia ada?" Another woman with two missing fingers piped up from across the room.

Nur glared at the woman and then turned back to Val. "She wants to know how many guns you own... you don't have to answer her."

Val glanced back at the woman; who was now shooting finger guns at Nur's grandmother gangster style. Nur's grandmother completely ignored her.

"I don't have any." Val answered truthfully.

Another woman was in the middle of a question about some superhero franchise from what Val could tell; when Nur's grandmother seized Val by her wrist!

Val yelped, as the strange old woman squeezed down, with a force that could juice a brick. Her hand seized, freezing into a gnarled cramp within her grasp. If that wasn't painful enough, the granny's palm and gaunt fingers felt like they were *on fire*... all but her rings, which stayed icy cold.

Val tried to wrestle her hand back; while Nur sprinted to grab something from one of the back rooms... but before Nur made it back, she began to croak. The color from her eyes disappeared, leaving a faintish white behind...

"*Dia akan merasakan daging iblis,*
dan akan mengetahui penderitaan yang belum diketahui oleh manusia.
Musim hujan kemudian membawa dua biji.
Satu cepat, satu perlahan, satu tinggi, satu rendah. Satu tetap, satu pergi."

Val gasped — smoke was seeping from her hand! She yanked it away, while the woman collapsed onto a pile of cushions conveniently placed behind her. Nur rushed back, bringing with her several pills and a syringe filled with something clear. After a few tense moments, Nur's grandmother began to stir again. Val peered around at the other woman; who to her surprise only seemed slightly annoyed at this outburst. Most of them hadn't even stopped sipping their tea...

"What was that about?" Val hollered, as Nur drove her back to her car. "What was she saying? Was it about me? What was that?"

"I — I don't know..." Nur sputtered. "I don't know if it was about you or not."

"What was she saying? Why did the other women not give a damn? Give me something!"

"I — I can't tell you for sure... all I know is my grandmother has some *prophetic* tendencies... she may have predicted that Amina would get pregnant this year."

"Did you know I dreamt about her last night? Did your grandmother mention anything about that?"

"She might have mentioned something strange this morning... but I didn't exactly know what she meant."

"What'd she see just now?" Val demanded. "What was she saying? I know you could hear her, she was practically yelling."

"I... I don't know." Nur lied.

"Yes you do — I know you do — now just tell me!"

Nur's face looked like a red party balloon. "She — She was just going on about some seeds, or something..."

"What seeds, like plant seeds — does that mean something — what about the seeds — what kind of seeds?"

"I don't know, it could mean anything." Nur stuttered. "She just mentioned two different seeds, planted in the rainy season — one, high, one low, one fast, one slow, one stays, one goes..."

Val could still feel Nur holding back. "What else? What else did she say?"

Nur shook her head, and turned a shade of scarlet Val wasn't sure was even on the color wheel. "That's all..."

"No it's not! What else did she—"

"*She said that you will taste the flesh of demons and know misery unknown to man!* That's what she said — there — are you happy?" Nur spat. "I have absolutely no idea what she meant by that..."

Val felt her heart stop. She was about to say something, anything, but no words found her lips. She slumped back down in the passenger's seat. They drove together silently all the way back to Khoo Hun Chhiau's car. She got out without saying goodbye, nearly leaving her enormous bag of strawberries behind. Val started the sedan and left the parking lot.

CHAPTER TWELVE

Val pulled into the Valet, and right on cue the men rushed to help her out, whisking the little car away. The frosty air had been a welcome relief from the sweltering heat, but by now she was starting to miss it. The chill just tensed her muscles more. She had stomped off all the way to her room, before realizing she had forgotten her key. Val huffed disappointedly, as Prince Diana's whimpers seeped through underneath the door.

"Don't worry!" Val wined back. "I'll be right back to let you out!"

Val hurried back towards the elevator, through the lobby, and up to the receptionist's desk; where the same squashed nose, pointed chin woman that had checked in Khoo Hun Chhiau was standing idly.

"Hi—" Val rushed, in the most polite voice she could muster. "I forgot my key card, can I get another one?"

The woman peered up from examining her chipped nail polish and shot Val an annoyed look. "Your name?" She asked snidely.

"Valentina Palacio."

"I don't have a Valentina Palacio in my system." The woman shot back.

"Oh, right... it's probably under the name Khoo Hun Chhiau?"

"I can't give out a key card unless the room is specifically under your name."

Val was losing her patience. "Look, my husband will be very upset to learn—"

"If he's your husband, then why is your family name different?"

Val glared into her black, careless eyes; loathing every cell in this woman's body.

"Look, I know you saw us walk in together the other day. Can you just give me the key? There's a dog in one of our rooms who needs to be taken out."

"I'm sorry — I can't."

Val let out an angry sigh. Not now. *Seriously?* Could the universe cut her some slack on this one?

"Can you just let me into the conference hall real quick? I can grab a key off of him."

The woman paused. Her face froze into a look befitting a much more audacious question. Val would've thought she'd just asked the Queen of England if she could walk one of her pet corgis. The woman's eyes dead-panned slowly up, and her jaw hung open enough for Val to spot the large wad of gum she'd been obnoxiously chewing on for this entire conversation. "Right now — really? There's no way—"

"I'll be in and out before anyone notices." Val whispered frantically, knowing full well that her crutches, old jeans, raggedy sweatshirt and sneakers would stand out from the black ties and heels clicking around. "Could you tell me where Khoo Hun Chhiau's supposed to be right now — which room he's in?"

"According to my files, he's scheduled to be in the main ballroom giving the keynote speech. I'm sorry, but we've had people sign up months in advance to get a seat at *this* specific lecture. The waiting list is longer than those who were even able to attend... there's no way I can let you in there... you understand, right?"

Val twirled back around and headed for a chair on the opposite side of the lobby. She plopped into it, and sat there silently; snacking on strawberries as she shot loathsome, heated glares at the front desk worker who'd so easily rejected her. After several agonizing minutes, Val heard muffled footsteps start draining out of the massive double doors. To her dismay, it took even longer for the crowd around Khoo Hun Chhiau to thin out enough for her to reach him. She had to elbow a scowling, eager-looking Chinese girl in the face to finally pull him aside and ask for the room key.

"I'll go with you." Khoo Hun Chhiau offered, looking a bit desperate to get away from the mob-like crowd. "I need to put my laptop up and get ready for tonight."

They trudged back up to the room in silence, politely avoiding any and everyone who clambered for his attention.

"So... you had an important presentation today, why didn't you tell me?"

Khoo Hun Chhiau shrugged. "It was in Mandarin, so I didn't need any help checking my grammar." He leaned in a little closer. "You already had enough to deal with — I didn't wanna give you one more thing to worry about. Anyways, how was your day? Did you figure out how to pick strawberries with just one hand?"

"Oh..." Val peered down at her bag of strawberries, which were half eaten by now. It seemed that *that* particular problem had become the least of her worries; but now didn't seem like a good time for him to hear about how she'd soon be eating demon flesh. "Umm, yeah, it went well..."

Khoo Hun Chhiau had caught something in her voice. He remained quiet, before switching into interrogation mode.

"What's wrong — did you cut yourself — did you fall?"

"No—" Val snapped. "I'm okay, stop it."

"No, tell me what happened, is everything all right?"

"Everything's fine." Val lied valiantly. "It's nothing, you just need to focus on whatever you're doing in that conference that's making people go crazy. What's that?"

"What's what?" Khoo Hun Chhiau asked, as they passed under the banister to his room, but it didn't take long for him to figure out the source of her confusion. All around them, gift baskets, large and small, had been perched on chairs, sofas, and nightstands. They waded through the mess, ogling at it all.

"I guess they found out which room was mine..." Khoo Hun Chhiau sputtered.

Val fretted through large, decorative boxes of dried fruits and chocolate truffles; reading through the few cards that were in English, congratulating him on being: *"such a devoted pioneer in his field";* and reminding him just how *"bright his future would be, if only he joined up with their firm..."*

"I can't believe this, they must have followed me to my room to figure out where to send all this... *assholes!*"

Val gaped at the large basket on his bed, which was big enough for her to crawl inside and sleep in. A whole family of teddy bears sat next to several board games; while large and small candy bars, lotions, and decorative soaps littered the bottom. In the very middle of the mess, a red card was sandwiched between a can of artisanal soda and the *smelliest* durian.

Khoo Hun Chhiau grabbed the card; scanning it, before scoffing, and turning a light shade of peach.

"Who's it from?" Val asked curiously.

"I'm not quite sure."

Val snatched the card from his hands. He tried to grab it back, but she ran around to the other side of the room, throwing the stinky durian at him as a distraction.

"Khoo Hun Chhiau — congratulations on all the success you are bound to achieve as a result of all of your hard work over the last several years. On behalf of our employers, the Wion group, we would like to give you this basket as a small token of our gratitude. We believe you would be not only a good fit for the future projects we'd like to pursue, but an excellent candidate for our leadership team. If you are interested, please meet with one of our Wion representatives in your attendance."

"Wow!" Val exclaimed proudly. "That's good — Isn't it? Do you have any idea which of these guys you're gonna pick? Do any of them stand out to you?"

Khoo Hun Chhiau shook his head and glared down at the floor. "I don't know yet, but the more everyone keeps bothering me, the more I just wanna die."

Val noticed how dark the circles around his eyes had grown since just this morning. It worried her seeing him like this.

"Well, let's rate all the baskets, and you'll join up with the firm that sent the best one. Oh look — this one has Battleship!" She held up the gray and black board game. "I'll teach you how to play — come on!"

Khoo Hun Chhiau rolled his eyes, but after just one round, he was hooked. The two of them sat there; eating snacks from various gift baskets, trying different board games, and making sure Prince Diana didn't steal any treats that would kill him. By cocktail hour, Val could have sworn she caught him smiling a few times.

"Okay," Khoo Hun Chhiau noted, "I'm gonna grab our drinks, are you okay here?"

Val leaned her crutches against her black armchair and nodded. "Yeah—yeah, I'll be okay."

"Good." With that, he hurried off towards the bar, parting the sea of men and women who were already beginning to crowd around him.

"It's a shame really..." A familiar voice pouted from behind her. "All of these top companies have sent their best recruiters, and 99% of them will end up wasting their time."

Val peered over just in time to see Scott taking a seat across the table, holding out a glass of white wine for her. She took it politely.

"Khoo Hun Chhiau is at the bar grabbing us a bottle—"

"Grabbing you a bottle." He finished. "He doesn't drink."

"Ah, right... well if you'd like some, it's only fair."

But Scott wasn't paying any attention to her now. His eyes were fixed on Khoo Hun Chhiau, who was now engrossed in a conversation with five serious-looking Chinese men. His hawk-like gaze only broke when Khoo Hun Chhiau began approaching their table once more.

"Ah, I see you've met the Ma group. They're in very *serious* merger talks with Match right now." Scott stressed. "Very bright group of men, very bright... well, did you see the Lee twins earlier? I heard that they blew a deal with some African dictator; word is one of them threw up on his daughter... crazy isn't that? Even crazier, he still got her number. I'll drink to that!"

Khoo Hun Chhiau grunted lazily back at him, as he politely sipped ice water. Val frowned. The dark circles under his eyes were making a comeback.

"Ah, and Mr. Mu over there—" he leaned in towards Val, "if he gives you a hard time, be careful not to kick him in the nuts, I heard he's into that."

Val winced — not only from the comment Scott just made, but because Mr. Mu had caught her staring, and had *winked*.

Scott went on and on, singling out various salespeople that were bound to approach Khoo Hun Chhiau, while pointing out seedy, if not downright disgusting details about them.

"Ah, and Mr. Salid over there, he gets the worst eczema. That's why he wears gloves most of the time."

"Actually—" A British voice cut in, in the form of the short, Chinese girl Val had elbowed in the face earlier. "Mr. Salid's found an ointment strong enough for his condition. I would know — my brother's his dermatologist." She lounged casually on the armrest of Khoo Hun Chhiau's chair, a little too close for Val's liking...

Scott scowled at the young woman. "Maybe your brother could set you up with a stronger anti-wrinkle cream. Your's are coming in early... maybe a prescription-strength one."

"That's not a thing dumb-ass." She snarled, before turning towards Val. "You must be the smart one out of the pair of you—"

"Oh, no, he's not my boyfri—"

But she wasn't paying any attention to her anymore. Her dark eyes were focused on Khoo Hun Chhiau, who was looking more depressed by the minute. "Oh my God!" She gasped, feigning surprise. She grabbed his upper arm; tugging on it playfully, before squealing, "Khoo Hun Chhiau — I can't believe you're here!"

Khoo Hun Chhiau's face was stunned, and unmoving. His jaw lay open. Val could have sworn there was a hint of pink on his cheeks. "Hey Morgan..." He mumbled.

"I've missed you so much — remember our old study group — oh my god, I can't believe my study buddy is here!"

Val cut her finger on the rim of her wine glass. *He'd had a study buddy before her?*

"What're you doing here Morgan?" Scott growled. Scott did *not* like this woman. Maybe Scott wasn't so bad after all.

Morgan flashed her badge at him. "What's everyone doing here? I'm here on some recruiting business for Wion." She turned back to Khoo Hun Chhiau, her body so close to his, she was nearly sitting on his lap. "Did you get our gift basket? I made sure it had your favorites in there."

"Oh, thanks." He said quietly, forcing his face into an appreciative smile.

"You have to meet some of my Wion colleagues, they're dying to meet you. Oh my god if you come work for us, we can be *work* buddies and *study* buddies. Come on — they won't take no for an answer."

Morgan had practically ripped his coat off from around his shoulders. He stood up to fix it, but before anyone could say another word, she'd dragged him away through the thicket of preying men, hoping to jump at the next chance at Khoo Hun Chhiau.

Scott had drained his glass in one gulp, and was shaking his head furiously.

"I fucking hate her!"

If Scott was angry, Val was livid. There was no point being here anymore. A tiny dart punctured her heart with every step he took away behind the other woman. She grabbed her crutches and started off towards her room, ignoring all the old, gross, men checking her out. Her crutches carried her down the hall, echoing off a high pitch *"Eech"* as they landed on the hardwood underneath. Before she knew it, Val was standing outside Khoo Hun Chhiau's door, a faded whimpering leaked out from the crack at the bottom.

"Okay, we can have one more walk tonight." Val obliged Prince, who was already holding his leash in his injured mouth by the time she opened the door. Val changed into her bedclothes, and the two of them were off into the night. Heading the opposite way down the hall, towards an emergency exit that led off into a quaint walking path.

The night was crisp and chilly. Val wrapped her robe around her waist even tighter, shielding her newly formed chest wounds from the sting of cold. The sky only had wisps of clouds. None solid enough to block the rays of the full moon; which bounced a twinkling light off the coy ponds scattered here and there. Eventually Prince came to a halt under a bushy durian tree to relieve himself.

"Lovely night, isn't it?" Someone slurred from over her shoulder.

Val whirled around. Ready to throw hands at any threat, but to her surprise it was just Scott stumbling towards her; peering up at the stars.

"That woman... that dreadful woman..." He mumbled. "Did you know I'd get the raise of a lifetime if I snagged him? Did you know that?"

Val shook her head. "How would I have known that?"

"Twenty-five percent! Twenty-five percent raise — and you don't even know my salary, but that's a lot. Trust me, sweetheart."

Val wanted nothing more than for Prince to hurry along with his business.

"That bitch Morgan Xiao... I met her a few times when I visited Khoo Hun Chhiau during his first years at Singapore National. She flirted with *every* guy — literally — every guy who came within ten feet from her, total pick me. But none so much as Khoo Hun Chhiau... if she blows this for me I swear—"

"Is that his ex?" Val asked quickly, regretting the question before it had even fallen out of her mouth, and onto Scotts beat red ears. He shot her a look of pleasant surprise.

"Oh... why do you want to know?" He teased. "Well, no, they never did date. Khoo Hun Chhiau has never been a *"dater"* of any sort, and trust me I tried... but she did hang around him quite a bit, hoping for the chance." Scott turned his attention to the pale moon and the surrounding blackness. "What do you see?"

"I'm sorry, what?"

"Up in the stars?" He asked again. This time a bit more softly. "You can see so many of them out here tonight. Come on... what do you see?"

Val didn't see the value in answering the futile wonderings of a drunken man. But Prince was still taking his sweet time sniffing a nearby flower, and she really wasn't in a rush to get back inside on a night like this. Truth be told, she didn't much like looking up at the stars. It stressed her out pondering the vastness of the universe, and how minuscule the earth was in comparison. She found herself picturing apocalyptic scenes, an asteroid striking, a solar flare lashing out, an alien invasion; more than a million different scenarios completely out of humanity's control would play themselves out in her mind's eye. It always led her down a depressing road, where she'd find herself trying to answer the most difficult questions... *What would she do in her final moments? Where would she go? Whom would she call? Whose arms would be wrapped around her... if any? How would she say goodbye...*

"I see chaos, death, and hopelessness." Val answered truthfully.

Scott gave her an incredulous look, but merely shrugged afterwards; demonstrating the kind of tolerance and respect only a drunk man can. "Interesting..."

"What do you see? Something maybe not so depressing?"

Scott gave a long, drawn-out sigh. He curled his glass beer bottle close to his chest.

"I see... I see... the unknown for now, but maybe not forever? Maybe one day, we'll unlock this universe's vast, dark secrets, and maybe it'll be a little less scary to us..."

Val paused, and nodded respectfully. They stared up into the stars, Val feeling a little more settled; until Prince Diana started prodding her leg. The impatient Prince's command to walk on once more.

"I better get going." Val yawned. "Don't stay out here too long... a tiger could get you."

Scott laughed, then hiccuped. "Yeah, I'd be some easy prey right about now."

Val wandered back down the path. With each crunchy step feeling just a little bit more hopeful about the world.

CHAPTER THIRTEEN

Val returned to her room, only to find Khoo Hun Chhiau retiring to his as well; looking thoroughly crestfallen. His eyes resembled two pool eight balls. The two packed up quickly the next day, checking out early enough to avoid most of the last-minute hoard of goodbye wishers, pining for just one more moment of his attention. They made it home in time to be beckoned inside by an ecstatic Yeo A'i, who offered the two of them an early lunch. One that Khoo Hun Chhiau wasn't allowed to refuse.

Yeo A'i's trip had gone well. So well in fact that Yeo A'i couldn't help but catalog every second of it with photos. So. Many. Photos… Val sat in her wicker chair, listening to Yeo A'i's play-by-play of the whole reunion for at least two hours, 'til she reached her point.

"My husband finally agreed to retire at the end of this year, so we're gonna move to London!" She blubbered excitedly, nearly prompting Khoo Hun Chhiau to knock his teacup off the table. "I already have a *ton* of buyers lined up waiting to snatch this house, but I've told them all that it was absolutely mandatory they wait 'til the end of December."

Val felt her heart disintegrate into thin air. Why exactly, she couldn't tell. It's not like she had any concrete plans to stay here after the year was up; but for some reason, Val felt empty. She strained an appropriate enough smile to hide all this regardless.

"Wow — Um — that's wonderful… I'm so happy for you, really…" Val forced.

Semua Tangan opened the following Monday, with only a few final touches needing finishing. Val dodged several painters on her way to her first class, as well as newly stationed police officers who patrolled the halls. If anyone needed to use the restroom, a woman officer escorted them to and from the bathrooms; while more armed guards stood outside. To Val's deep, *deep,* dismay, the guard assigned to patrol her hall was none other than Officer Yusef.

"I can't believe this is all Captain Jano gave me to defend myself!" He gripped that afternoon to anyone who would listen, as he twirled his colorful children's slingshot between his fingers. "Everyone else gets a side piece and a real grenade, and all I've got is this stupid piece of shit that couldn't take out a fly, and a smoke grenade?"

But even his smoke grenade privileges would be quickly revoked, after one particularly windy afternoon. Officer Yusef swore he caught a blur of grey outside Val's window, and promptly hoisted it into her classroom; barricading Val and her whole class inside while he radioed for back up. It came in the form of an incensed Principal Arif, who forced him out of the way to evacuate students. Half of whom were nearing toxic smoke inhalation.

As all the teachers were well aware, the Friday night town hall meeting couldn't come fast enough; where the future of Semua Tangan, if any, was up for debate.

City hall, an imposing English colonial house that had been fully restored, sat in the middle of the town's main street. Val and Yeo A'i spotted a few free seats near Amina, which must have been saved over threat of death — considering how cramped the wide auditorium was now growing. The two of them squished in next to her, Val making a particularly pointed attempt to avoid Nur's eyes, which darted away at the sight of her.

A short, scrawny man, with a head that rolled forward in age banged on a gavel.

"Order — *Order!*" He croaked.

The hum from the crowd quieted. All eyes fixed themselves upon the wooden podium.

"Ehem—" He cleared his throat and spoke with a voice that rattled. "The council has decided that Mayor Osman will henceforth preside over this town meeting. I call Mayor Osman up to the stand."

Val watched, as an older, casually dressed Malay man, with thick-rimmed glasses shuffled onto the stage, holding a curious mug of coffee in his hands. It had Principal Arif's face plastered on its side, surrounded by the words *"World's Best Principal."*

"Mayor Osman?" Val demurred. "Is he related to Principal Arif?"

"That's her husband." Amina whispered. "But she's on the town council too, look at the seat next to his."

Val glanced over to the line of town council chairs at the front that faced the audience. Sure enough, there was Principal Arif, seated to the right of the now empty seat. Her lips were so tightly pressed together, they could have formed a vacuum seal.

"Why does she look like that?" Val whispered again.

"Like what?"

"Like... she's angry, or frustrated, or something?"

"Oh — *that*... you'll see."

Val turned her attention back to Mayor Osman, who was shuffling through several loose pieces of paper, looking worried.

"All right—" He commanded. "As I'm sure many of you are well aware, we have gathered here today to discuss the future of Semua Tangan and its possible relocation—"

"*No!*" Several high pitched voices cried out from the back. Val swirled around in her chair to get a better look at the group of young women, each of whom dawned grey sacks.

"She's the divinity of Semua Tangan!"

"The children are blessed to be in her presence!"

"A true goddess amongst us mere mortals!"

"We must keep the balance!"

Mayor Osman let out a sigh of annoyance. He glared at the group, like a father would at their most embarrassing child.

"Ladies of the Monster fan club — we urge you to wait your turn to speak once the floor is open—"

"How dare you mock our faith!" The most prominent amongst them, a heavy set, beady-eyed woman, with dyed, fire-red hair objected. "We are the proud congregation of *The Daughters of the Eternal Mother* — a legitimate religious organization that worships our fierce queen — protector of *her* realm. *She* lifts our spirits, and hears our prayers—"

"Oh for Pete's sake Peh Si — I taught you, and all your silly little friends here when you started this ridiculous club at school!" Principal Arif snapped from her chair. "You only worshiped *her* because *she* tormented that poor girl you-lot bullied endlessly. And you — Farah — I keenly remember just how frightened you were when you *actually* caught a glimpse of *her*. We had to phone your mother to bring you a new skirt after you wet yourself! I can't believe you galavant around with this group of deranged women!"

A girl in the middle, and a little to the left of the group, hid her pink face behind her hands.

"Sit down and be quiet... all of you! This isn't some silly game, we have actual students who need protection. If none of you are willing to act like adults and contribute *reasonable* solutions, leave!" Principal Arif finished, pointing a bony finger toward the back doors.

The girls mumbled amongst themselves, before unfolding extra seats, and plopping themselves down at the very back.

Principal Arif nodded toward her husband. He took the hint that it was his cue.

"Now — as we're all very well aware, the city budget has recently taken quite a large hit, due to a few unwise investments by our former town treasurer. Most notably, in his very *generous* contribution to the cryptocurrency known as *Crocodile Coin*..."

No names were mentioned, but Val caught several eyes glaring at the back of Mr. Elmsworth's head. He shrunk down a little in his seat.

"Luckily for us — very luckily — we have recovered nearly half of our funds' previous value. However, we've already spent most of that on Semua Tangan's most recent remodels..."

"Why don't we convert the old tire factory into at least a temporary school?" Someone from the crowd yelled out.

"That was our first idea too." Mayor Osman agreed. "Granted, it would still need a great deal of work, but there's been a very unfortunate snag to that plan…"

"I'm not selling it!" Officer Yusef piped up from the very right-hand corner of the room. "I bought it for a very reasonable price, and I'm gonna make a lot of money… you guys'll see…"

The whole crowd grumbled. Mayor Osman slapped his palm to his forehead.

"Damnit Yusef… what poorly planned enterprise have you decided to squander your late father's fortune on this time? It surely can't be worse than even our own government's squanderings…"

"Hey—" He shot back, "as a proud owner and co-inventor of Crocodile Coin, I resent that mischaracterization… but no… my new idea is more innovative… more self-inspired and represented…" He flipped his collar, and ran his fingers through his hair. "I am converting it into a music studio. I've already put down several million into the latest recording tech."

Val watched, as Mayor Osman's face turned white, then red, then purple. His temple veins throbbed furiously. He took off his glasses and rubbed his eyes.

"In what ways does this town require a recording studio? How's *that* more necessary than a school? Have you seen Killer Wiz Akeem — or whomever the young people are listening to nowadays walking around here? Or have I just missed him?"

"Killer Wiz Akeem is gonna be nothing compared to the next star on the scene… you all can start calling me *King Yusef* — that's my rap name. I released my new single on sound cloud last week. It's called, *"Shooting Monsters with my Glock."* He mimed.

"It should be called shooting teachers!" Mayor Osman exploded. His voice ringing around the auditorium so loudly, Val covered her ears. "At least that would be more accurate!"

Officer Yusef ignored the outburst, instead opting to stroke his flimsy go-tee. "You know what… I would be willing to sell you *that* particular investment of mine for a good cause, at a discount…"

"Great — *Great...*" Mayor Yusef swore in exasperation. He waved his arms around, and let them fall heavily onto the podium in front of him. "How much? What's your price?"

Officer Yusef shrugged. "Mmmm... I would say... an even one billion ringgits sounds fair? Don't you think—"

But there would be no more haggling. Mayor Osman lunged from the stage, while several police officers leapt to their feet to defend the scrawny man. Officer Yusef bolted out of the room faster than Val reasoned his twig-like legs could carry him.

Mayor Osman took a moment to collect what was left of his patience, before moving forward once more. After several deep breaths and a nearly hemorrhaged forehead vein, he continued.

"There are a few more options on the table that we can discuss..."

"Why don't we just put the girl students with our boy ones?" Another parent shouted. "It would make picking up and dropping off so much easier, and probably save the town money in the long run."

It was the dad's turn to grumble. There were murmurs of *'not my daughter'*'s and *'I don't trust those hormonal teenage boys'*'s.

"Yes, we've considered that option as well, but unfortunately the boys' facility is nowhere near big enough for all the students to fit together. I've been informed by the fire department that the classroom size would be a fire hazard." Mayor Osman replied, crestfallen.

"What about online schooling?" Another parent chimed in. "There's no need for a building then."

"I am not staying home with my kids!" Someone shouted out from the back. "They're demons I tell you — worse than whatever monster's roaming that school — I would never—"

"You're just worried they'll ruin your morning binge!" Another parent shot back.

A brawl broke out between the parents. Several chairs, and the people sitting on them were knocked over. It took six police officers to tear the two women and their husbands apart.

"Okay — *Okay*, everyone calm down!" Mayor Osman commanded. His hair now ruffled and messy from how many times he'd rubbed his fingers through it. "As much as I hate to say it, that woman is right. We can't expect parents to stay home all day with their kids for eighteen years!"

"Well I can't keep half my men posted at Semua Tangan thirty hours a week!" Jano spoke up. "Our police budget has exploded — we can't keep that up either!"

The crowd began to rumble once more. Mayor Osman dismissed the town, and people poured out from the doors; bickering amongst one another which bad option would be the most feasible. In the end, it seemed doing nothing was all they could do at the moment. Val shuddered. A long shower sounded nice after that display of humanity at its most petty. She was reaching for Yeo A'i's car door handle, when a question arose in her mind.

"Is this how all the town meetings go?"

"What? Oh, you mean like that?" Yeo A'i sighed. "Honestly, in all my years attending them, that was one of the better ones if you ask me."

CHAPTER FOURTEEN

The next month was the most hectic yet. It seemed each day was trying to top the next. Parents openly fought in the pick-up line, to the point that teachers had to step in, dragging them apart after hands were thrown. Val had to beat back two warring moms with the help of her crutches, which were getting less and less use as the days wore on.

The Daughters of the Eternal Mother were giving everyone a headache, no one more so than Principal Arif. They picketed and protested outside the building day and night. On more than one occasion, the guards had caught them sneaking onto campus, supposedly offering sacrifices of dried fruits and playing cards by chucking them into the forest behind the school. As if all that wasn't enough, Officer Yusef had taken to using her body as target practice for his slingshot.

"Can you please remind Jano to take that *damn* toy from him?" Val gripped at the Wednesday night gathering, while *"The Bachelor"* India was dramatically choosing between his final two — a pair of identical twins.

"I'll try," Amina simpered, as she twisted Val's hair into a long double braid, "but he's been so busy lately. Even if I get him to agree, he'll probably just forget."

"You could just try taking it away from him yourself." Parini offered. "He probably weighs less than what... fifty kilos? I bet you could take him. Maybe if you recruited a few of your students to help..."

"That's great advice — assault and disarm an active duty police officer. Why don't you just go ahead and handcuff yourself? March right down to the jailhouse. Do you want to lead her to it, or should I?" Tan Soan mocked.

Parini shook her head and rolled her eyes. "What do you think, Nur? Do you think Val should risk taking a toy from a man-child or keep getting trash pelted at her?"

"Oh — What?" Nur stuttered, her attention keenly focused on the fight that was breaking out on the television. The Bachelor had very artfully told the two women that he might as well marry them both, as they're identical. "Oh... uhh both sound good." She replied carelessly. The twins were now beating the poor man with their heels.

Parini rolled her eyes. "I bet it'd be easier to snatch it from him than it would be my own baby."

"How's he doing by the way?" Amina asked. "Did you get any more sleep this week?"

"Mhmm maybe a little, but he's going through this weird staring phase... it creeps me out honestly."

"It can't be that weird... can it?" Amina shrugged. "Don't babies stare a lot anyways?"

"You'll see." Parini grumbled.

"Well, maybe by my birthday party he'll have grown out of that." Tan Soan grinned. "All your cards are in the mail by the way." She turned to face Val. "You need to look extra cute, my brother is gonna be there. I've already talked you up to him... don't make me regret my choice of words... I told him you could win a Nina Dobrev look-alike contest. *Win,* is what i said. Not loose, not come in runner up... reserve September 20th on your calendars people!"

Everyone's attention had now turned to the sobbing twins, who were now hugging and crying in each other's arms. Val caught sight of Nur, curled up onto a corner armchair, snuggling a blanket between her legs. Things had remained awkward between the pair ever since that fateful prophecy had been spoken by her grandmother. The tension was starting to rest more uneasily in her chest. Val got up and sat down next to her.

"Hey..." Val Whispered. "Ummm... how have you been?"

Nur shrugged. "Oh, um, I've been all right... and you?"

'I'm okay." Val rushed. "I just wanted to say I'm sorry for overreacting the other day in the car... that wasn't cool of me."

"Nah — Nah, I get it." Nur faltered. "I shouldn't have yelled that you would — what was it? Know misery unknown to man?"

"And taste the flesh of demons." Val joked.

"Right, right... well anyways, maybe I should have broken that to you a bit more gently. Not exactly my best bedside manner."

"I suppose not."

The pair watched on, through the bawling and bruises and tears; until Val broke the silence once more.

"So, you must have gone to Semua Tangan around the same time as those Daughters of the Eternal Mother? Is that right?"

Nur nodded her head. "Yep."

"What a bunch of nuts!" Val swore. "Were they like that back in your day too?"

"Worse, they were like fanatical teen groupies. It was bizarre." She stared off in the other direction, looking at nothing in particular. "I used to hope that they would grow up and drop the act, but some people never really grow up now do they..."

"Who was the girl Principal Arif was talking about in the meeting? Who started their obsession with the monster? She said someone was tortured — do you remember that?"

Nur's cheeks turned pink, and her lips pursed together. "Yeah, um, she was talking about me..."

"YOU!" Val gasped, causing the other three girls to snap out of their Bachelor trances, but only momentarily.

"Yeah." Nur shrugged. *"She* tortured me, and tried to drag me into the forest with her, but I got lucky. Principal Arif and the other teachers caught up with me just in time... I could have disappeared forever!"

Val grabbed hold of Nur's soft, plump hand, and squeezed. "Nur, I'm... I'm..."

"It's all right." Nur wavered. "I'm here now, she didn't get me. I just make a point to do what I can for Principal Arif when she needs a little backup every now and then... that's why I volunteered to chaperone the field trip this year. Who knows what would have happened to that poor girl if I hadn't been there to at least delay *her* a few seconds."

Val remembered back to that day — how she had glared at Nur through those red, glowing eyes, with a fury that seemed reserved especially for her. It made more sense now.

"Well, I'm glad you're not dead." Val said cheerfully. "Or missing in the woods somewhere."

Nur giggled. "Thanks."

The Bachelor season finale ended, with many tears on and off screen. Val caught a ride home from Tan Soan, and tried her best to keep Nur's story at bay from her dreams.

It wouldn't be long until Val found herself face to face with another set of identical twins. This time standing in the doorway of her classroom, accompanied by Principal Arif.

"Class — I'd like you all to meet your two new classmates — Dhia and Damia."

The class waved to them shyly, a few even sharing tepid greetings back. Both of the girl's round, pudgy faces glowed at being put on the spot.

"Let's all give them a proper Semua Tangan welcome!" Principal Arif finished, before pushing the girls through the doorway and darting off down the hall.

There was a brief moment of silence. They stood there in the doorway, unmoving.

"Oh—" Val remembered, "you two can take those two seats in the back over there."

For the first few days Val kept an eye on the pair, watching as other students approached to say hello and introduce themselves, or share some helpful tips — bring your own lunch on Wednesdays, don't stand too close behind Mr. Elmsworth, hide your sodas and gum around Ms. Nadar, don't stay after school gets out... never walk alone... Val felt sorry for them at first, she remembered how horrible middle schoolers could be to one another. Transferring in the middle of the year, into *this* school, should come with a free therapy session.

Val's sympathies didn't last though. It didn't take long for her to notice that the two would glare, giggle, and gossip between the pair of them; staring and pointing meanly towards the direction of other girls. A week passed by, and Val caught them stealing chairs as students were about to sit down, causing them to tumble to the floor in a heap. Another week and they were throwing trash, dirtying up Val's classroom. Ms. Nadar didn't miss the opportunity to point it out during a staff meeting. A few more days and they were pulling girls' ponytails and hijabs. The rate of their debauchery was only escalating.

Val watched a soggy candy wrapper fly through the air. It hit little Zara in the back of her head. This had been the fifth ball thrown so far in her direction. *That* crossed the line. *Not* little Zara. Val was just about to set them up on a date with a toilet brush, when Wani stood up from her desk, grimacing as she faced them.

"Maybe you guys shouldn't be eating so many of those..." Wani teased. "Pigs are forbidden in your religion. You probably shouldn't be turning yourselves into them."

"Wilbur!" Eng ki snickered. "Willlllbur!"

"Girls settle down now." Val stressed.

The twins quit chuckling to themselves. Their beady black eyes narrowed in on Wani.

"At least we aren't little rats, who hide behind our friends to fight our battles for us."

"We don't scurry down the halls, flinching at every small noise like something's gonna get us... what kind of small... weak... powerless person could *that* be?"

Val watched Zara's cheeks flush scarlet. She tried to pull Wani back and hide her own face into the crevice of her elbow in one.

"Don't you two have better things to do right now than waste everyone's time?" Eng Ki seethed.

"Like eat slop and roll around in mud? There's a puddle behind this building I can show you if you'd like."

The twins almost jumped to their feet, but instead stumbled back against their desks.

"Careful Wani, I hear pigs can run up to eleven miles an hour. We might not make it." Eng Ki sassed.

Dhia had had enough. She picked up a stapler, and chucked it right at Zara's head — it hit dead on — she fell to the ground, and wailed out in horrible pain.

"Fucking Bitch—" Wani cried as she spat into Dhia's face.

Dhia lunged at her — Val watched in frozen panic as Eng Ki tried to defend her friend, but then was swung at by Damia. The four of them tussled on the floor, forcing students to dart aside. Val grabbed Zara, and pulled her out of the way of the commotion. She screamed for Officer Yusef, who unfortunately was too busy with that *stupid* toy... after several tense seconds a hoard of officers rushed in. Quartering off the rest of the girls, and pulling the other four off of each other, and onto their own feet.

"To the Principal's office!" Officer Yusef declared proudly, like it was his first time catching anyone committing any sort of crime ever. The police officers dragged the girls out the door. Val followed behind, helping a quietly sobbing Zara hold her wound. The four girls swore, kicked, and spat at each other the whole way down, 'til they reached a worn door with a gold nameplate, reading: *"Principal Arif."* Officer Yusef kicked it open, barging in on an important meeting with the city council.

"Principal — we've brought in a couple of brawling students! What should I book them on? Assault? Battery? *Attempted murder!?"*

Principal Arif took a moment to assess the sight in front of her. Once she had, she scowled up at Officer Yusef and rubbed her temples stressfully. "What happened?"

Val explained the situation as quickly as possible. Fighting off the girls as they interrupted her to add their own side of the story.

"Then Dhia threw a stapler at Zara! See — look at her head!"

Val led Zara over to Principal Arif, and gently removed her hand from the side of her head. Blood dripped down in messy glops.

"Goodness!" Principal Arif swore. "We need to get you to the hospital immediately. As ironic as it sounds, that wound might need a couple of *actual* staples."

"I only threw it cause Wani called my sister and I fat pigs!" Dhia cried. "They started it!"

"You guys started it!" Wani shot back. "They've been bullying Zara ever since they got here, we were just standing up for her!"

"They keep throwing trash at her!" Eng Ki snapped.

Principal Arif turned back to Val, letting out a long, exasperated sigh. "So, who exactly is telling the truth here?"

Val shook her head, trying to remember everything that was just said. "Well... technically, all of them are telling the truth."

"I see." She said calmly. "Well, the four of you will all be joining Ms. Val and myself in detention tomorrow. You two," she pointed at the twins, "for bullying your classmates, and yes, I said *classmates*. This is not the first time I've heard of your malicious shenanigans — and you two," she glared at Wani and Eng Ki, "for that horrible display of religious bigotry. The pair of you should've known better than that, considering your third little best friend here whom you two claim to have been *valiantly* defending shares these girls' faith. There's no justifying any of your actions. Go and grab your school things, I'm sending all of you home early." She motioned for Val to bring Zara toward a chair in the center of the room. "I'll be calling your parents first."

The girls collected their stuff from the room. Val and the guards making sure to keep them well enough apart the entire time. Val spent the whole of the next day wondering what exactly would be in store for them. She knew non-toilet cleaning detentions couldn't be held on the official school compound, but it still surprised her to find the six of them pulling up upon the trash-filled lawn of city hall.

"All right — gather round." Principal Arif called, while handing each of them a long, wooden stick with a pointed metal spike at the bottom. "You'll use these to pick up the garbage left last night by a group of... *civic protestors.*"

"What were they protesting?" Wani pried. "Why do we have to clean up their mess? We didn't make it?"

"It doesn't matter—" Principal Arif snapped, but Wani, or any of them, only had to make a cursory glance to find several posters, reading, *"Daughters of the Eternal Mother"* strewn about amongst the beer cans, broken shot glasses, stereo cords, and party favors. "My husband is in the middle of tracking down these hooligans and fining them the proper amount for their trouble as we speak. Just use the end of these sticks to pick up the trash — *it's not rocket science!"*

The afternoon sun dolled out its own version of a punishment. It beat down on their backs, making the day drag on. At times Val felt they would never finish cleaning up the mess those women made. Those weird, weird women... one pile would vanish, and a new one would appear even larger than before. The only respite was the sight of a familiar woman walking down the street, accompanied by a young Prince at her heels.

"Principal Arif," Yeo A'i trilled. "So lovely to see you, what're you doing here?" She asked in feigned curiosity, as she sneaked a wink at Val.

Principal Arif shook her head. "Just cleaning up another mess." She griped, while wiping sweat from her brow.

"I found a ruby necklace!" Eng Ki hollered from the other side of the lawn.

"And I found a cell phone!" Wani cheered.

Val caught the twins glaring green-eyed at their two companions. To Val it was only fair, as the twins had been taking long seated water breaks in the shade, and hadn't been doing any of the cleanup.

Principal Arif waved her hand in the air cavalierly. "We'll deal with that later."

"You will deal with that now!" A gruff voice ordered from a few meters away. A big-boned woman stomped over towards the three of them, standing a little too close for comfort in Val's vicinity.

The vein in Principal Arif's temple began its regular course of beating furiously once more. She growled her reply.

"Peh Si — would you care to tell us who exactly was the cause of all this mess? Could it be you and your friends amongst that silly little cult..."

"We are not some silly little cult!" Peh Si seethed. "We demand respect — *and* the right to pray to *our* goddess on *our* sacred sights, during *our* holy mother's full moon... we will not stop until *our* requirements are met!"

"Your little rituals will get you and all your friends killed... or is that what you want? Are you secretly hoping your little monster god will come crawling out of the forest, taking with *her* the weakest amongst your friend group? Is that what you *really* want?"

A twitchy smile at the corner of her mouth betrayed her intentions. "If one of my sisters is willing to offer herself up as a sacrifice to our mother, then who am I to stop them... and who are you to stop us from living our sacred truths? This country was founded on religious tolerance and—"

"You're sick—" Principal Arif hollered, "if you were the only one offering themselves up, I would gladly let you, but you're putting very emotionally disturbed, very vulnerable people in danger with your twisted antics!"

"My sisters are led by no one but themselves and our mother." Peh Si declared proudly. "Our mother knows who the weak are amongst us... that's why *she* chooses *her* prey so well. Maybe one day, when all the weak are expunged from our midst... the ones not willing to go the distance to do what must be done... the ones who are too fearful to stand up for themselves... then will *she* bless the rest of us with her own immortality... and we'll all become our own mothers!"

"Shut up — Shut up — *Shut up!*" Principal Arif roared, causing her glasses to fog, and her temple vein to throb with so much vigor, Val swore one more sentence from this lunatic would break it. "You're mad – you are absolutely mad — you know that? You're a danger to your friends, to your family, and the students of my school. If I catch you there one more time, I'll have you arrested. Do you understand me?"

Peh Si didn't wince, or frown... in fact, she even shared an eerie, half-curled smile. "You will do nothing to get in the way of my sisters and my mother. Besides, I came here to city hall for reasons other than aging you... that cell phone and ruby necklace are *not* your property."

"Wonderful!" Principal Arif cheered sarcastically. "Absolutely wonderful — tell me, should my husband make out the littering fine to the *deluded-daughters* or to you directly?"

Peh Si peered around the handsome, yet filthy front lawn suspiciously, eyeing her options.

"How much is the fine?"

"Mmmm, I don't know? How much are a smartphone and necklace full of Burmese rubies worth? Plus the cost of manual labor to clean up this mess..."

Peh Si glared at her."You will see me and my sisters again... " She growled.

"Looking forward to seeing you in handcuffs then." Principal Arif seethed after her. Val watched Peh Si's plump behind giggle slightly with every stomp she took away from them.

"Soooo... we get to keep them?" Wani asked hopefully.

"Finders keepers." Principal Arif grunted, as the girls' high-fived. Val caught Yeo A'i's eye, the two desperately scrambled to calm Principal Arif back down.

"Did I ever tell you about the time my own daughter got detention?" Yeo A'i blubbered happily. "It's the silliest story... gosh, she mustn't have been any older than these girls!"

"Mhhm..." Principal Arif mumbled, her eyes still lingering on the diminishing dot in the distance causing everyone so much trouble.

"Well, it happened during health class. My girl and her friends were learning a bit more about human anatomy than they were ever familiar with... on that specific day, they were learning about the consequences of having unprotected sex..."

Prince Diana started voicing a low, deep growl.

"Of STDs in particular."

The growling grew louder. He bared his teeth.

"Well, unfortunately, a few of them were a bit scared to say the least from what they saw. And the only way their poor teenage brains could process it was by having a bit of a laugh... so, they started drawing."

"Bark!"

"On each other."

"Bark Bark!"

"In sharpies."

"BARK — BARK — BARK!"

"And so that's how my precious daughter and her friends spent a week of detention with genital boils on their foreheads. We were livid then, but now all us parents can't help but laugh about it whenever we run into each other."

The barking was becoming incessant and deafening now. Prince tugged violently on his leash! *"BARK — BARK — BARK — BARK — BARK — BARK!"*

"What in the bloody hell Prince—" Yeo A'i swore, but the sound of Wani's desperate screams shook everyone — Dhia was on top of Wani —the two lay prostrate on the ground — Val watched Dhia try again to stab the poor girl with her spear.

"Not again—" Principal Arif gasped, but there was something different about this fight, something not quite right... as the adults ran to separate the two, Yeo A'i doubled back. Val caught sight of Damia now advancing on Eng Ki. Val tackled Dhia, and forced her to lie prostrate on the ground, while Principal Arif and Wani pinned her arm down. Both of them together struggled to separate her fingers from around the spear. Out of the corner of Val's eye, she caught Yeo A'i and Eng Ki performing a similar strategy. Once the spears were free, and thrown several feet away, Val felt Dhia convulse violently underneath her. Her pudgy body shook, as if she were seizing — seizing *bad*. The colorful parts of her eyes disappeared into her skull...

"What's going on?" Val cried out.

"I don't know—" Principal Arif yelped, "you wait here — Wani help hold her there!"

Val watched Principal Arif run to check on the other three, who by what Val's shaky eyes could make out, must be dealing with the same thing. Principal Arif's eyes grew wide and frightened. Her small feet dashed off towards the school van.

"Envy—" An unfamiliar, raspy voice croaked from Dhia's mouth, sending shivers down Val's spine.

"What the hell—" Wani cried.

Dhia's eyes retreated back down from inside her skull... only this time, they were no longer the black they were before, but a fiery crimson, that danced in the chaos of it all.

"*Envy — Hatred — Death!*" The voice croaked once more, sounding even more terrible and hoarse. "*Man lusts pointlessly in vain, billions of greedy, mortal hearts return to ash, a waste of earth's time... more valuable as food for insects than one pump of dirty, filthy blood!*"

"What the fuck is she saying?" Wani cried. "Dhia, If you're in there, wake up — wake up!"

Principal Arif rushed back over to them, kneeling at their side, carrying with her a basket full of random items.

"Okay, I gave the vial of holy water and a few amulets to Yeo A'i to try her luck. Let's see what I have left for this poor soul over here... Val, keep her held down, Wani I want you to read these scriptures as best you can right here."

Wani shared a concerned look, but obliged, reading from a book in what Val assumed must be very broken Tamil. Principal Arif cut open a sack of burnt spices, and tossed it over Dhia's face and chest, causing everyone to cough profusely.

For several minutes, Val held Dhia down, Wani prayed and Principal Arif danced and sang ceremoniously. From the few glances Val stole away at the other group, it appeared Yeo A'i and Eng Ki were chanting something she couldn't quite make out from a sheet of paper, while sprinkling water from a small glass vial onto Damia. Val clung onto Dhia, foam seeped from her mouth, as she thrashed around! Val felt Dhia's veins pulsate so furiously in her arms with each chaotic laugh, she worried for the girl's poor heart.

"It's not working…" Val cried. "Nothing's working!"

She wasn't quite sure what it was that made her do it; most likely just the desperate fear of waiting for someone to die in your arms and having no other options… but Val forced herself to stare into those manic, ruby-red eyes, and beg.

"Please—" Val mouthed breathlessly, her eyes giving away her own vulnerability. *"Please…"*

She could have hallucinated… it could have been a trick of the dazzling sunlight that beat down on their backs… but Val swore for a split second, she caught a hint of something other than raging, fiery, anger. Something other than the revelry of chaos and utter loathing in those blood red eyes that focused in on her, piercing her soul… Dhia's eyelids drooped closed. When they flickered open again — tired, baggy, and near lifeless — they were black once more.

Time was of the essence — the group lugged the twins' limp bodies to the van, and the seven of them sped off in the direction of the hospital, with Principal Arif behind the wheel. They reached the emergency room just in time. Val was more than relieved when the paramedics were finally able to take control of the situation, letting at least her and Yeo A'i have a small break. They let Principal Arif and the girls explain the shit-show to the doctors.

"Hey." Yeo A'i sighed breathlessly.

"Hey… you alright?"

"Yeah…" Yeo A'i lied. "You?"

"I guess so." Val lied back. She watched her hands tremble in her lap. "Was that a—"

"Possession?" Yeo A'i interrupted. "If that's not, I don't know what is."

"Damn." Val swore. "Did Damia… say anything?"

"Oh? That nonsense about mortal hearts being bug food? Yeah, she was going on about that too…"

"How can *she* possess two people at once? I mean, isn't that impossible? You saw *her* red eyes too?"

"Yeah, I did." Yeo A'i shrugged. She stared down the corridor at the two girls being wheeled away. "Who really knows what's possible and what's not..."

They ambled down the hall to the girl's room and watched nurses hook up IVs and heart monitors onto the now slightly stirring twins. The medical staff whizzed around them; calling out phrases in medical jargon Val didn't have the slightest idea of how to interpret. What was the code word for demonic possession? Surely *this* town would have one by now.

"We should call their parents." Yeo A'i said quietly.

"I already called them five minutes ago." Principal Arif groaned. "They should be here any minute."

There was a knock at the door, causing everyone to tense. They readied themselves for the horror of watching a mother walk into her worst nightmare. Principal Arif took a deep, shaky breath, before opening the door... Val watched her face drain of all color, at the sight of the mob of young women waiting on the other side of the banister.

"No—" Principal Arif cried out, but it was too late. The whole of the Daughters of the Eternal Mother barged through into the crowded room, encircling the twins. Showering them with makeshift gifts, praise, and unnecessary attention.

"Sisters—" Peh Si sang triumphantly. "Sisters — gather round! We're blessed to be in the company of those who have been bestowed with the highest honors anyone can receive. These mere children have had their souls united with our mother's."

"These children almost died!" Yeo A'i cried out, with a vigor and emptiness Val had never heard from her. "You guys need to get out right now — how'd you even find out about any of this?"

Peh Si smirked at all the anger she had conjured. "My sisters are everywhere. We watch, whisper, and carry on..."

"Nonsense—" Principal Arif spat. "Farah's mother works the front desk at city hall. She probably just messaged her that she had seen something. If there weren't so many children around, I'd have a few words to whisper to you right now... you are so full of—"

"Nah-ah-ah—" Peh Si pestered playfully. "Like you said, there are children present."

"We don't care if you swear!" Eng Ki pleaded with Principal Arif. "You know what, I'll say it — you're batshit crazy!"

"The bitchiest, craziest bat — one with rabies — *and* COVID!" Wani chimed in.

"You should be put into an insane asylum!" Eng Ki finished.

Peh Si flinched at the outburst. It was clear to Val she had no witty comeback. Instead, she turned back to the small crowd of frenzied women. "Sisters — as you can see, these two are desperately upset... and who could blame them? It must be *so* disappointing to be passed up by our mother for their twin classmates."

"I spit on your mother!" Eng Ki cried. "I spit on *her* and fight *her* off every day! *She's* nothing but a bully to my friends! I would rather die than let *her* anywhere near my soul! Your mother hates me, and nothing makes me prouder!"

"More proud..." Wani whispered.

"Same fucking thing!" Eng Ki screamed. "God I fucking hate English!"

"All right — that's enough!" Principal Arif gripped. "Everyone out — everyone get out of the hospital right now. The twins' parents will be here any minute. We need to give them some time to be by themselves."

Peh Si ignored her, opting to turn back to her followers once more. "Before we leave, I want you to remember these girls... what *powers*... what *wisdom* was imparted onto them from our mother? What wisdom could be imparted onto *you* if you just let *her* in... this is a sign that we need to be more persistent — more devoted than ever. If *she* chose to share with these two strong, yet unfaithful, naive youths, then how much more likely are we to be chosen next?"

Principal Arif, Val, and Yeo A'i finally herded the women out the door, and the hospital security team finished the job. Under Principal Arif's orders, Val and Yeo A'i drove Wani and Eng Ki back to their houses. The van jolted to a stop a few houses down from Amina's.

"I can be let out with her." Wani informed them. "I was supposed to be picked up here by my parents anyways."

Yeo A'i nodded. The two retreated back to the safety of their home.

CHAPTER FIFTEEN

The twins didn't show up at school the next few days, or for the next few weeks afterward. Word around Semua Tangan was that after Principal Arif explained everything that had happened to the twins' parents, they left town; waiting only long enough for their girls to be discharged. Val didn't blame them. Nobody deserves to go through that, even the shitiest of kids, but she couldn't help but feel relieved. The mood in her classroom had shifted back to what it once was. Val could tell her students shared in her respite, even little Zara was daring a smile every once in a while now.

So it came as a shock one afternoon after several unusually quiet weeks when something did happen to dampen her students' spirits once again. It happened after the last bell had rung, dismissing class for the rest of the day. Val watched her classroom be let out from the banister under her doorway. Zara, Wani, and Eng Ki passed by her, giggling amongst each other. The sight of the three of them enjoying their youthful goofiness brought back memories of her own middle school days, with her own little friend group. She smiled after them, watching as they made their way down the narrow, crowded hall... when Val's eyes met *hers*.

She lingered lazily, sitting casually on the side of the hall, going completely unnoticed by everyone but Val. *Her* red eyes staring right back into Val's green ones. That horrible smile... with its pointed, shark-like teeth, and lack of lips... Val's jaw dropped at the sight of it; but nothing could prepare her for the single, jagged, stiletto nail, stretching a foot long that extended from her pointer finger. *She* swirled it around playfully. Watching and reveling in the now morphing expressions Val's face must have been making — from fear, to revulsion, to wonder, and finally to disgust. All while little Zara skipped past *her*, laughing hysterically at some joke Eng Ki must have made.

Val wanted to call out to her, to say something, but it was too late — with a flash, *she* had slashed Zara's backpack nearly completely in half. Zara's belongings came tumbling out, spilling onto the hard-tiled floor.

In a blink, *she* vanished. Val searched for where *she* went, but ultimately knew there was no point. Val's eyes instead took in the scene in front of her. Wani and Eng Ki were peering around their surroundings intently, each of them grabbing for something in their pockets. To Val's surprise, they didn't seem as confused as she felt at that moment... in fact, they seemed more prepared, than disturbed...

Val watched them curiously. The two reminded her of Killer Wiz Akeem's bodyguards, as they watched, waited, and grabbed onto Zara unexpectedly. It all felt eerily familiar... only this time, instead of screaming girls rushing from every direction, there was just one monster who struck without one. After the girls had had a good look around, presumably judging that the coast was clear, they knelt down to help Zara with the rest of her books, and scurried off. Rushing her towards the front doors as quickly as their little feet could carry them.

"And then *she* just disappeared like that!" Val ranted to a distracted Khoo Hun Chhiau, who sat lazily on her floor, looking over a printed-out copy of his finished thesis. "I mean why would *she* do that? Out of all my students, why does *she* have to go after cute, little, innocent Zara? Why?"

"Well, *she* is a monster." Khoo Hun Chhiau droned back. "It's kind of in their nature to go after the innocent and cute, isn't it? Besides, it sounds more like *she* was trying to get inside your head... and considering that interaction you two had at the twins' possession, I'm not surprised. Maybe that freaked *her* out as much as it did you, and *she's* trying to figure you out now."

Val frowned. Khoo Hun Chhiau was the only person she had confided in about that particular moment; when she had chosen to beg, instead of actively exercise *her* from the twins. It stayed with her, haunting Val's loose thoughts in her spare time. Was it just a coincidence? Was *she* just getting bored? Or was there more to it...

"What do you mean *she's* trying to figure me out?"

Khoo Hun Chhiau shrugged. He put down his paper to tug a rope out of Prince Diana's mouth. The two were now as thick as thieves. Every day, Khoo Hun Chhiau played with him outside in the back garden for at least thirty minutes before even thinking of starting his work. It had become a part of their nightly routine for Val and Khoo Hun Chhiau to take Prince for long evening walks. When it was dark enough that people wouldn't see Khoo Hun Chhiau out with some random woman, but also not so late so that the mosquitos would swarm them. Val even caught him sneaking Prince some of his own food. She knew it would inevitably break his heart to see Prince moved across the world from him.

"Well... my guess is it's probably not very often that *she* gets spoken to directly like that, much less asked upon to do something. I mean from what you've said, it sounded like everyone else was just trying to expel *her*, and you were the only one to simply *ask* her to leave. You may have been desperate, but you weren't mean... you might have shown her a bit more vulnerability from humans than she had ever seen before. Just a few months ago, I helped launch a rocket straight at *her*... but it sounds like what you did probably threw her off even more."

"But why was *she* messing with me like that today?" Val persisted. "Why was *she* bullying my favorite student right in front of me?"

Prince yanked on the rope. It slipped from between Khoo Hun Chhiau's hands, stinging the ends of his fingers. "Well geez — I don't know?" He winced sarcastically, sucking on his newly formed battle scars. "What did you think *she* was gonna do? Casually walk into your classroom? Take a seat at one of your students' desks, and just have a nice, pleasant chat? Do you really think that's exactly *her* style? Do you really think *she's* that naive? What would you have done if *she* had done that? Would you still not have completely freaked out, and tried to hit her over the head with your largest textbook?"

"Okay — *okay*, I get it." Val snapped. "I see your point, but why this specifically? Why exactly did *she* try to get inside my head in this way?"

"I don't know." Khoo Hun Chhiau sighed. "But it sounds like it's the only way *she* knows how to confront any person. Seeing how people react to shock or torture can teach you quite a bit about someone... how empathetic they are... what makes them tick... that's my best guess."

Val shrugged. She was already tired of thinking this through from so many different angles, and it had happened less than four hours ago. Val hung a dress recently dried from the laundry onto one of her hangers. Taking a moment to consider if this would be the outfit she should wear to Tan Soan's birthday.

"So..." Val said shortly. "I saw Tan Soan put you in the group chat for her birthday on Saturday. Are you really coming?"

"What — Who?" He mumbled. "Oh, that girl... I think I was invited, but I can't come. I have a very important meeting with Scott in Singapore that morning."

"Scott? Your buddy Scott? What's he want from you now?"

"Same thing as last time. I fly out of Penang Friday."

Val frowned. Her eyes cast down onto the floor. She didn't want to admit it to anyone, much less herself right now, but her heart had done a bit of a backflip when she saw his name added to the *"Tan Soan's Bangin' Birthday Bash"* chat. After their three weeks together over the break, evenings revising his thesis didn't seem like enough time anymore. A whole day spent in Georgetown with him sounded absolutely wonderful.

"Well, that's a shame." Val simpered, fFlipping her long, chestnut hair back behind her shoulder casually. "You're gonna miss Tan Soan trying to set me up with her twin brother. *"Did I mention he's a doctor?"* Val mocked.

It was Khoo Hun Chhiau's turn to frown now. He paused for a moment, pursing his lips in thought; before quietly asking, "What time exactly is the party Saturday?"

Val hadn't seen a stormier Friday afternoon than this one. Rain droplets the size of quarters splattered the windows of Semua Tangan. Class had been dismissed for the day, and a rare lull made Val desperate to head home as soon as possible. But before she could make it out of her hallway, a voice from the opposite end of the corridor called her name.

"Ms. Val — *Ms. Val!?*"

Val turned around, and caught sight of a waving, soaking-wet Principal Arif, dripping puddles onto the floor.

"Can we meet in my office for a second?" Principal Arif called once more.

Val looked longingly in the other direction outside. It had completely stopped raining by now, but for who knew how long?

"Um... Yeah, yeah, I can do that." Val nodded. Trying to hide the disappointment on her face.

She hurried over to Principal Arif. The two marched down the hallways until they came across the wooden door that led into her cramped office. Val scootched her body around the other side of the large desk, into a space that could really only fit a chair, and not a whole person sitting in it. Val scrunched her arms and legs as if she were back on the flight here from Arizona, as the sound of heavy raindrops started up again outside.

"Alrighty — Ms. Val." Principal Arif started breathily. "So, in light of all this chaos, I haven't really had much of a chance to look for another English teacher to replace you next year, since you were only signed to a one-year contract."

"Oh—" Val faltered. Truth be told, she hadn't even thought about next year's plans. Val realized now that she should have started looking for a job in the states months ago if she were to go back according to her contract.

"I'm not gonna lie to you Val," Principal Arif said candidly, ",under these circumstances, I really don't think any new teacher would be willing to come on board with us. It's hard enough finding good English teachers under even normal circumstances, and well, these circumstances aren't all that normal, are they?"

"Um, No..." Val mumbled. "I guess not."

"After everything you've witnessed here, I fully understand if you want to finish your contract and be done with it. But... if you were to stay on... say, at least one more year with us... I would very much appreciate it. This school would very much appreciate it." She looked over her thin teacher spectacles, and stared at Val intently, almost gravely. "Mr. Elmsworth has enough problems trying to control his class of girls. Adding double his normal class size to the mix would send his already struggling heart into cardiac arrest... trust me, you would be saving me one more headache..."

"Another year?" Val mouthed breathlessly. This surprised her, but the more she thought about it, the more it made sense. "Um — yeah, sure, I'll go ahead and sign up for one more year."

"Great." Principal Arif beamed. She clapped her hands in front of her and rubbed them together. "I'll get the paperwork over to you sometime next week. But before you leave, we need to sort out exactly where you'll live next year."

She had nearly forgotten to think this part out. Val found herself going days at a time forgetting about Yeo A'i's move. She had decided instead of selling her home, she would turn it into an instant hotel for tourists. Her latest project. The house was morphing into a place of homage for bespoke furniture and neutral tones as they spoke.

"Yeah, I guess so." She said sadly.

"Well." Principal Arif started again, frantically looking for a certain sheet amongst the sea of loose papers. "I normally would just give you a stipend to find a new place, but as all our school budget, plus some, has gone to this year's *"redecorating"*, Mayor Osman and I have a granddaughter around your age who has a spare bedroom at her apartment. She owes my husband and I a *big* favor... I'll give you her number so you two can meet."

"Yeah, all right..." Val said cautiously, already knowing that whatever place came next wouldn't be nearly as homey as her second-floor bedroom; that she had come to love and cherish so much.

Val woke bright and early Saturday morning, feeling that nervous, excited, trepidation, a child feels before spending the whole day playing outside with their very best friends. She threw on a light, flowy sundress over her swimsuit, and jumped into the back of Nur's crammed SUV. Getting squished in between a very downcast-looking Jano, and Parini's husband.

"What's got them down?" Val asked no one in particular.

"Oh, those two?" Amina huffed. "They're just pouting because they have *the pleasure* of spending the day with their *wonderful wives*, and sometimes they don't get to choose who else may be tagging along."

Val's heart skipped a beat. Were they talking about her? If not, who? "Who's tagging alo—"

"It's not fair — it's bad enough putting up with Tan Soan's tone-deaf snipes at us every conversation — but her brother?" Jano snapped, pointing at himself. "Let me tell you, Fuaad here and I had to suffer through her twin *every year* in primary *and* secondary. He was the annoying little twerp who *always* had to win at *everything* — he could never let anything go. And now you're telling me at the last minute that he's some fancy cardiologist In Georgetown, and I have to spend the whole day with him?"

"You're the youngest Police Chief in our town's history." Amina seethed back. "How's *that* not an accomplishment worthy of bragging rights? What do you expect me to do? Ask Tan Soan to uninvite her *twin* brother to her birthday party. Which is basically *his* birthday party as well—?"

"Yes." Jano said quickly before Amina could finish her sentence. "Yes, that's exactly what I want you to do. I'd rather my body become target practice for Yusef's confiscated rifle—"

"*THAT'S SO STUPID CAUSE YUSEF WOULD MISS EVERY TIME!*" Amina yelled. "You're saying that you would risk a *riskless* situation rather than go to this — that's a worthless declaration. This is why he's a doctor and you're not."

"I—" Jano started, but stopped. Opting to let his eyes do the speaking for him, which stared daggers. "Psh — whatever — I just wish Khoo Hun Chhiau could've been here. He could've shut him up."

"He is coming." Nur said quietly. "You didn't see the group chat? He messaged us last night. He said he would be a little late to brunch, but that he would make it."

"YES!" Jano whooped, high-fiving Parini's husband over Val's head, who looked equally delighted. "This might not be so bad after all."

Val enjoyed the drive. The SUV wove through a thicket of rainforest trees, past several construction sights, and down a narrow, modern bridge with baby blue water below them and blue sunny skies above. They reached Penang island, and pulled into a trendy-looking shopping and restaurant complex, entirely built from repainted neon and pastel shipping containers. Everyone stumbled out from the car and headed straight for one of the little cafes in the back.

"Hey!" Tan Soan trilled, as everyone arrived. "Everybody come — come — sit. Val, you sit here."

Tan Soan grabbed Val by her shoulders. Marching her straight towards a seat across a handsome man with an unnatural hairline, and strong, model-esk facial features... too strong... too model-esk... was he a cardiologist or plastic surgeon? His eyes swept over her face and body quickly. Seemingly eating the image of her up, and taking a little too much delight in it...

"Vaaal, this is my brother Ken." Tan Soan sang. "Ken this is my friend, Val, from the states."

Val suppressed a chuckle at his name. He looked exactly like a walking Chinese Ken doll. "Hi, nice to meet you—"

"Nice to meet you too!" He beamed, yet not a single line creased his face. He stood up to shake her hand eagerly. The group settled into their seats and ordered their Nasi lemak's, teas', and french fries.

"So," Ken proceeded curiously, as he poured Val a glass of mimosa, filling it to the brim. "What's it like moving away to such a foreign country? Do you miss home?"

Val took a long sip of her drink. She had already recognized this man as something else, besides a child's play doll by the time she had sat down in her chair. He was a *fuckboy*. Val was *tired* of fuckboys.

"I miss my mom and my grandparents." She replied truthfully. "I'm hoping I can save up enough next year to fly them over here for a visit, but overall, no, not really. I thought I'd miss my friends back home more..." she peered around at the friend group she had in front of her, feeling truly grateful for each and every one of them, "but these people aren't so bad I guess!"

Amina and Jano scoffed. Nur playfully nudged her in the ribs.

"Man, I'll tell you what though." Ken shrugged. "I wish I was working in America right now. Imagine... a sea of all those fat, clogged, hearts, with their owners having no other option but paying me to buy them a few more years... god I'd make so much money."

No one wanted to touch their food after that. An awkward silence lingered in the air; until Ken himself decided to break it.

"So, Jano, Tan Soan tells me you've been demoted — I mean *promoted* — to Police Captain. Tell me, do you have any new leads on that serial defecator? He's gotta be pretty old by now... my grandmother remembers when he first struck her neighbor's house *decades* ago. It wouldn't be that hard by now to find him in a town with the population of... what is it now, five... six thousand people? Or has that case gone cold?"

"Seven thousand, nine hundred and twenty." Jano enunciated, before glaring at Amina. "And yes, actually we did catch HER in a sting operation last year. It was Ms. Lou — the one with the little bakery. We were lucky we had someone on our force who happens to be an expert in profiling criminals... he pointed out that with that type of criminal history, we should be looking for someone with a chronic anger problem. And of course, we all remember how she'd pelt her own customers with stale buns when they'd take too long."

"Wow." Ken mocked. "What fantastic, important police work. Now tell me, how exactly did you narrow down the list of senile, angry, old people? How'd your team go about setting up this sting operation of yours? What's the protocol for you policemen when you catch someone... shitting themselves unlawfully? Is there something in y'all's manual? Something like that—"

Ken's words died in his mouth. His eyes followed a mass moving behind Val that she couldn't see. The empty chair to Val's right was pulled back, and filled by a familiar presence.

"Sorry I'm late..." Khoo Hun Chhiau said quickly. Not making eye contact with anyone.

"No, it's fine, we're just glad you managed to fly back so quickly." Tan Soan beamed. "Did you take a taxi here from the airport? I hope they didn't overcharge you. We already ordered and ate a bit of our own meals, but the club doesn't open up for another little bit. You have time to get something from the men—"

"They didn't overcharge me." He said shortly. "And it's fine — I'll just steal a little off of Val's plate."

He grabbed for a slice of pizza. Khoo Hun Chiau had nearly stuffed it in his mouth, when Ken slapped his hand, and let out an obnoxious *"Tsk-tsk-tsk!"* Khoo Hun Chhiau peered up at him, confused.

"We — Val and I, actually decided to share OUR meal. There really isn't enough for you. I'm sorry."

Khoo Hun Chhiau stared down at Ken, then towards Val. It was the most surprised and alarmed she had ever seen him. Val tried to give him *"I'm sorry"* eyes, but it did nothing to soothe the poor man.

Khoo Hun Chhiau ordered a large burger, stuffing it down within seconds of it being brought to the table.

"You know—" Ken started. "If I were you, I'd be more careful with that. That's exactly how I end up seeing most of my patients."

"Ohh, that's right." Jano perked up, pointing with one hand at Ken, and the other over his chest. "You're a cardiologist... is that right? That's the *"word"* for a heart doctor? Isn't it? Am I getting that right?"

Ken nodded in zealous approval. "Yup — and you're right. That's the word for it."

"So if you're a cardiologist, that must mean you have a doctorate right?"

"Yes — that's exactly what it means." He beamed.

"And Khoo Hun Chhiau here almost has his *second* doctorate? What does that make him — a *double* doctor — what's the word for a *double* doctor? Is it like black belts, when you get enough of them can you call yourself a master? Does that make you a doctor, and Khoo Hun Chhiau a *master* doctor? Is that how it works — or is it something different?"

Ken's ears turned beet red. Val could see his jaw implants grinding his veneers.

"No, that's not how it works at all…"

There was another awkward pause 'til Parini rushed to change the subject. The rest of the meal went by peacefully. A North Korean, South Korean, DMZ type of peace. Every now and then, Ken would say, or do something particularly flirty, and Khoo Hun Chhiau would react as if Ken launched a nuclear missile.

"If you really like the water, you should come out with Tan Soan and I on our father's catamaran. It's docked here in Penang. We should have eaten lunch on *"The Blur"* earlier. That's her name, because it's so dreamy and relaxing sailing her, that the day just feels like a blur. You know?"

"It's not peaceful in the slightest." Parini whispered into Val's ear. "When I went on it last year, Ken yelled at me for spilling some tea on one of the chairs. I cried for two hours afterwards. That's how I figured out I was pregnant you see, extra emotional and extra seasick at the same time."

Val's giggles were drowned out by the loudspeakers from the outdoor club that surrounded them; which from what she could gather, was supposed to be a mashup of reggae/latin vibes. Either way, the drinks were fruity and sweet, the weather was nice and sunny, and Val was just thankful to be out here, having a good time.

A remix of a popular Spanish song blared behind her. Ken sashayed right up to Val, performing what he probably thought was a good imitation of Latin dancing.

"So Val, I heard you dated a certain famous rapper… can you throw it back as well as his backup dancers? Were you one of his backup dancers?" He asked a little too excitedly, whole offering out his smooth, unblemished hand to her.

"I can salsa, but I'm not an expert or anything." She said truthfully, while thinking through her options. Val turned back towards Khoo Hun Chhiau. Shots fired at the border. All color drained from his face. Val could tell he was about two seconds away from slapping that hand into outer space.

"What's wrong?" Ken asked, feigning sincerity. "Are you gonna ask anyone to dance Khoo Hun Chhiau? Ohhhh, that's right. You're… *you*. My bad, *totally* forgot, and you're a police officer. How bad would it look if you got caught dancing with an *American* girl? Oh well… nothing you can do about it." With that, Ken snatched Val's hand, pulling her off her high stool and dragging her away.

Val tried to keep a bit of distance between her and Ken by focusing more on teaching him the basics, with plenty of room in between; but that wasn't enough to stop his hands from dropping to her hips, or from sliding too low for comfort down her back. Every now and then, Val would spot Khoo Hun Chhiau craning his neck, watching them like a hawk. A tomahawk.

To Khoo Hun Chhiau's relief, not more than twenty minutes later Tan Suan declared that she wanted to head over to the beach. Val declined Ken's very generous offer of sitting on his lap for the duration of the ride; and a short drive and boat ride later, they made it to monkey beach. A secluded strip of shore with turquoise water and turquoise sky. Monkeys ran up and down the water line; searching for bits of trash and spare food, while the group stripped into their burkinis, bikinis, and swim trunks.

"For the last time Jano," Amina snapped, "I am too pregnant to get in there and play with you guys. This swimsuit is already too tight for my belly, and someone has to sit with our stuff so that the monkeys don't snatch our things."

"Come on!" Jano pouted. Are you really gonna be one of those *"I have fun watching"* wives."

"But I do have fun watching."

"But you would have more fun if you got in for a little bit. Pleeease... just five minutes. *Pleeease?*"

Amina rolled her eyes. "Fine!" She surrendered. "Just five minutes though."

"Hey—" Ken teased happily, pinching Val's hip as he ran by her. "I'm gonna beat you so bad at water basketball." He pointed over towards the water, where two floating hoops were tethered meters apart.

"I don't know, I was on the JV team for three years in high school. I was considered for MVP... almost." Val lied.

"Oh — you're so feisty — come on!" With that, he grabbed her hand once more and pulled her down towards the water.

The game of water basketball descended into chaos. They decided to split up males vs. females, and already things were getting very heated.

"Stop — *Stop!*" Ken whined. "That was a foul — foul! You elbowed me in the collarbone, that's this bone right here—"

"Shut up—" Nur hollered. "I know what a collarbone is — you're not the only doctor playing here." She snatched the ball from his fingers, and lunged towards the other team's basket.

Val nearly jumped into the thick of it all once more, but instead felt someone grab her from around her waist, and lug her several meters away; around a line of rocks that stuck out from the shore.

"What're you doing?" She scrambled frantically once Khoo Hun Chhiau had set her down within a caved-out area. "What the hell was that all about?"

Khoo Hun Chhiau caught his breath. Val watched him check around the corner from them, making sure they were both completely blocked off from everyone else's view. Jano had stepped on a starfish. Amina's eye was bleeding, and Parini broke a nail... no wait, that was

Ken. It seemed nobody had noticed their swift disappearance. "Sorry... Sorry... I just wanted to see how you were doing?"

"I'm fine!" Val huffed, as she settled down onto an underwater rock at the rear of the little cave. Her own voice jumped off the boulders that surrounded her on all sides; except for where Khoo Hun Chhiau stood at the mouth, grasping onto the rocks on top. "I'm perfectly fine — are you doing okay?"

He nodded and looked away.

"You're lying to me."

"I am not."

"Yes you are, what's wrong? Tell me. Did everything go alright with Scott?"

"What? Oh, that? Yeah, everything went fine..." He looked fearful, and agitated. Choosing to glance away toward the vast Indian ocean instead of at her. The sun hung high over the horizon, making the water around them shimmer. "So... are you gonna date him now?"

"Date who?"

"Ken!" He shouted a little too loudly. "I mean, are you gonna see him again? Do you like him?"

Val already knew the answer to that question — a resounding no. But anger was starting to boil in the pit of her stomach. "No, I don't like him, but why do you even care—"

"Do you like me?" He said quickly, almost so quickly that Val wasn't sure if he was actually saying those words. For a man his age, this was an oddly childlike question...

Val gritted her teeth, and took in a long, deep, breath, before answering. "Yes." A youthful, excited energy pulsated through her body. "But what does that matter? You have your values and I respec—"

It all happened so fast, that in her later years, Val could only recall the blissful energy that ran through her veins. She felt Khoo Hun Chhiau's arms sweep around her hips, and pull her tightly into his own chest, kissing her with the longing and desire Val knew he buried deep within him. Val's heart raced, her stomach performed a whole acrobatic routine, and her legs turned to jelly as they wrapped around his waist;

losing their strength, and grip. With one hand, he caught her, with the other, Khoo Hun Chhiau gently let his calloused fingers run down the middle of her stomach, creating a euphoric electricity that could power a thousand cities. It was all too much... it was all way too much...

"Damnit Jano — I told you those damn monkeys would be after our things!" Amina swore.

The shriek broke the two of them apart. It took a moment for both to recover and compose themselves. Val wanted nothing more than to stay in that little cave forever, but also didn't wanna be *that* girl — sneaking off on someone else's special day. When they did make it back to the beach, Khoo Hun Chhiau came up with a quick story about his flip-flop breaking, and everyone else was too busy fighting off the monkeys, no one thought to ask.

The rest of the day passed by in a happy haze. After a tense standoff where several monkeys came at Jano holding sticks like baseball bats, the rest of the group used him as distraction bait to grab their things; moving somewhere the monkeys were hopefully kinder. They weren't. Val and Khoo Hun Chhiau never got another chance to sneak away, but it was more than enough fun riding on the back of his jet ski; where she at least got an excuse to grab onto him one more time.

By the time they were making their way back on the boat, Ken had fully realized he had lost. He moved on quickly, trying to impress a very annoyed Nur, whose patience and politeness were wearing thin. But Val wasn't paying close attention. Everything else was far from her mind... the sun beamed down warmly, her hair whipped around wildly, and specks of water splashed her face with every little bump of the open-air boat. She had never felt so free, so peaceful, so happy she had chosen to come here and stay. It was the best decision of her life.

Val was more than delighted to cram into the back seat of Nur's van next to Khoo Hun Chhiau. They lazily drove back to town, winding their way back over the bridge and into the trees that swallowed them whole.

CHAPTER SIXTEEN

"Are you sure you want to do this?" Yeo A'i asked nervously as they climbed the rickety stairs to the second-floor apartment. "I've heard things about this girl that would make your skin crawl. Word is... that she murdered the Raja's family cat! I mean don't they say serial killers start on animals?"

"Well, I might as well look." Val faltered skeptically while yanking at her shoe, which had gotten stuck to a metal step thanks to the strangest gooey substance she had ever laid eyes on. "Besides, are we even sure that story is really true?"

"No, it's true." Yeo A'i testified. "I watched the trial at city hall, it was all that the town could talk about for a while. Well, that is until they caught Ms. Lou..."

Val's eyes swept the outside of the apartment, hoping the old adage, *"you can't judge a book by its cover",* would prove itself more true now than ever. The yellow, chipped paint stood out from the trees that surrounded it. Several roof shingles were missing, and the smell of garbage lingered in the air around her.

"Well... I guess it's now or never?"

"I guess so." Yeo A'i surmised.

Val took a deep breath and wrapped on the hollow, unaligned door. It creaked open a few inches. Two dark, suspicious eyes peered out from the other side.

"Hi — Hello," Yeo A'i sang politely, "I'm Yeo A'i, and this is Val. Your grandmother told us we should swing by today around this time."

The girl's eyes shifted back and forth between the two women like an owl. She slammed the door abruptly; the lock on the other side fiddled before the humble entry reopened all the way this time, revealing the source of the putrid smell.

Val instinctively took a deep breath, and crossed the threshold of the doorway. They entered a short hallway that opened up into the living room; which, if not for the black sheet curtains hung over the large windows, would be a bright open space surrounded by nature. Instead, she had brought *nature* inside with her. Several cramped, dirty, bird cages sat and hung in every little nook and cranny. The feathered creatures hopped around, squawking, pecking, and pooping freely.

"Is that a pheasant?" Yeo A'i pried appallingly. "Where did you get that? Where'd you get all these birds? I didn't know they sold those types? Did you catch them from outside and bring them in here?"

Principal Arif's granddaughter froze. Val finally got a good look at her, since she stood in the only spot where a curtain had slipped a bit on its thumbtacks. She was a conventionally pretty goth; with heavy black makeup, a matching black hijab, and black skinny jeans under a loose-fitting band t-shirt. She wouldn't have been out of place at Val's own high school... or at a psych ward. Her face contorted in rage, her nostrils fumed, and a pronounced underbite made her jaw tremble.

"I need to protect my babies..." She hissed, cocking her neck towards the cramped kitchen.

"So you did." Yeo A'i snapped back, shoving her hands on her waist. Val stepped away to take a cursory look inside. The stove, microwave, and table were stained a rainbow of colors, most prominent of all, a suspicious white. That had to be bird shit. The refrigerator leaked a vomit-inducing smell of rotten food, while a small, yellow bird gnawed on the wires that were barely holding the fire alarm in place. But the creepiest features of all were the flickering fluorescent lights. They hung from their half-chewed cords low enough for Val to bang her head on.

"I must protect my babies from the monsters." The girl hissed again. "They prowl around, and stalk my children..."

"You mean house cats." Yeo A'i fumed. "What you mean to say is house cats. Those are people's pets. Look, I know that cats can threaten native bird life. So the whole town came together to spay our cats to make sure we don't have too many — and since we all did that, you agreed you wouldn't go after them. But then you went and murdered that poor Raja kitty anyways."

"She was no kitty!" The Osman granddaughter fumed. "She weighed at least fifty pounds!"

"That's insane!" Yeo A'i spat. "You're insane — this whole place is insane! Val, do you wanna take a look in the spare bedroom real quick? I've had about enough of this dump."

"She's not allowed in there, no one's allowed in there... ever."

"Where would she sleep then?"

Principal Arif's granddaughter nodded towards an old couch. Val plopped down on it, coughing profusely as a plume of dirt rose around her.

"Oh my god—" Yeo A'i hollered as Val dragged the two girls apart, then Yeo A'i out the front door and back down the stairs, swearing the whole way.

"I hate that girl." Yeo A'i seethed, as she drove furiously down the streets back to her own house. "God I hate her — and her creepy little bird den. That place should be condemned. You know she went to school with my daughter? I don't know what her deal is, her parents and siblings are absolutely lovely people, but *that* one is just a psycho."

Val chuckled.

"You're laughing now, but we need to figure out another place for you." Yeo A'i whipped out her phone. "I'll message Principal Arif right now."

Before Yeo A'i could reach her painted fingertips into her purse, her hand retreated to the wheel, stomping on the brakes furiously! Val felt her body fly, and then be caught by her seatbelt — she crashed back into her seat. Yeo A'i had just nearly missed what appeared to be a rogue protester marching in front of the police station; along with several other enthusiastic sisters...

Val and Yeo A'i climbed out of the van — scurrying past the small throng of people until they were able to reach near the front; where an adamant Peh Si was chanting into a megaphone.

"Move out of our way — We want to pray — Move out of our way — We want to pray!"

Val caught a glimpse of Jano, seated at a desk in the front, cradling his head in his hands. Officer Yusef whispered something into his ear that caused Jano to roll his eyes and wave a bothered hand. This gesture was interpreted as a resounding yes to whatever his request was. Before anyone knew it, Officer Yusef was outside, lugging paper mache balls and chocolate candies with his handy little slingshot.

"Christ!" Jano cried. He grabbed Officer Yusef by the back of his uniform, shoving him behind him; much to the dismay of the protestors who were only inches away from dealing with him themselves. "Look — you guys can pray to your mother in your own homes, or somewhere else — but it's too dangerous for the police to let you do it on *her* own territory! Someone could get very *seriously* injured or hurt! How do you guys not understand that?"

Val caught the same, sinister twinkle in Peh Si's eye that she had had a few weeks before. It made Val's stomach twist. Peh Si held up her microphone to the crowd once more, ready for this exact moment.

"Our mother calls out to us — *she* calls out for us to trust *her*, even when we mere mortals don't understand, even when it seems dangerous."

"No — No — No *she* does not!" Jano retorted firmly. "Your mother... look, she wants to be left alone. *She* doesn't want to be bothered. *She* told me and my whole station that very bluntly a few months ago."

"These people defiled our mother! They never trusted that *she* knew what was best... if they did, they would have left *her* to do *her* business... weeding off the ones *she* sees as weak... it was fate that Semua Tangan was placed there. What else could it be? We are honored *she* chose our community to sift through so that our stock will be stronger. If only our city council and police station allowed *her* to do *her* bidding, who knows what fortune we would see. Only the strongest of our daughters would birth forth an even more promising generation after theirs, 'til all that is left is the unblemished — the most perfect amongst us — those who are worthy and able to live forever — like our mother — with our mother. What other town could stop them? What other city, nation, or empire could bring down the immortal? Yes my sisters, sacrifice is hard, but it's necessary. It's our only hope. If we don't, we'll become progressively weaker, until we die. A chain is only as strong, as its weakest lin—"

A tomato slammed into Peh Si so hard that red tears fell down her cheeks. Everyone swirled around for the source, but it wasn't hard to find. Officer Yusef tried to hide the slingshot behind his back, but it was too late — a swarm of angry women descended upon him. Jano and the rest of the officers were caught up, trying to salvage what was left of the poor man's bloody face.

If Officer Yusef looked bad when Val left the protest, he looked ten times worse the next day at school. Both of his black, shifty eyes had swelled so massively, his eyelids only separated into two little slits. There were terrible scratches across both his cheeks, a few teeth were missing, and If Val's eyes weren't deceiving her, his nose had shifted. Val had half a mind to recommend another profession to him. Maybe his rap game was stronger than his policing skills...

He used every excuse in the book to avoid the Daughters now, so it was no surprise to Val when he didn't join his fellow cops that fateful day a few weeks later. They tried holding the cult members back, but it was futile. Around one o'clock, only a few minutes into her final period, the whole class was drawn to the large windows that looked out onto the vast courtyard; where the Daughters of the Eternal Mother had succeeded in breaking through the ranks. Several of them stood in a semicircle, completed by the forest in the back.

"Am I late?" Officer Yusef grunted, pushing aside her students so that he could get a look for himself. "Have they started doing their... you know? What are they doing exactly?"

"Shouldn't you know?" Eng Ki sassed. "Shouldn't you be down there trying to stop them?"

Officer Yusef scowled at her, even sticking his tongue out a little. "Eh little girl, someone has to be the lookout..."

"Not if they've already gotten past you guys." Wani chuffed.

Officer Yusef waved the girl's sassy comments away with a flick of his wrist, turning his attention back to the now-growing crowd of worshipers at the threshold of the forest. Val could see them clearly, first standing, then crouching, before lying in child's pose on the ground; with their arms out in front of them, and knees tucked underneath.

"Mother—" Peh Si yelled as she stood at the very front towards the forest. "Your daughters are here — your sons are here — we've brought you the finest gifts — the purest perfumes, diamonds, rubies, jade, silver, and gold."

Val peered into a few of the prostate hands of the worshipers; which were turned up, and holding various items within.

"Halt — freeze — stop this silly nonsense right now!" Someone screamed.

There was a commotion at the back doors of the school. Policemen followed by Ms. Mawar, Ms. Dian, and Principal Arif rushed towards the group at the edge of the forest.

"Mother — we ask you to come out and accept our offerings — not only of those things within our hands, but of our hands themselves — we offer you our bodies — we offer up your judgment of our hearts, souls, and minds unto you, to do as you wish. You alone can judge us, you alone see which of us are weak, and which of us are worthy of carrying on... we are ready! Come, mother — come out of your home — come out of your dwelling place — hide no mor—"

No one really expected it, not even the Daughters of the Eternal Mother it seemed by the way they murmured amongst themselves. They let out a collective, horrified gasp, before shushing up so quietly, Val could hear Officer Yusef's annoying breath over her shoulder. There was a rustling in the trees as *she* appeared, walking out of the forest on two feet; staring down at the curious scene around her.

Peh Si scrambled to bow down in front of *her*, while at the same time kicking out the sacrifice from the small, fragile young girl behind her. This must be Peh Si's intended sacrifice. Every body trembled as *she* passed by. Taking long, strident steps, as she moved from person to person, occasionally stopping to examine what they were holding within their hands. *She* peered down at her gifts with both confusion and boredom, but mostly contempt...

"No!" Principal Arif screamed. She tried to break free from the officers' grasp. "No — please — don't touch them!"

No attention was paid to Principal Arif by *her*. *She* continued, walking eerily along. So human-like, yet so demonic. Finally she stopped before Peh Si's outstretched arms at the front. *Her* eyes lingered on the strange, erratic girl for a few moments... *she* took one last, final look at the scene around her, before peering down at Peh Si again. Val watched in aghast interest, as *her* eyes morphed; from a curious pondering, to a shocked, angry scowl, and then ultimately, to a furious, seething stare that shook *her* whole body. *She* clenched her fists so tightly together, that her long, stiletto fingernails cut into her palms, causing a black oozing to drip down from them, staining the grass below.

"No!" Principal Arif cried out once more. She broke free from the police officer's grip, sprinting like a mad woman toward the scene of the soon-to-be crime.

Peh Si began to quiver so violently, that Val could make out her shaking from the safety of her room. She wasn't sure what to do herself in this situation... should she shoo the girls away that pressed on her from all sides? Should she jump down from the window and join Principal Arif? There wouldn't be enough time!

She took her long, mangled foot, and turned Peh Si's face over with it, 'til her head was sandwiched between the soggy ground and her sole. What exactly Peh Si mouthed to her, Val couldn't make out from such a distance. Whatever she'd said, it did nothing to change her fate... *she* hissed down at her, with all *her* pointed teeth bared; coming face to face with the woman before her hand swiped across Peh Si's throat, and blood splattered across the nearest worshipers. *She* snatched the body up and swiftly retreated back into the forest... Peh Si's last cry still echoing in the wind...

CHAPTER SEVENTEEN

To say that Peh Si's disappearance was met with grief and outpouring would be a lie. A few of the most devout Daughters of the Eternal Mother held a small vigil outside the police station one night; but besides her own parents, siblings, and a few other blood relatives, most people were relieved. By the next week, most of the cult members were vehemently denying their affiliation with it amongst their peers.

"And then, when I asked him to give me his statement, he told me that he was with his mother shopping for groceries." Khoo Hun Chhiau gripped as an old rerun streamed in front of them. "I know damn well his mother lives in France. My Grandad sold her house!"

Val chuckled quietly to herself, pulling the oversized fleece blanket over her shoulders. "Are you guys gonna look in the forest for her? What's next?"

"Psh—" Khoo Hun Chhiau scoffed. "That land back there goes on for hundreds of miles. We sent a chopper over a few days ago, but it came back with nothing... We did a review of the crime scene though. It looks like Peh Si was still alive when she was taken. Her cut had to have been shallow, or else we'd have seen more blood. Who knows... maybe *she'll* let her go once *she's* had her fun..."

Val simpered at the thought. She droned back to the TV show playing in front of her. They had just sent in the final edits of his thesis and were now celebrating with some junk food, but she'd rather celebrate another way.

It frustrated her the lack of moves Khoo Hun Chhiau had made. Ever since he kissed her that day in the cave, there hadn't been anything else from him. Even now, only the edges of their thighs touched as they sat in silence, watching TV.

"Let's play a game!" Val said out of nowhere, growing bored with the episode. "Oh — let's play *The Embarrassment Game!*"

"What's that?" Khoo Hun Chhiau growled.

"You don't know it?" Val smiled devilishly. "We used to play it all the time when I was in middle school. It basically goes like this: I say something to you that I think will make you feel really embarrassed, and if you show any signs that you're flustered, say, if your cheeks get red, or you get really agitated, then I win that round. Then it's your turn. Come on, pleeeease!"

Khoo Hun Chhiau rolled his eyes, but ultimately gave in. "Fine, you go first."

"Yes! Okay, um, remember that day that you had to find flip-flops to go on a walk with Prince and me? Well, your toenails... they looked like claws."

"Psh—" Khoo Hun Chhiau scoffed, shaking his head, but catching himself before going any further. He took a few moments to think of a rebuttal. "Alright, remember that very first time I saw you, not at Jano's party but that night the power went off at Semua Tangan?"

"Yeah?"

"You made the dumbest face when I shined my flashlight at you." He jeered, contorting his face, mocking her.

Val's mouth dropped but she closed it, deciding it would be best if she just squinted her eyes at him.

"Okay, okay, remember that party? Everyone acted like you had the absolute *worst* social skills, then you literally stalked me home."

"I didn't stalk you — I was making sure your ass didn't get run over — or lost!"

"Op—" Val smirked. "I just won this round."

"Damn!" Khoo Hun Chhiau swore while looking away, pursing his lips in deep thought. "Okay, okay, well if we're being honest you fart in your sleep. A Lot."

"I do not!" Val snapped.

"Yes you do!" and I've witnessed it first hand, all those weeks I slept in here taking care of you. Honestly, some nights were so bad, I had to open the window. Oh — what's that — a frown — and you rebutted me. Do I sense a little agitation? Does this mean I win this round?"

Val inwardly seethed. He was right, he had won. Val shook her head, thinking over her options. How was she gonna get him back? How would she come out on top?

And then it hit her.

Val pushed herself up from the floor, and straddled Khoo Hun Chhiau's lap. Brushing the tips of her fingers lightly along his arms, 'til she reached his shoulders.

"You know," she whispered, "I've been waiting for you..."

Khoo Hun Chhiau gulped but didn't move.

"I've been dreaming about that cave..." She teased. "It's driving me crazy... are you trying to drive me crazy? Is that what this is?"

Khoo Hun Chhiau shook his head, his stern face contorting as he tried to keep his composure. He peered down towards the floor, but Val tipped his face back towards hers with a light finger under his jaw. Their lips only kept separated by wisps of air. She began unbuttoning his shirt, gently.

"You know... if you want this to stop, please, say something. Just tell me, and I'll stop it right now."

He remained silent.

"Why've you led me on this whole year?" She whispered into his ear, as she began to unbutton her own shirt. "Why'd you do that to yourself? Don't you want more from me? To be honest, I've wanted more from you..."

The last button came undone, and her bare chest took Khoo Hun Chhiau by a happy surprise; judging by the disturbance underneath her. His eyes drank her in. His chest heaved with heavy breaths. Val wondered if this was the last shred of his self-control.

Val scooted down a bit lower, while unbuckling his pants and pulling down his trousers. "I'm gonna stop unless you tell me otherwise..."

Khoo Hun Chhiau remained silent, for a moment his body seemed to go limp. He stared across the room at the blank wall, most likely trying to imagine paint drying on them.

"Okay." Val sighed. She began to refasten his belt.

Khoo Hun Chhiau caught her wrist, his grip firm, and stiff. His eyes darted back, meeting her own intently. He nodded.

Val pulled everything back, and let her hand rest on his stomach. It trembled at her touch, as she performed the oldest trick in the book.

CHAPTER EIGHTEEN

"And then he just sat there while I walked around, *butt naked,* cleaning up his mess he left in the garage." Amina griped. "THEN, his dumb ass *"ACCIDENTALLY"* hit the garage door opener. What if one of the neighbors had seen me? What a scandal! How would I ever teach again after something like that? Val — *Val!* Are you listening?"

"What? Oh — yeah, sorry." Val simpered, as she realized she'd been staring directly into the sun for the entirety of the story. To Amina's credit, she wasn't actually paying attention. She'd rather gotten lost in reminiscing from the night before, and the night before that, and the night before that...

"Jano really needs to learn where to draw the line on his pranks sometimes." Val said convincingly enough. "Imagine the trouble your kid will get up to with those genes."

Amina huffed while kicking a rogue soccer ball toward a student who had missed the goal. "I don't know what to do with that man sometimes. He's been working overtime at the station so much lately, he needs a way to get some of that stress out." She glanced back at Val, and her tone grew more pointed. "Speaking of Jano, he told me that Khoo Hun Chhiau has been acting a bit strange lately."

"Really? How so?"

"Oh, nothing too odd..." She said suspiciously. "He just says he seems a bit more relaxed, that he's been smiling more... He's not exactly a smiler now is he..."

Val felt her cheeks glow.

"So, how exactly are you two doing? Are you guys, I don't know... getting a bit closer? Are you two more than just friends now?"

Val covered her mouth and looked away. The truth was they had gotten more than a fair bit closer. Each night he came over now would always end in passionate lovemaking. The sounds of which that escaped her mouth made Val desperately thankful she was halfway across the world from her grandmother's earshot. The physical intimacy was always followed by snuggles, and deep, meaningful discussions about life, love, god, childhoods, loss, grief, and happiness. There seemed to be no limits to their range...

"Mhmm." Amina sassed. "That's what I thought. Look, I get that you want to keep this under wraps, my near scandal would pale in comparison if word got out... but tell me everything. How deep has this gone?" She peered around, making sure the nearest child was out of earshot. "Are y'all being... safe?"

Val rolled her eyes at this question. She wanted to say yes, but the honest answer was that it'd slipped her mind completely.

"Remind me to go see Nur about that..."

"Well you better, or else you're gonna end up like me in nine months, just you wait. And how would you hide something like *that* next year? With this one—" she pointed at her belly, "it only took one time — I swear!"

Val made a mental note of that, but her train of thought was broken by a sudden commotion in the halls behind them. A familiar couple of parents slammed the school's front doors so forcefully, one of the windows shattered. Val and Amina swiveled around on their trusty little bench, watching the deranged parents drag a sobbing Zara behind them toward Principal Arif's office.

Val and Amina jumped up and sprinted towards them! They stopped halfway down a near-deserted corridor, meeting Principal Arif halfway.

"Excuse me dear—" Principal Arif apologized to a student that she tried to shuffle away. "What's the meaning of all this? What's going on here?"

"We should be asking you those questions!" Zara's dad seethed through gritted teeth. "Show her Alya!"

Zara's mother pulled the sobbing girl, who fought her every move toward Principal Arif. "No — please — you don't understand!" Zara cried.

"What exactly is all this?" Zara's mom screamed as she pulled Zara's clothes from side to side; revealing several long, jagged scars down her arms, legs, stomach, back, across the back of her neck, and the most chilling of all, down her spine. Val's stomach lurched.

"No — *Wait!*" Two high-pitched voices cried from down the hall. "You guys don't get it!" Eng Ki cried.

"It's — It's not what you think!" Wani panted as she reached them. "Well, what exactly are you thinking it is, cause maybe—"

Zara's mom pulled her face real close to Zara's. The vein in her temple throbbed furiously, as she whispered her next words. "Tell us... who did this to you?"

Zara made eye contact with her mother for only the briefest of moments, before returning her gaze to the floor. All the poor girl could do was sob.

Zara's dad whirled back towards Principal Arif, his voice quivering with rage. "I want a detailed investigation, completed by the police on all the teachers and students who could have possibly done this to my child."

"It wasn't a student—" Eng Ki objected.

"Or a teacher—" Wani cried.

"It was... It was... It was..."

"What're you trying to tell me, Ms. Eng Ki—" Zara's dad screamed in her face, "are you gonna give me that nonsense that it was *HER* again? Zara's already tried that lie today. I have half a mind to have you and your little friend here investigated first. Did you two teach her this lie to keep her quiet? Is that what this is!"

"No — please — stop! All they've done is help me!" Zara cried, as Principal Arif stepped in between the two.

"Sir, I understand your frustration, but could you please try and calm yourself down." She pleaded. "These two are still just kids after all — please don't yell at them like that."

"I should have you charged for gross negligence!" He screamed in her face. "This has all happened under your roof — you're the Principal here — what did you know of any of this?"

A gleam of guilt sparkled in Principal Arif's eyes... she looked away, before returning his gaze. "Admittedly, I knew nothing... and this right here might be the most egregious mistake in the whole of my professional career..." She wiped away a lone tear that fell from her eye. "I am so sorry about this whole situation, of course we'll begin a full police investigation into this matter immediately. Let me call the Chief here to get your daughter's full statement personally, as well as yours and your wife's. I'll go ahead and call my husband down here as well—"

"Tell them to meet us at our house." Zara's dad snapped. "I don't want my daughter, or the rest of my family anywhere near this place — for who knows how long, maybe forever! You can have her teachers email her classwork to my wife."

Val could tell Principal Arif's instincts were to try and change his mind, but she faltered; instead opting to go with a subtle: "That'll be alright..."

The next week was a whirlwind of questions, questions, and more questions, by a myriad of different police officers; oscillating from surface level, to very serious with no buildup in between. *"What exactly was your relationship with the student? What kind of student was she? Did you notice any suspicious behavior by her classmates? Do you have any suspicions yourself on what could've been the cause of it? Did you ever see any self-mutilating tendencies? Do you think she just went fucking psycho one day and did it to herself?"*

"What?" Val snapped at a thoroughly taken aback Officer Yusef, who had taken it upon himself to do a bit of rogue police work. "No — of course not — stop it."

Officer Yusef scribbled some notes, before slamming his little scratchpad closed.

"Fine!" He seethed. "If you don't want to cooperate with my *enhanced* interrogation techniques, then I'll find someone who will." His combat boots squeaked as he swirled around. Stomping away down the hall, into the silence.

Val shook her head, grabbed her bag, and left for the front entrance as well. The last class had gotten out well over twenty minutes ago, and she was in no mood to be caught up alone here.

She walked past the first open hallway, turned left, and shuffled down a flight of stairs. Val was almost at the front doors when something out the back windows caught her eye...

There, in the middle of the courtyard, behind the statues of the Holy men that stood as imposing, and eerie as ever, was the hut she had seen in her dream several months ago. Smoke poured upwards from a small, stone fire pit; where the same, young, Orang Asli girl, was cooking a stew in a large pot; humming quietly to herself. Val could see the same Malay boy, crouching behind a bush; enthralled by her beauty as he watched her.

A coconut fell from a tree above him, landing on his head. He cried out in pain, and fell to the ground. This startled the young girl, who at first glance screamed at the prostrate boy; lying half hidden, half in her view. But after a few moments, she came to her senses and dragged the poor boy near the fire; nursing his bleeding head until his consciousness returned. Hours went by, then days, then weeks, and gradually the girl's own love for the boy matched his own. Val could tell that by the time the middle-aged man returned from where he'd been and the boy had scattered, her stomach had already begun to swell...

Val remembered what came after that. She tried to turn around and head for the doors, but a force kept her glued to the spot... she now faced the Holy men once more, and felt that same, cold, strong hand on the back of her neck, forcing her down... except it was *stronger* this time. Val fell to her knees, her palms pressing into the floor in front of her. She struggled to stay in even a tabletop position.

"Ms. Val, am I interrupting something?" Officer Yusef asked incredulously.

The force broke. Val found herself scrambling up to her feet again, trying to catch her breath.

"What — what — oh — I don't know..."

"Hmm..." Officer Yusef murmured to himself, as he examined Val up and down suspiciously, offering no help whatsoever. He scribbled down something in his little notepad once more, before turning back towards his official post outside the classroom. Val darted out the double doors; trying to both make sense of what she had just seen and force it from her memory...

CHAPTER NINETEEN

"Where are you taking me?" Val teased playfully, as Khoo Hun Chhiau drove through the winding hills on the opposite side of town. "You're not kidnapping me are you?"

"Psh—" he scoffed. "If I were actually kidnapping you, would I have let Yeo A'i and her husband see us drive off together? Honestly that's the first rule in kidnapping 101. Don't be the last person seen with the victim, much less by more than one witness."

"What's the second rule?" Val pressed. "Don't kidnap someone you're dumber than — because then they'll be able to trick the kidnapper? In that case you choose the wrong victim."

"Oh, you think you're smarter than me?" Khoo Hun Chhiau scoffed.

"More smart." Val teased. "See, in English *smarter* isn't actually a word. But I get it, it's not your first language."

"Or my second, or my third."

Val rolled her eyes.

"Or my fourth, or fifth?"

"Humph."

"Remind me, what were your two doctorates in again? Was it posting pictures on Instagram and being annoying?"

Val shoved his shoulder while he chuckled to himself. She peered at him with squinted, snide eyes, before they lingered out through the front window again. They had entered a new-build neighborhood of matching, modern, two-story houses.

"We're almost there."

They pulled into a house near the end of the road. A *fancy* one. All white, two stories, koi pond, the whole shabang. Khoo Hun Chhiau rushed to open her car door. Val crawled out, in awe of the place.

"Damn!" Val swore. "You must have some rich friends."

"Not exactly." Khoo Hun Chhiau murmured. "Come, I want to show you the inside."

"We can just walk in?" Val asked, confused. "Unannounced? Are you sure the owners won't mind?"

Khoo Hun Chhiau tugged at Val's arm. "No they won't mind. Trust me."

Val followed behind reluctantly, trying her best not to gape at everything around her. A pair of big-ass doors opened up to a bare living room, dining room, and kitchen. The back wall was completely covered by floor-to-ceiling windows, which had a view of the wild valley below, all the way to the ocean. The sunset was only moments away from setting over the horizon, causing a myriad of colors to paint the sky above.

"Oh my!" Val squealed. "Oh my — Oh my — this is beautiful!"

Khoo Hun Chhiau rested his hands on her shoulders, gently squeezing them. "It really is."

Val nearly forgot to ask what the fuck was going on.

"So... what exactly are we doing here?" Val pried. "Who lives here? Where's all the furniture?"

Val gazed around the empty rooms; searching for some signs of life but finding none. She could feel Khoo Hun Chhiau's chest rise behind her. He took in a deep breath, and held it.

"I bought this place." He said, monotony.

The words went through one ear and out the other. She turned around to look up into his stony, fixed eyes, that told no lies.

"What?"

"Well, uh..." Khoo Hun Chhiau started, "I should probably explain... a few months ago, my dad agreed to sell his house and give me the money, as long as I allowed him to live with me."

Val thought back to the one occasion she had seen his family house; which, if memory sufficed, was more of a hobbit hole than a house.

"Oh... uh, well, congratulations, but, if you don't mind me asking, how'd you afford a place like this?"

Khoo Hun Chhiau stared at her, then towards the ground. "Well, I know schooling is a lot for some, but it was covered for me by scholarships... I saved up a bit working at the police station since I lived with my dad, and was paid by the university to do my Ph.D. work and teach—"

"But that wouldn't be enough for this?" Val pushed back. How many bedrooms does this place have — five?"

"Six."

"*SIX!*" Val gasped. "How're you gonna afford a mortgage on a place like *this* as a police officer?"

"I'm not gonna be a police officer anymore." Khoo Hun Chhiau shot back. "I put my two months' notice into Jano yesterday, starting January first I'm leaving to work for Scott's firm — MATCH."

"So, you got a new job?" Val asked quietly.

Khoo Hun Chhiau nodded and pointed over to the kitchen. "The details are in that book over there..."

Val spotted the white binder. She shuffled over towards it, grabbed the cardboard notebook off of the kitchen counter, and flipped through it quickly. The salary section explained everything.

"Jesus Christ—" She swore. "Well — umm, congratulations, really, if anyone's earned it it's you. I mean it, congrats."

Khoo Hun Chhiau tried to hide his smile but couldn't. "Thanks." He said softly.

Val turned back around towards the rest of the house. "So... how're you gonna use these bedrooms?" She asked playfully. "A gym, a man cave, a woodshop room?"

Khoo Hun Chhiau started pointing at the rooms aimlessly, starting with the one downstairs. "I was planning on giving the first floor room to my dad, one would be a home office since most of my work would be from home, one will be a guest room, two would be for my future children I guess, one would be my bedroom, and one... we could call your room."

"My room?" Val chucked, pointing at herself. "What do you mean my room?"

Khoo Hun Chhiau shrugged and took another long pause again. "Well, I heard from Yeo A'i about that trip to Principal Arif's granddaughter's house, and, and... I heard it went badly." He said matter of factly.

"It did." Val snapped. "And?"

"Well, have you looked at any other places?" He asked, his tone raising.

She hadn't, truth be told it had slipped her mind. Everything was slipping her mind now-a-days.

"No, but... I mean, what would people say? You're a cop?"

"Only for a little while longer." Khoo Hun Chhiau reminded her.

"But—" Val stammered, "what would people say if they knew I was living with you? Couldn't you get into trouble—"

"Not if you're my wife!" He said boldly.

A surge of blood rushed to Val's cheeks, which turned scarlet. Instinctively she turned away, towards the dazzling sunset which was now halfway past the waterline. Out of all the possible words in all the languages this man knew, these were the last ones she'd expected right now... it was all so fast... but at the same time, not as fast as it should feel. They had only been secretly together for a month, and had shared their first kiss a few weeks before that...

"Look..." He muttered, shakily, losing all boldness. "I didn't mean it to come out like that, but what we've been doing is... not how I do things. I feel *ashamed*. Happy, but ashamed. This wasn't how I was taught things were *supposed* to happen. We should probably start making some plans..."

Val's head raced a million miles a minute. What was her life anymore? How was this happening? Of all the things that'd happen this year... fighting off a demon, dodging stampeding elephants, hallucinations, possessions... *mariage?* It took all her effort to say anything at all.

"Things — things don't normally move this fast where I'm from—"

"Things don't normally move this slowly where I'm from." Khoo Hun Chhiau countered.

"My — My family will not be happy about this."

"Nor will mine."

"I don't have a car, or a scooter." Val faltered.

"I'll buy you one then. A car, not a scooter. You said you liked those... what were they called again? Range Rovers? We can go into Kuala Lumpur and see if they have a dealership there."

Val scoffed at this bold promise, then remembered just how minuscule of a dent a measly Range Rover would be to his new budget.

"That's... That's crazy!" She turned back towards the view once more, silently seething. "So since you're feeling guilty about having your fun with me, you're trying to feel better by *bribing* me into marrying you?"

"I — I — didn't—"

"You're just gonna spring all this on me without any warning — without any indication — without asking me for any input in any of your plans — and it's all okay now because you're *rich* all of the sudden!"

"You don't understand! I—"

"Do you really feel that badly about us being together?"

"That's not it at all!" He protested frantically. "You don't understand, I asked because this is what I want!"

Val winced, and gazed up towards his downcast face; which she couldn't help but cradle within her hands. He fumed silently for a few seconds, before pulling her into a firm, engulfing hug; bending over so that he nuzzled his face into her neck. This gave Val so many chills, she had half a mind to drag him upstairs and christen the new master bedroom on the spot.

"This... this is what I need... I've never *wanted,* never *needed* something, *someone,* so badly in my whole life. I just... I just..." he faltered, searching for the right words. "I just want you with me."

Val choked up at this. Her cheeks flushed even more violently, and her eyes swam with tears.

"I want to be with you too." She cooed. "It's just a little overwhelming is all."

"I understand." He croaked softly. "This is a lot."

"This is insane." Val heaved. "This is... this is..."

"Whatever it is, there's no point in fighting it, or delaying it, or letting other people get in the way..." he growled, through the silence.

Val took a deep, calm breath in, then nodded. Sealing the deal with a kiss on his forehead. Together they turned back around to watch the sun dip slowly below the horizon.

CHAPTER TWENTY

"A little to the left." Amina commanded from her tanning chair; while Val, Nur, Tan Soan, and Parini dropped a heavy garden fountain on Nur's toe.

"Seriously!" Nur swore, grabbing her foot. "We agreed to help you with some *"light gardening work."* That doesn't mean moving a three-hundred-pound fountain all around your yard. You're wasting away your pregnancy sympathies very quickly."

"You guys are almost done, I just wanted to see where it'd look best... and I'm thinking just a bit more to the left will be perfect." Amina cheered.

"It'll look perfect right here," Parini fumed, "right here exactly. Not an inch more to the left."

"All right, all right, now you guys can get started on my orchids. They're not very heavy I promise."

The girls rolled their eyes, too tired, hot, and sweaty for any humor. It was the Saturday after the last day of school, and Val thought she'd chill today. Boy was she wrong.

"I'll go grab the lemonade from the kitchen." Tan Soan panted.

"And while you're at it, can you grab the mini handheld fan?" Amina called from her chair as she stretched her legs out in front of her lazily. "It's getting a bit too hot out here for me."

"For you?" Nur cried. "Seriously?"

Amina brushed her aside once more. "So Val, is Yeo A'i all packed for her big move yet?"

Val nodded her head. She had helped pack, organize, and ship so many cardboard boxes the blisters on her hands stung with even the slightest touch. It wasn't just Yeo A'i's stuff she had been packing up. Val and Khoo Hun Chhiau had been slowly getting her own things together as well...

"Yup," Val said quickly, "it's all ready. She's so excited, I don't think she can move fast enough. I swear, sometimes it's like she's in two rooms at once, and her mind is somewhere else entirely."

"That's kind of how I would describe her on a quiet day." Nur smirked. "I can't even imagine her now."

"Ms. Val — Ms. Amina!"

"I saw her facetiming at the dentist one time."

"Ms. Val — Ms. Amina!"

"I've seen her do that while driving too, very dangerous."

"Ms. Val — Ms. Amina!"

"She better not try any of that with me next time she comes in for a pap smear..."

"MS. VAL — MS. AMINA!" The rogue voices yelled, diverting everyone's attention away from Nur's rant towards the two, young, familiar girls sprinting down the street; running like a tiger was chasing them.

"That, that can't be—" Amina groaned.

"I think it is." Val sighed, already exasperated just by the sight of them.

"Hmph, what in the world do they want?"

The girls kept screaming and running 'til they knocked over the three hundred pound fountain.

"Ms. Val — Ms. Amina," Eng Ki started, "Zara," She panted furiously, "Zara — Zara — Zara's in danger!"

"Danger?" Amina perked up. "What do you mean? What're you talking about?"

"We went to visit Zara a few minutes ago, she lives a few blocks away from here, and she... she wasn't right." Wani wheezed.

"What do you mean she wasn't right? What's wrong with her? Is she sick?"

"Does she need a doctor?" Nur chimed up.

"No—"

"She was — She was — She was—"

But Val already knew the answer before Eng Ki could get the words out.

"She was possessed!"

The two girls looked at each other and nodded.

A chill ran down everyone's back. Val grabbed Wani's forearm and brought her close.

"Are you sure?" Val asked gravely.

Val watched Wani's eyes begin to panic, then swell with tears. She nodded at Val. *"Her* eyes, I remember those eyes."

"They were red!" Eng Ki cried. "They were red, and angry, and horrible!"

"Where is she?" Amina asked seriously. "We can run to her house real quick, I'll call Principal Arif—"

"She's not there anymore!" Wani cried. "She's at the school, she left her house and said she was gonna walk into the forest and never return!"

Val nearly threw up. "How long ago did she leave?"

"I don't know!" Wani cried. "About twenty minutes ago? She might have made it by now, it could already be too late!"

"Parini—" Amina commanded, "go inside and call Principal Arif. Tell her to meet us at the school ASAP." She pushed herself up from her chair, with great difficulty as her stomach was now the size of a dinosaur egg. "The rest of us will hurry to the school. There's a shortcut through the trees over there, it's faster to run that way than to drive the street way."

"I brought some stuff we can use in my backpack." Wani added.

Val sprinted in front of the pack, hurrying through stray vines and roots. There were no thoughts right now, only panic, only dread.

They made it out of the brush. Val found herself dead across the street from Semua Tangan. The group crossed the street quickly, rushing for the front doors, when they found an interesting scene blocking their path...

"No, you can't shoot me with that stupid slingshot, I work here! I'm not some intruder trying to rob god knows what from a girls' school!" Ms. Dian chastised a thoroughly upset Officer Yusef.

"You whipped around that building so fast I didn't know who you were. For all I knew you could have been a kidnapper or something."

"There are no children here!" Ms. Dian seethed. "We're done for the year, where do you think the rest of your colleagues are? Why do you think they only sent you in for the day to guard the entrance?"

"Well, you could have been, you know... *her.*"

"What's a slingshot gonna do against *HER?*" Ms. Dian hollered. "In what universe does a children's slingshot have an actual chance against *HER?*"

"It would buy me time—"

"It would make *HER* hate *YOU* even more, and secure your death sentence. I'll tell you that much!"

"Ms. Dian, Ms. Dian—" Amina cried as they ran up to the pair, "Ms. Dian, this is urgent, have you seen a young girl around twelve or thirteen years old come through this way?"

Ms. Dian cocked her head. "No, I haven't. Why? What's going on?"

An SUV pulled up right beside the group, parking in the specified *"Principal's parking"* spot. "I'm here—" Principal Arif rushed. "I'm here, I'm here, Ms. Dian, I've just got off the phone with 999. We have a real crisis on our hands, have you seen—"

"These people just asked me that question, no, I haven't seen anything. What's going on?"

The front door whipped open behind them. A panting, white-faced, Ms. Mawar poked her head out from the other side. "Call the police, come quick, *Help!*"

"What's going on?" Ms. Dian cried as everyone pushed past her through the front doors, into the entrance hall. Where beyond the statues, through the windows, in the middle of the back courtyard, was a silently jerking Zara. Her body lay prostrate on her back; the grass around her soaked with her blood!

Val scoured the girl's body for the wound, but It was *every* wound. Every scar she'd incurred throughout the year had opened up, and was now gushing her life force away. Standing above the carnage was *her*, with her arms outstretched at her side, like a magician performing his final trick.

"NO—" Eng Ki screamed, while taking the charge and running outside through the double glass doors first. She lunged for *her*, but was caught in mid-air, frozen for a few seconds in time and space until *she* threw her back. Eng Ki hit the windows on the second floor, cracking them. Her body fell back down on the lawn below.

"*You bitch!*" Wani screamed from the top of her lungs, ready to lunge next — but Val caught her just in time — falling with her behind several recycling bins which burst into flames just as they hit the ground. The heat stung her skin. Val looked around, she'd provided enough of a diversion for the rest of the women to grab Eng Ki and pull her behind a bench.

"What in the world is going — OH MY GOD—" Officer Yusef screamed as he lingered onto the scene in front of him, desperately scrambling for some useful cover. Ultimately he decided to hide with Val and Wani behind the bins.

Val watched whatever the fuck was going on in front of her. *She* held out her hand, and the metal bench hiding the rest of the crew crumpled like loose foil wrap. Val felt Wani squirm against her.

"Let me go — *Let me Go!*" She screamed. "I have something that can help — please!" She broke free from Val's grasp and unzipped her backpack.

"Give us the girl!" Principal Arif cried out from another bench. "The police are on their way, we don't want another repeat of a few months ago!"

This was *not* the right thing to say. Val waited for Principal Arif's body to crumple just like that metal chair, but something else caught *her* eye... *she* looked behind herself. There, in the opposite corner of the court yard, the silhouette of a fat man running slowly behind *her* cast large shadows behind himself. *She* caught him not even halfway across, throwing him into one of the flaming trash bins.

"Ouch! Oh — no — no — no — no — no!" Mr. Elmsworth grunted, as he frantically patted the fires out while the rest of them helped. Val was just surprised he was actually conscious and moving.

"Shit—" Wani swore, "you're making me lose my concentration." She pulled the fattest stack of fireworks Val had ever seen from her book bag, handing them down the line. "Okay, we need to plant these in the ground towards *her,* then on the count of three, we need to light them up, tip over these bins, and run for it. I'll run and grab Zara, the rest of you—"

"No you fucking won't!" Val shrieked. "You'll run with these two towards the nurse's office, and make sure you get everyone else's attention so they follow as well. I'll grab Zara and follow behind."

"Fine." Wani agreed. "By the way, Officer Yusef, your fireworks are aimed at Zara. Point them up a little bit. Actually if you could just give those back, I'm sure–"

"Hey—hey—hey, they're mine now." He huffed while slapping her hand away. "Trust me, if there's one thing I'm an expert in, it's playing with fireworks... these will hit *her* right in the chest, trust me."

"If you say so." Wani cried. "On the count of three — one — two — three!"

The four of them tipped the flaming trash bins over, then ran. There were three seconds of absolute silence. Officer Yusef, Mr. Elmsworth, and Wani ran across the yard to the building to their right; shouting for the rest to follow. Val beelined it directly for *her* and Zara. Val made it halfway when she felt her body freeze within *her* telepathic clutch. Val knew at any moment her body would soar through the air, through any number of bulletproof windows, easily shattering both glass and bone alike.

A deafening crack rang around her, the grip vanished and she hit the ground. Fireworks soared through the air, hitting their mark. Dozens at a time shot out from the ground, raining sparks everywhere. Val had no clue where *she* was, but there was no time to look. She army-crawled her way to Zara's limp, chilly body; dragging it alongside her until they were far enough away from the melee to change positions. Val threw Zara over her shoulder, and sprinted faster than she ever had in her life, towards the direction of the side door held open by an apprehensive Principal Arif.

"YOUUUUU!" A wretched, demonic voice hissed. "YOUUUUU!"

Val ran faster, knowing at any moment it could all be over. All their efforts for nothing. The last seconds of her life would be spent running like prey from predator. She felt the cold fingers reach out, the claws well past the front of Val's shoulder. *Her* actual, physical grip would surely take them both...

A stone pebble soared over her shoulder, hitting *her* in the face. Val looked over at the defiant Officer Yusef, and his trusty, silly, stupid little slingshot.

It was just enough to get through the doors, which slammed shut behind her. Val dropped to the floor, as a raging, raggedy, wretched, screaming *her* pounded the outside for several moments, before silencing completely.

"I upgraded the whole nurses' station here over the summer to panic-room level security." Principal Arif grunted as she and the rest of the girls laid Zara down on the nurses' cot. "All the doors are made of five-inch titanium. It'll take *her* some time to get through that, but I'm not sure how much..."

"Where are the police officers?" Ms. Mawar gripped. "I called them at least five minutes ago, they should be here by now?"

Officer Yusef grabbed his walkie-talkie, speaking into it with profound clarity. There was no response from the other side.

Val grabbed her phone, and checked her messages. Only one came through from Khoo Hun Chhiau.

"We've just received word that there's a major problem at the school. As of right now we're running into some unusual supernatural difficulties... that is how I can best describe the situation. We cannot break through.

I know you're there. Please message me if you're able. If not, please keep yourself hidden 'till you can get out. Please... please..."

"What's this mess that Jano is messaging me about the Holy men setting up an unbreakable barrier around the school grounds?" Amina gripped. "I swear that man has gone crazy!"

Everyone crammed in around Amina, looking over each other's shoulders to catch a peak at what the message described. Val read something along the lines of *"six points of equidistance encompassing the entirety of Semua Tangan, where each of the Holy men have materialized and are now chanting ritualistically."*

"They're doing it as a warning." Principal Arif chimed in. "They don't want anyone else becoming subject to *her* wrath. They know a full-scale invasion might just make *her* mad enough to eviscerate the whole town."

"We need to worry about that later—" Nur cried, while desperately searching around the room for medical supplies. "If the police can't get through, then that means an ambulance won't be able to either. Principal Arif, I need sutures and blood bags quick—"

"Ohhh, right—right—right, okay." She fretted. "I know we have sutures in the emergency kit, but as for blood bags I'm afraid we only have needles and the bags themselves, no actual fresh blood."

"Of course you all wouldn't have fresh blood, what school would? Well then, someone's gonna have to donate some of their own then. Do we know her blood type?"

"Let me check her nurses' file, let me see here... it says that she's AB negative."

Eng Ki jerked on her cot, slapping her arm.

"You are thoroughly concussed ma'am. That's gonna be a strict no from you."

"Well what about me?" Wani cried. "I can give her some of my blood."

"You two are too little to give any of your blood. I'm sorry, but no children. Who else wants to volunteer?"

"What about me?" Amina chimed in.

"You are way too pregnant. As your personal OBGYN, I am strictly forbidding it."

"I would, but I'm O positive and I don't think they can give to any of the negatives." Principal Arif chimed in.

"You would be right then." Nur said quickly as she stitched away at Zara's wounds; which had slowed their bleeding, but only because she didn't have much blood left to lose. "How about you, Ms. Mawar?"

"I'm O positive too."

"I'm anemic." Ms. Dian chimed in. "So I don't know if that rules me out or not?"

"That does, that's why I'm ruled out too."

Everyone turned towards Mr. Elmsworth, who faced the ground.

"I have hemophilia, which means if I get cut—"

"You won't be able to stop bleeding. I understand, and what about you... Officer Yusef..."

Everyone switched their gaze; focusing narrowly in on Officer Yusef, who didn't seem to hear the question.

"I, ummm, I'm AB negative okay, but I am very, very afraid of needles. So I guess I'm out too—"

"Oh no—" Nur cried. "This girl is moments away from death. So help me I will pin you down and extract your blood myself!"

"Everyone started moving in on Officer Yusef, ready to corner and hold him down if necessary... that was until he went off.

"Please, please, please no!" He cried. "Look, I didn't want to mention this, but I took a little trip to Thailand last month, and well, I did some... *unseemingly* things... with some... *unseemly* people... a lot of people... and now I have some suspicions... *unseemly* boils... in some... *unseemly* places... you're a doctor! Why don't you check it out for me real quick—"

Everyone groaned, and jerked to stop Officer Yusef from unbuckling his pants. Val covered Wani's eyes.

"Stop!" Nur cried. "Okay, okay you've made your point. If you don't buckle that belt back up this instance, I'll beat you with it myself.

There's absolutely no way I'm letting a drop of your *filthy* blood get anywhere near this poor child's body." She shot him one last loathing look of disgust. "If we get out of this alive, I'll refer you to a urologist."

"Thank you!" He cried. "Thank you — thank you — thank you!"

Nur sighed, while suturing up the last of the major gashes along Zara's back. "And you—" she asked Val. "What's your blood type? For the love of god please don't tell me you've had malaria in the last twelve months or something."

Val shook her head. "No none of that." She sighed. "But I'm B negative, so doesn't that mean I can only give to the other B's?"

Nur's eyes lit up in a frenzy. "Not at all, you can give to all B's and AB's — including AB negative, you're a match! I might need to take a bit of extra blood from you than a normal person would usually donate though..."

Val gulped. She, like officer Yusef, was a coward. She *hated* needles. Really *really* hated them. For a second she wavered, but it only took one look at Zara's tiny, pale, withering, body to change her mind.

"Okay... what do I do then?"

"Just—" Nur arranged a chair for Val to sit in. "Just sit in this chair and lie back a bit. I'll sort out the rest."

Val did as she was told. Nur ran around the room, sanitizing equipment and ordering everyone else in and out of her way. After only five minutes all the needles and tubes and bags were set up, ready to go.

"Okay, you're gonna feel a pinch in your arm. I just need you to squeeze this ball and relax."

Val tried to breathe easy as the long needle pierced her vein, but it was gross, and weird. She squirmed as the tube stretching across her arm warmed with her blood. Val watched in morbid curiosity as it flowed smoothly, filling the bag. Every ten minutes or so, Nur would stop by and replace it with a fresh one when it had filled."

"This is probably the last bag I can take from you safely before you pass out from shock." She said skeptically. Nur grabbed the third and final bag from her, unhooking her arm from the IV. "Please don't—"

Val tried to stand up, but just fell back down in a shivering heap, puking all over the floor.

"Get up just yet..." Nur sighed. "Everything's fine, that's a perfectly normal reaction, nobody panic."

Ms. Mawar dug through a cupboard labeled *"Diabetic"*, and handed Val something in her hands. "Just sip this juice. It's a good one, mango flavored, my favorite."

Val nodded, as her trembling, pale fingers tried their best to clutch onto the little box. She took a sip, it tasted sweeter than anything she'd remembered drinking.

"You look terrible." Ms. Dian teased while patting Val hard on the shoulder. "It really looks like you transferred some of your own health into that girl."

Val peaked over at Zara, who, although still pale and exhausted, looked much more at ease. Val watched the third bag of blood seep into her veins, sighing in relief at the hints of color returning to her cheeks.

CHAPTER TWENTY-ONE

They waited hours for something, anything at all to happen, but there wasn't a peep from their phones. Every now and then Val could have sworn she heard a helicopter flying high above them, but never the sound of it landing.

"*T — T — Time?*" Eng Ki yelled. "What *T — T — Time* is it? I'm hungry!"

Principal Arif glanced down at her phone. "It's half past nine." Her brow furrowed, and her tone grew even more pointed. "Look, I don't want to alarm anyone, but we really shouldn't stay here through the night... we need to make a break for it."

At these words, every body tensed up, even Val's faint, weak one. They all knew that she was right, but no one wanted to be the first to bring it up. There was silence, until Val piped up from her cushioned seat, wrapped in the nurse's quilt. "We need a plan..."

"Right." Principal Arif replied sternly; as if she were now a military commander. "We will pair the weakest with the strongest. Nur — you and I will keep charge over Ms. Zara here, while Ms. Dian takes Eng Ki, and Ms. Mawar watches out for Amina — now don't give me any attitude here Amina! You are very pregnant and that alone is risky enough for you to have help. Officer Yusef, you will stick by Mr. Elmsworth, I am well aware of the arthritis in both your knees. You've never spared me a day without hearing your grunts up and down the stairs. Make sure you safely escort him out of here. She turned to Wani and Val, "and you two... you two will watch out for each other."

Val and Wani made nervous, frightened eye contact with one another, before nodding. The next hour consisted of the group trying to makeshift defense materials out of the nurse's office, which went poorly. The only thing of any help at all was a cane that Mr. Elmsorth took for himself.

"Alright—" Principal Arif began as she leaned in towards the steel door. "Once I unlock this, there will be no turning back… we stay together as best we can, no matter what. Do you understand? And under no circumstances do you leave your buddy behind."

Everyone nodded in agreement. Val's heart pounded with what little blood she had left, making her dizzy.

"One… two… three — go — go — go!" She whispered.

The group tiptoed into the deserted, dark hallway, trying their best to not even breathe too loudly. They turned the right-hand corner at the end of the corridor. With the front doors now in sight, everyone sighed in relief.

"Okay, almost there, we just have to get through the *OH MY GOSH RUN — RUN — RUN NOW!*"

Val whirled around. At the end of their hallway, a dark shadow with red eyes leapt on all fours across the ceiling. Not even gravity was a match for *her*. *She* made it straight for them.

Val felt Wani's hand grip her forearm. The eleven of them booked it down the hallway so fast, Val could barely keep up. Every movement was slowed. This was *not* the time to be slow.

Val felt a shadow pass above her head. Just as they were about to reach the front entrance, *she* dropped dead center into the middle of the foyer; growling, huffing, puffing, and pacing in front of their way.

Everyone squeezed into a tight mass. Val watched Principal Arif and Ms. Dian move to the front, while Mr. Elmsworth and Officer Yusef pushed her aside for the rear.

"We have more fireworks!" Principal Arif lied, her voice trembling. "And if you don't move out of our way right now we'll use them!"

She remained silent and still for a moment, a stillness beyond humans. Then, something sprung her back to life. *She* let out a loud, long hiss, and leapt for them!

Everyone ducked down, and closed their eyes. Val felt hands go up around her reflexively... but nothing happened... after several shakey seconds, a horrible, panicked, shriek rang out around them. Val squinted her eyes towards the source...

She was suspended in mid-air... twirling and tussling, screaming and crying, howling and cursing, while the six Holymen surrounded her with their hands raised. They stood there, rooted to their spots, chanting and singing. Each in their own tongue, each their own prayer...

"*Our Father who art in heaven...*"

"*Bismillah...*"

"*Ooommmm... Ooommmm...*"

Val tried to move, but she was frozen. She felt for Wani's arm again, helping her up as everyone raced for the door.

"*OUR FATHER WHO ART IN HEAVEN...*"

"*BISMILLAH...*"

"*OOOMMMMM... OOOMMMMM...*"

She rose higher and higher into the air, twitching feverishly. It was like they had cast an invisible net around *her*. *Her* head almost hit the ceiling when *she* let out a terrifying, deep-chested, rattling roar!

The Holymen fell to the ground! Val realized *she'd* broken free of their spell! Val grabbed Wani, and ducked behind a nearby decorative sofa. *She* hit the ground — *her* fist along with *her* feet, cracking the stone floor where *she'd* landed. A deafening shockwave rang throughout the entire hall.

Granthi Balnoor, Daoshi Yang Pha, and Monk Ho Kla rematerialized before the front doors, chanting once more. The Sadhu leapt to his feet, conjuring from behind him a sandstorm of burnt spice. Val grabbed Wani, and ducked, making sure to cover her eyes and mouth.

The world went red and black. Wind and particles stung their skin. Turmeric filled every canal. Val felt like ants were crawling in her ears, all her cuts burned.

After several minutes, the sand storm ceased; but another storm was already brewing. Imam Haruun struck from the left, sending what could've been all the bees in the world hurdling in every direction.

They stung everything, finding nooks and crannies in Val's tattered clothing that not even the spice storm could. Val tried batting them away, but gave up. There was no other option than to get out!

Val tried once more to book it for the front doors, but *she*, now covered in a reddish hue, blocked her. At the sight of the pair, *she* lunged in their direction! The priest stood several paces away, and just before *her* claws were about to dig into Wani's neck he summoned a tsunami behind himself. All Val could do was grab onto Wani once more, and let the tidal wave of holy water take them.

It swept them away, carrying them down the hall. The wave rose, ten, twenty feet; one mighty current. The two were carried around the corner, then smashed into a wall. Val prayed everyone was alright, but what's a prayer in a battle.

"Wani, Wani!" Val cried. "Please stay still, it'll be much easier if you don't fight me."

"I can't swim." Wani cried.

"Just try and hold your breath, and let me hold on to your arms. It's easier for me to hold you up when you're not—"

But a force yanked Wani under the water.

"No!" Val screamed. She dove under in blind hope, searching with her hands. One found the back of Wani's head, the other something much, much more foul...

Val struggled against the creature, doing her best to separate Wani from its grasp and push her up to the surface. Wani drifted off towards the side. The creature rammed Val's body against every wall she could. Val found herself choking on water, gasping for air where there was none, whirling down a flooded hall she had walked every day for the last year, next to a literal monster; and this is how she very well might die.

As if a chasm opened up underneath, the water vanished. Val found herself falling through nothingness 'til her body slammed into the ground; the force of which made her throw up. Her first breath pierced her lungs like a knife. Her second breath felt no better, but she was alive.

"Wani!" She coughed. "Wani!"

Her hands felt around the floor, while her eyes adjusted to the room again. To Val's surprise, Wani was right behind her, sprawled on the floor, puking into Val's hair.

A thunder of footsteps ran past.

"Get up—" Amina screamed, her voice ringing around the barren corridor. "We can't come get you right now — too many injuries — Yusef is unconscious — Professor Elmsworth is carrying him — Ms. Mawar broke her ankle — get up — grab Wani — now — hurry!"

Val's body had never felt so sore before, but she knew now was it. After this, who knew what sort of plagues the Holymen would perform? What horrors *she* would throw back at them? They were only ten meters away from the front doors. Every footstep and movement felt like agony, but Val persisted. She grabbed Wani by the forearm, forcing her upright; then booked it to the foyer one more time, bringing up the rear. Nine meters away. Eight meters away. Seven meters away...

A shrill pierced the air. Val felt her eardrum rupture.

Six meters away. Five meters away.

Every glass window shattered all at once, spewing flecks everywhere. Val felt tiny cuts run down her cheeks, neck, chest, arms, and legs.

Four meters away. Three meters away.

The sound of flat feet sprinting across the cracked floor crept up behind them.

Two meters away. One meter away.

Val felt Wani slip from her grasp, yanked away once more — by *her!*

Everyone else had already escaped through the now empty door frames. Principal Arif turned to look back over her shoulder, and sprinted back toward the trio.

She dragged Wani back so viciously, Val heard a wrist snap and Wani's cry. Val lunged for them, tackling *her* to the ground. *She* released Wani, and Val kicked her towards the front door. Principal Arif grabbed her, before starting for Val.

"Go—" Val cried. "It's too late — get Wani and *GoOOUUUU—*" She screamed in pain, while *She* forced Val up in the air, then slammed her body into the floor.

Val caught a glimpse through her watery eyes of Principal Arif's struggle. In the end, she did what she was told; forcing a sobbing, screaming Wani out of the building, beyond Val's line of vision.

It was just the two of them now, in the silent, dark foyer; which was now an empty shell of what it had been. Everything was destroyed, ripped apart, turned over, and insect ridden... except for the statues; which stood as imposing and gaunt as ever in their spot near the back.

She noticed where Val's eyes had crept. Val knew *she* had... for in the time Val's eyes had lingered, *she* had leapt off her, using her telepathic force to move Val to the center of the room, in front of the stony Holymen one more time. Val stood there, nearly as frozen as the statues, before *she,* clutching Val's head in her long, spindling fingers, forced it down. Next came her back; which after the day she'd had, couldn't even put up a fight. Val found herself bent over, staring at the ground, when *she* knocked her down again, back into that familiar tabletop position... and then finally into child's pose, with her hands stretched out before her.

"Greed — Envy — Lust!" *She* rattled, in that same, horrendous, crackled growl that sent shivers down Val's spine. *"But most of all, HATE AND FEAR! That is what the people worship!"*

Val felt like her arms would rip off from the rest of her body. Like her spine would soon be ground into powder, but there was no moving, no release.

"P—P—*Please!*" Val cried. "I don't want to hurt you — just let me go!"

"*PAIN!*" *She* cried out once more, lowering her face now so that it was even with Val's. Those horrible, crimson eyes and jagged teeth seemed exaggerated somehow. The only thing bringing some temperance was the strangely sweet aroma of her breath. *"You humans are masters of pain — you bring pain upon this world — upon your enemies — you're neighbors — your friends — but no one more so than yourselves!*

In man's eye, there will be no worse victim than himself. His grief is guilt not of the other, but of not being perfect himself; while demanding perfection from everyone around him! There's nothing you love more. All you need is someone and all you want is more!"

"Please... please..." Val cried out one last time, her voice nearly giving out. "Just let me go..."

"NOOO!" She screamed manically, flipping Val over so that she was lying on her back now. *"NOOO!"*

Val tried to fight *her* off, but *she* was on top of her now. Both of *her* long, cold fingers clenched tightly around Val's throat, *her* stiletto nails cutting into her skin. Val tried to push *her* away with all her might, but *she* was too strong. Val scrambled around frantically, kicking, scratching, thrashing, trying to release herself, but it was no use... Val felt the life begin to drip from her. There were no Holymen here to save her now. Her eyes searched frantically around, for something, anything... she examined the strange body above her... the skinny, muscular neck, the bony, skeletal shoulders, and the forceful, beating rhythm that protruded from the left side of *her* chest...

Looking back, Val couldn't ever pinpoint what made her do it. Whether it was some stroke of genius or something much more instinctual... but at that moment, Val ceased pushing *her* away — causing *her* body to tumble onto Val's. Val buried her face into *her* chest, and sank her teeth into *her* beating heart! A piercing shrill that made Val go temporarily deaf filled the room, along with Semua Tangan, the whole town, and quite possibly all of Malaysia... but Val wasn't focused on that. Instinctively Val took another bite instead, and concentrated on the sweet, delicious, familiar juice of a fruit that gushed from her mouth... something she had eaten a thousand times growing up. Something that reminded her of her own grandmother... the sweet... sweet juice... of a mango...

Val's eyes rolled into the back of her head, and a moment later *she* was emerging from the same plot of earth, a fresh babe... knowing nothing... wanting something... wanting... *help? She* felt the innocent, sacred, beautiful naivete of childhood for only the briefest of moments. That is, until the woman arrived... the woman who had brought *her* into this world, but was not *her* mother... her face contorted, and twisted in fear, and anger... and rage! Her calls for help would echo in *her* ears for millennia. The men who came to the woman's aid hurt *her*... cut *her* skin, pierced it with sharp rocks and spears, trying to end *her* life when it had just begun!

She overtook them all, and ran; and then had to run back because the men there tried killing her too. Eventually *she* went back to *her* earth, left alone... to be? To die? But *she* didn't die... *she* kept living, and living, and watching, and living. *She* watched the humans hunt — and build — and destroy — and love — and lust — AND HATE — AND KILL — AND CRY — AND CRY — AND CRY! The only thing worse than knowing everyone wanted you dead, was not being able to kill yourself for dozens of years — hundreds of years — thousands of years — *tens of thousands of years!* The anguish, the despair, the fear of being alone forever and forever more. Who would hold *her* like mothers hold children and husbands hold wives? Who could stand to be in *her* presence without trembling and begging *her* for their lives? Who would see *her* for her? For once, who could *she* see as someone?"

Val's eyes returned to face forwards. She flipped over, vomiting up what was now a disgusting volcanic ash. *She* was crying, withering, and crawling away, the floor around them gushing with *her* blood! Val tried to move towards *her*. To help *her*. To maybe stem some of the flow... but before she could do anything, a flurry of police officers moved in, shooting bullets at *her* while *she* fled!

"*No!*" Val cried. "*No — stop it — please — don't hurt her!*"

CHAPTER TWENTY-TWO

Val wasn't certain what happened next. Everything was a blur. She was on a stretcher, then in an ambulance, then finally in a hospital room, getting pricked by more needles.

Yeo A'i was the first to see her. She fretted nervously, asking a million questions a minute. Her little body trembled so forcefully Val had to calm her down.

"I'm so sorry I wasn't there to help!" Yeo A'i cried. "Tell me, is *she*... is *she* really dead?" Yeo A'i's eyes dropped to the floor. "I overheard some of the officers saying there was a lot of... uh... blood, or something on the scene?"

"I don't know." Val answered truthfully. The thought of *her* actually being dead punched Val in the stomach. After everything she had just seen... heard... felt... Val didn't want *her* to die like that. In fact, Val didn't want *her* to die at all...

There was a tussle out in the hall. A few seconds later Khoo Hun Chhiau burst into the room, still in his vest, rifle, and combat boots. His eyes were swollen and red, his jaw locked. Val watched the tears swell and fall down his face, as he collapsed onto her. Nearly squishing Val all over again.

"I'm so sorry!" He cried silently. "I'm so sorry!"

Val gently hugged him and scratched his back. "What for?"

"I should have protected you!" He sobbed. "I should have found a way to get to you... I should have found you sooner!"

"What? You don't think I can protect myself?" She teased.

"Stop."

The curtain was yanked aside once more. To Val's surprise, it was a very concerned-looking Nur who entered this time.

Val couldn't get the words out fast enough. "How's Wani — Eng Ki — Officer Yusef? Is everyone alright? Did everyone else make it out okay? How's little Zara?"

"Fine, fine." Nur said quickly, a little too quickly. "Everyone's fine, Officer Yusef is recovering from the anaphylactic shock from his bee stings. Eng Ki is getting treated for a cracked skull and concussion, and Zara's not great, but she's improving... she'll be okay... but I'm here to talk about *you*."

Val brushed her aside. "Me? I'm tired, but that's all. Got a few stings of my own, but I'll be okay."

Nur shook her head. "I, uh... I have some rather surprising news to share with you." Nur glanced nervously from Khoo Hun Chhiau to Yeo A'i. "Would you like me to ask everyone to step out of the room first?"

"What is it?" Val asked, annoyed. "Just tell me, whatever it is, it's probably not that embarrassing, is it? Did I break my tailbone or something? It feels quite sore..."

"You're pregnant."

The room fell dead silent. Val felt Yeo A'i grasp her hand. Khoo Hun Chhiau's face drained of all color.

"I'm... I'm sorry?" Val asked. Dazed. Her mind reeling a million miles an hour. "I'm what?"

"You're pregnant. We aren't quite sure how far along you are, and after today's ordeal I have no clue if your baby survived... we'll need to do a sonogram to see what it's looking like in there, but you're definitely pregnant. I'm gonna go get some equipment so we can get a better look at things."

Nur left the room. Khoo Hun Chhiau collapsed into a chair. Val fell back into her pillow, crying silent, petrified tears.

"I... I..." Yeo A'i stuttered as she fretted with the bed linens, tucking Val deeper underneath their embrace. "What in the world is on your clothes?" She coughed, while trying to get the taste of something out of her mouth. "That tastes dreadful!"

Val peered down at her tattered t-shirt. A gray, familiar-smelling ash had settled itself deep into her fabric; where just moments ago *her* blood had soaked through.

"Oh, I don't know. It's…"

"You know what that looks like?" Yeo A'i sleuthed. "It looks like dust from buildings that have blown up. My husband and daughter were covered in something similar years ago when they watched a building demolition; and considering what the state of the school must be in now…"

"Yeah." Val lied. "I guess that could've been it."

They sat in silence once more. Nur returned a few moments later with an intimidatingly bulky machine. To everyone's surprise her baby was perfectly fine. Yeo A'i brought her home for a bit, doting mercilessly before Khoo Hun Chhiau swept her away to his new house, halfway up the mountain. Still bare, but with a fancy, white sectional couch taking up a decent portion of the living room.

Val collapsed onto it, sprawling out wide, letting her body sink into its leathery chill. Khoo Hun Chhiau threw a blanket over the top of her. Val snatched it, pulling it close to her body. She watched him walk away, feeling a newfound coldness towards him she couldn't quite explain…

"What?" He asked harshly, startling Val.

"What?" Val snapped back, rolling her eyes, forcing her glare elsewhere.

"What is it? What's wrong? What happened in there? You've been acting weird since — since—"

"Since hmmm, I don't know!" Val snapped, even more cruel and harsh this time. "Maybe since I had to rescue a bunch of kids from a m-m-onst… from… you know. From that… from that…" Val's heart sank to its lowest point in her remembered life. The breath escaped her lungs. When it returned, it came in the form of raspy, angry sobs. "From *HER* — FROM HER!" She wailed. Her dripping wet eyes found Khoo Hun Chhiau once more; only this time, they didn't see her lover, her best friend, her soulmate, they saw the men chasing *her* away, cutting *her*, *b*urning *her*, *s*tabbing, piercing, spitting at *her* savagely. An endless string of men. Their faces blurred together, in a morph that now rested over Khoo Hun Chhiau's own in her mind's eye.

Khoo Hun Chhiau rushed towards her. His arms outstretched as if to swallow her in them, but she flinched away, briefly catching the pain in his eyes.

"What's wrong with you?" He wailed. "What did *she* do to you? I, we saved you from *her*, *a*nd, and..."

"You saved me from *her*?" Val cackled maniacally. "You made her *her!* You, and all your friends — and relatives — and everyone! This is all *your* fault! Did you ever once think to just, I don't know, ask *her* to stop? Did you ever think once to maybe sit down with *her,* and see what *she's* like? What *she's* really like? In ten thousand years has not one person here even *thought* about that?"

"What're you even talking about?" Khoo Hun Chhiau yelled back. "What do you mean? Are you saying that we should've just gone up to *her,* waved a friendly hello, and just asked her politely to *stop trying to kill people?*"

"That's exactly what I'm saying," Val cried, "and more, no one has ever been kind to *her. She* has never experienced a single shred of decency in her endless life. How do people expect *her* not to turn into a monster?"

Khoo Hun Chhiau paused. The hairs on his arm raised, like a cat ready to pounce. "So..." He started quietly. "What you're telling me, is that I, and the rest of my teammates, should have walked into that school tonight, and just asked her politely, to *not murder the woman I love — more than anything or anyone — the woman who's carrying my unborn child! Do you really think that little of me? That I wouldn't do everything in the world to protect my future family?*"

He collapsed onto the couch next to her in a fit of tears. Val's heart sank once more. Val climbed on top of him, holding him close to her chest. He tried to push her away but ultimately gave in, sobbing into her bosom.

"I'm sorry!" Val apologized profusely. "I'm so, so, so sorr—" but her voice cut out, as she caught her own reflection in one of the windows.

Only this time, it was different as well. Val saw in her own reflection the faces of women past... women who looked back at *her* own countenance in horror, in fear, in a cold-hearted terror. An unspeakable, supernatural fright. A *primal* fright. Some grabbed their children, hiding them behind; while the worst of them offered them up, as if to appease her in some twisted, perverted sacrifice. Val heard the thousands of following screams echoing in her head like a manic chorus, but even louder was the frozen, silent emptiness of those who couldn't even find it in them to make a sound. Their pale, hollow faces etched themselves so deeply in *her* mind's eye, they haunted her dreams like ghosts. Anger, she could take one day at a time... but utter revulsion cut deeper than any knife.

Val turned away, weeping profusely into Khoo Hun Chhiau's arms. Harder than she had ever wept in her whole life. So hard, that Khoo Hun Chhiau was caught off guard through his own cries, and began comforting Val instead.

"Shhh... it's okay..." He cooed softly.

Val spent the night switching between breathtaking sobs, and recounting her story back to him. Val told him everything, processing it all herself. Beginning with the back-breaking work at Amina's, to the warning the kids gave her, to the fireworks and rescuing of Zara, and giving up so much of her blood. To the battle of the Holymen, and finally, to the horrible, tragic, loveless story, that was the tale of *her*.

CHAPTER TWENTY-THREE

That February night was a strange one. Chilly and windy, like the cusp of a monsoon. The skeletal remains of Semua Tangan stood bare, surrounded by a rainforest that seemed ripe to take it back into her arms once more.

A quarter moon guided Val's path. She crossed the yellow *"do not enter"* tape that surrounded the complex. It was a waste of plastic, no one dared come anywhere near here for months now.

Val passed through the once grand double doors, into the bare foyer. A musty smell of mold and spice filled Val's nostrils. Buzzing sounds echoed where a beehive had taken residence behind the statues, who's silhouettes and shadows danced in the moonlight. A cold, familiar chill nearly made her turn back at this point... but Val pressed on. Forcing herself to do what needed to be done.

The center of the first courtyard directly behind the entrance hall still bore the burn marks of fireworks and human blood, but new grass was starting to poke through. Val passed this too, but not before glancing up at her old school room; which, like all the other rooms, was a mess of water damage, overthrown desks, and the silent history of children's mischief. Val couldn't help but crack a smile.

Val reached the edge of the forest. By now it had encroached itself much closer to the school's closest courtyard. It was a wild, beautiful, terrifying, sight. Val felt it could swallow her up any second.

"I know you're here." Val said loudly into the trees, and the blackness in between them. Her voice cracking with every word. "I know you're here, and I know you can hear me. I just want to talk... please."

There was a cold, still silence, that could almost pass as peaceful. For a moment Val felt a brief requiem of relief. Maybe she was wrong. Maybe they wouldn't meet. Maybe *she* was gone...

The moment lasted only briefly, 'til Val felt that same prickle of terror that let her know that *she* was near, and *she* was watching... a slow, gray shadow moved behind her. Val turned around, and was met by those same, fierce, crimson eyes, as *she* crawled on the ground slowly, circling her, examining Val's every move. A quiet growl trembled in the air.

Val's heart stopped, as it did every time she was in *her* presence. For a moment Val had forgotten everything she had planned to say. It was as if the words that she'd rehearsed a thousand and one times vanished from her mind... but something deep within her pressed her forward.

"I... I am no threat to you." Val started, her hands trembling. She raised them in the air in front of herself. "And... and I think you know exactly why I've come... or... at least you've had some feeling... or something that I would come back. I'm here to bring you a peace offering, from the humans, to you... from me, to you..." Val gulped a fat lump down, before pressing forward. "I... I know the pain, and suffering, we, including myself, have brought upon you, and... and..."

Val gazed into her red, curious, sad eyes, before continuing.

"On behalf of all humankind, I am sorry. I am *so... so... so* sorry." Val cried, her voice completely breaking now. "I am so sorry, we are so sorry, for the pain, anguish, and hurt we and our ancestors have put you through. We were wrong... I was wrong. I never gave you a chance."

Val watched, as *she* watched her back. *Her* countenance morphed, from curiosity, to empathy, to pain, to anger, before finally to bitter acceptance. There were no words, only the eyes that met her's once more.

"We... I understand that you'll never fully forgive us for everything we've done, and that's okay... but if I do what I'm about to do, I need you to promise to never harm another human ever again. Do you understand that? How do I know that I can believe you?"

It was curious the way *she* trusted Val just now. Val understood the magical, spiritual, empathetic tug of whatever you want to call it that brought her here to this very spot helped the two of them form the semblance of a strange faith in one another... but even then, Val knew that *she* still didn't quite know exactly what she was doing here. Trespassing on *her* land. *Her* safe haven. *Her* only refuge... just to be standing in *her* presence at this moment was a miracle in and of itself.

"You can stay here, even if the school reopens, but you just have to promise me you'll never hurt anyone ever again. Do you understand that? Now, I'll ask again, how do I know that I can trust you? I know you can speak, what do you have to say?"

She crawled up to Val. *Her* shadow nearly lagging behind in *her* speed as they came face to face. *She* pulled out the same, jagged, stiletto nail Val had seen once before. A cascade of shivers ran down her spine, as *she* dragged it down *her* forearm, all the way to the palm of *her* hand. Blood seeped down onto the ground around them. *She* held out *her* hand, waiting for Val's.

Val took a deep, shaky breath. This was it. Her shirt lifted briefly, revealing the small, rounded lump that was now a source of so much pride and joy. *She* glanced at it, before digging her nail into Val's shoulder, causing her to cry out in pain and nearly jerk back, before forcing herself still. *She* dragged it all the way down. Each ensuing inch more painful than the last, until she reached Val's palm. There was a sudden, brief relief, before *she* seized Val's hand in her own, cold, wet ones. Grasping it firmly, before pulling *her* body in close...

"*I promise...*" *She* hissed, into Val's ear.

Val was nearly sent into another fit of chills. All the blood drained from her face, but a strange, soothing warmth ran down her arm, tracing the line *she* had just drawn... Val peered down at it incredulously, wherein the fresh wounds wake a jagged, silver scar a centimeter thick shimmered in the darkness.

Val stood there gaping for several seconds before gathering her wits about her once more. She nodded to *her,* forcing out a stern, "I promise too", before pulling out the seed of the most delicious mango she had eaten in the last three months; of which, there had been quite a few, considering mangoes were her pregnancy craving. From her other pocket she retrieved a small glass vial, filled with the ash that had accumulated on her clothing that fateful night. Val bent down, and dug a small hole in the ground. She placed the seed within, before burying it, and emptying the vial of volcanic cinders on top.

Val took a deep, slow breath, as she gazed into the red, cold eyes that stood before her. Those red, cold eyes that had seen, and heard, and felt, so much pain. So much injustice. So much of the worst in others... a soul that had the courage even now to dare to hope, to even try for something more...

Val's tears tumbled down onto the small lump of raised dirt, faster and heavier than she had expected them to. It only took a minute for it to be soaking, and by the time Val was done remembering the worst in herself and her fellow man, a small puddle had formed. Val pushed herself back, and sat down on her behind; wiping wetness from her face.

The two sat there in silence... while the rain forest in front of them danced. Almost as if every tree, every leaf, every bush and bug were a part of a never-ending ensemble cast; performing a play just for the two of them. A chilly breeze swept across the courtyard. Val felt her eyelids begin to drift down, when a loud *crack* broke the ground where they were sitting — nearly bursting Val's remaining ear drum. Val searched around for *her* frantically, only to find that *she* had sprung into the treetops above in shock. Val felt her heart pound as she crawled on the ground in front of her...

The light from the moon shined down on *his* countenance... *he* rested in the dirt, as if *he* were a man dead in *his* wake. Only now this was *his* birth. *He* opened *his* red eyes, and pushed himself up until *he* was face to face with Val; who did her best not to cower in *his* presence. Instead opting to offer her newly scarred hand to help *him* to *his* feet.

Val helped *him* stand up on legs that shook briefly, before finding their footing remarkably fast. *He* looked around at his surroundings curiously, before staring back down at Val. Searching her face for answers...

Val felt that familiar crawl up her spine, letting her know that *she* was behind her, and it was time to leave. Val walked away, back towards the school. Only glancing back when she was nearly at its back doors again, to see the two standing face to face with one another silently. In the distance, it reminded Val of what she and Khoo Hun Chhiau must look like from that same stretch, since their respective heights nearly matched up perfectly. Val turned away once more, heading back into the night.

Epilogue

Val watched the toddler try again to push himself off the ground, and walk the few steps up the back patio away from his mother's arms. He was nearly thirteen months now, and every step he took brought Val more joy than the last.

"Good job sweetie!" Val cooed. The child merely gave her the tiniest smirk of satisfaction before returning his focus to the task at hand.

Val took in a deep, satisfied breath, and placed her hands on her hips. She surveyed her back garden and the valley below once more. The sun had been up for several hours by now, but a light mist had brought with it a rare, Saturday chill; that reminded her of that day nearly two years ago now, when she had set things right.

After much arguing, haggling, and full-on fist fights by dueling sides, the city council finally agreed to repair Semua Tangan to its former glory; on the sole condition that if anything were to happen regarding *her* again, that would be the last bail-out. Val didn't worry about this though. She had returned to campus a few months before from maternity leave, and in that time had experienced no supernatural pricks, visions, irks, feelings, or fights play out around her whatsoever. Val had even slyly grilled one of the newest facility members, Ms. Bombo, to figure out if she had experienced any new teacher hazing. Which, minus an upsetting encounter with a slingshot from the school's newly appointed security guard, she had not.

That isn't to say Val hadn't seen the last of *her* in the slightest. About a year and a half ago, Peh Si was found roaming down the main highway aimlessly. Much worse for wear. Her matted hair was filled with twigs and leaves. The scar on her neck was black and infected; and her ass was way less jiggly, since she'd lost a good twenty kilos. Val heard that she now suffered from a bad tendency to ramble, but then again when did she not.

Every now and then, Val would peek out her class window, or look out from her lunch bench spot; past the gossiping teachers, and Ms. Dian and Ms. Mawar bustling about, over the children at recess playing a soccer match, to see two pairs of those same, crimson eyes; peeking out from their dark canopy of trees; watching those below. Beforehand, the sight of this would have sent Val into a frenzy; a demon, picking her prey. Now though, it was a source of comfort; a guardian angel, protecting her own secrets, her own vows.

A lurch of morning sickness panged her chest. Val grabbed her now slightly swollen stomach as the feeling passed. Just a few days ago, Val had figured out she was once again pregnant. Khoo Hun Chhiau would be returning from his work trip to Mumbai any moment now, and Val couldn't wait to see the look on his face. She'd already told her own family back home as well as Khoo Hun Chhiau's father, who she'd grown quite fond of. His silent, cheery mood helped everything feel more peaceful, and was nice company. Val watched him perform light aerobics in the very back corner of their garden.

Every now and then Val and Khoo Hun Chhiau would notice the ignorant stares that would shoot their direction. But over the last two years there had been a slew of even odder couplings than herself and Khoo Hun Chhiau... Nur and the young, kind, robotics technician, that so reminded Val of a dorky friend of hers from high school. Principal Arif's granddaughter and Officer Yusef. Tan Soan and the firstborn son of the serial defector... but none more surprising than that of Ms. Nadar and Ken. Val couldn't believe her eyes when she opened up the *"save the date"* letter of their wedding announcement; but it explained Ms. Nadar's slightly less unpleasant mood as of late. The other day even, Val had accidentally bumped into her at the grocery store as she left the produce section; and instead of the usual tongue lashing that she would've expected, Val was met with a knowing, polite nod towards Val's stylish shoes. She might as well have declared all her apologies to her on the spot. Val's students had been whispering about how many soda bottles and gum-packets they had gotten past her lately, and now Val knew why.

The day was young, her family even younger, but Val was satisfied and fulfilled.

Acknowledgements

First, thank you, thank you, thank you, to everyone who read this book. I appreciate it more than you could ever know. I hope you enjoyed reading Mango as much as I enjoyed writing it. I would also like to thank my mother, Lisa Brown, for editing my grammar; as well as my wonderful friend Andrea for creating the cover art for my work. Last but not least, I would like to thank my incredible partner Ross, whose constant devotion and support made this book possible.

Author Bio

Paula Brown is the author and illustrator of the children's book *Daddy's in jail,* as well as the horror novel *Mango.* She was born in 1994 in Houston Texas, and started her world travels at the age of twenty-two, where she passes the time on planes, trains, and everywhere in between by writing. You can follow her travels on Instagram: @paulabawlla

For more of Paula's published work, visit amazon.com

www.ingramcontent.com/pod-product-compliance
Lightning Source LLC
LaVergne TN
LVHW041914070526
838199LV00051BA/2610